CUTE MUTANTS

VOL 1: MUTANT PRIDE

SJ WHITBY

To You-Know-Who (no, not that one)
for believing in me when nobody else did

CHAPTER ONE

S o this is my life: I fall asleep browsing Crunchyroll and twenty minutes later some asshole is shaking the entire house. At first I think it's a dream, but irl things are moving in a way that is not at all natural. I let out an unflattering screech. It's drowned out by Summers, who has leapt off my bed and is running in circles, yapping his mutt-yap.

"Summers, you idiot," I say. He is adorable, but he is not a good listener.

I scowl at the ceiling, pissed off at a universe that seems intent on ruining my night. I've been sleeping like crap lately. Being stricken out of the blue with inexplicable and strange powers seems to have that effect and—

There's a thump from the wall by my head. I have no idea what it's supposed to mean—maybe there's a poltergeist in the house? I give an answering thump anyway because hey, maybe the ghost is friendly. I fumble my phone up from where it slipped down by my neck.

There are a bunch of random notifications, but nothing about an earthquake. I flick on the torch and wave it around the room. It's hard to tell if anything fell, because I have a lax attitude toward tidiness and my room already looks like an earthquake has pitched a fit. My lamp's still swaying. A car alarm blares in the street.

Pear appears in the doorway. Not a literal pear. My life may be surreal, but it's not one of those cursed YouTube clips that everyone freaks out about their toddlers watching. It's Pear short for Parent, like Mum is short for Mother.

"That fucking dog," they say.

Summers quits barking and leaps all over Pear, licking every patch of bare skin he can find.

"That felt big right?" I squint in the bright light coming in from the hallway.

"Woke me up." My parent is something out of a cautionary tale when they're disturbed at night. Which is better than the partially reanimated corpse they are in the morning until they sniff out some coffee grounds.

Voices carry from the street outside, people loudly guessing at the Richter scale like they'll get a sticker for being right.

I roll out of bed and grab the first enormous hoodie I can find, then shuffle for the front door.

Pear and I are about four steps out of the house when the dude across the street yells out to us. He's sitting on a deckchair in the entrance to his garage, drinking a beer. The suburbs, ugh.

"The Taylor girls," he says and I'm like, *haha, oh you dummy.*

"Not a girl," Pear says, flexing those Janet muscles. They don't look exactly girlish, head all new-shaved and with the big leather coat that's exactly the one Spike wears in *Buffy*.

But dude across the road is like, "Sorry, I meant Taylor *women*," in this sarcastic voice, and there is no prize at all in life for being a dumb motherfucker, but this guy is trying. Neither of us wants to talk about they/them at midnight. He's looking at my bare legs sticking out of the hoodie that only goes down to mid-thigh.

I'm over this already.

Our street is a little weird. At one end are slumpy little bungalow houses like ours and Drunky McGee's across the road. Then, starting from next door, it's all McMansions with gables and balconies and spa pools and fancy dogs with proper names for the breeds. It's like our street has a wrong side of the tracks halfway down it, and that's where we live. Except come earthquake time, we're all shaken down to the same level, just sleepy-ass people in their sloppy nightclothes in a state of *ugh what the fuck.*

We wander down and find half the neighbourhood gathered outside house number fifty-two. People are spilled all over the front lawn and out onto the street. The house has big windows and a second storey and this fancy arch entranceway. Every single bit of that has been wrecked. All the house lights are on, and the family is standing shaky and teary in the middle of everyone. Summers greets the neighbours with his usual indiscriminately joyful level of enthusiasm, i.e. the polar opposite of me.

It's disconcerting how badly their house is damaged, when ours is just fine.

The nice lady from next door to us has her shit all the way together. She's made cups of tea for everyone and her grown-up kids are passing them out. The little kids from the quaked house are crying, which I totally get. It's bad enough being woken by an earthquake, without having your own house messed up. Cups of tea don't go down so well with them, so I jog back to our place to find something better.

"Evening, pretty lady," Drunky says. I give him the finger and he cackles at me. I stop walking, but the guy's still laughing. I can feel my pulse beating in my neck. Fuck this guy. Like what even is up with him? Why does he have to sit there and act like this?

I glare at him, and I feel this twinge in my head. There's something listening to me.

This is the weird new thing I can do, the *powers* thing. It's not actually that super—in fact, it's a bit embarrassing, but here goes: I can talk to objects. Ordinary, boring household objects. Except only some of them listen to me, and it doesn't work all the time. I'm still figuring out the details. Right now, I can sense that the deckchair he's sitting in is sentient. There's a thread of awareness running between us.

"Go fold yourself," I snap, but I'm not talking to the dude.

The chair jerks and then collapses, scraping its legs and falling to the ground. The guy tangles up with it and his head hits the concrete. He howls and thrashes about, completely stuck.

The chair is all panting and breathless. "Hey, did I do good?"

"You're the best folding chair ever," I tell it, which is maybe a low bar, but shrug emoji.

My supervillain inclination satisfied, I let myself into the house and rummage around in the kitchen. There's no damage here. The cupboards are messy, but just regular-for-us messy. It takes a minute for me to find a family size bag of M&Ms. When I go back out the front door, the guy is gone, deckchair and all. The garage door is shut.

I run back to number fifty-two, where I become the focus of attention.

"Thank you," the mother says, all super enthusiastic, like I fucking saved them from the earthquake myself. "That's honestly so kind of you." She has tears in her eyes and it's weird and awkward, so I stare at my feet and hold out the M&Ms.

The kids stop crying long enough to snatch the bag right out of my hand. They start gorging on sugar. I beat a hasty retreat from conversation and wander off to look at the house up close. This big crack splits it right down the middle, to where a dirt trench runs through the lawn and out into the street. Where it stops, there's a splintered patch of asphalt with a couple of holes and lines zig-zagging out. It gives me the creeps, honestly, like this part of the world has been deliberately broken.

We do get earthquakes here—there was a big one back when I was a kid. Buildings fell down, people died. It was pretty terrible. Pear and Dad were still together, and they both came to school to collect me. At first it seemed like a big adventure, but the adults turned up grim and crying. Mostly I remember having to use portaloos and getting water from trucks. My worst memory is from an aftershock. I was sitting at the table eating when the house started rattling, and I started crying because *obviously*. The shaking got worse. Pear screamed at me to *get under the table right fucking now*, so I cried even louder and finally slid under the table seconds before a bookshelf fell right where I'd been sitting. I was curled up sobbing, surrounded by books, while Pear and Dad shouted at each other over whose fault it was that the shelf hadn't been secured. Fucking earthquakes, I swear.

This one tonight is different. I've never seen such a specific earthquake, like the planet deliberately said, "Fuck that house at number fifty-two, Imma mess it up good," but that would be supremely freaky. Right?

My brain is blinking at me going *hello Dylan, this is a clue, you dummy*. But my mysterious powers are a fluke and couldn't possibly be part of anything larger. It's not like they're contagious.

And then my brain says *oh well, life is weird, there is bizarre shit on the internet everyday ho hum*. Then I'm derailed over a sudden anxiety about being on the street with all my neighbours where everyone can see my thighs. This makes no sense, because they've been able to see my thighs this whole time but as soon as it occurs to me, my brain is just thighs thighs thighs. Fuck you, brain. Why can't you be nice to me for once?

I tug the hem of my hoodie down as far as I can, and flip the hood up over my short black hair. I wander over to the splintered patch of asphalt and kick at it. There are no further coherent thoughts in my head, because it's well past midnight and I'm zombie tired.

I yawn and walk over to Pear, who's staring into space. I nudge against them, and they pat my hood absently. Although we're both sleepy, we manage to get Summers back home with only minimal cat chasing and property invasion. Once we're inside, Pear lies down to moon over their phone. Their very special friend is away, which makes them oh so emo. I swat them with an overlong hoodie arm and wander down the hallway to bed.

Because I've been up and out, I now have to go through the nighttime routine all over again, which is a significant downside of my new ability.

"Dylan!"

"Hey, Pillow."

"What were you doing out of bed?" Pillow asks comfortably.

Then because Pillow started up, my giant candle chimes in, along with the glow-in-the-dark unicorn clock I've had since I was six, my shower-friendly Bluetooth speaker, the porcelain cat Dad brought back from Vietnam, and my comfy beanbag seat.

Every single one of them wants attention. It's like that old American sitcom I saw a clip from on YouTube, where everyone has to say goodnight to everyone else i.e. extremely fucking aggravating.

"Goodnight, Clockadoodledoo," the candle says.

"Sweet dreams, Candy my love," the clock says in return.

"Meow," the cat says, because she's trying to pass as real.

"Sleep well, Bluedude," the candle says.

The speaker plays some very slow music that sounds like Pear's godawful nineties shit, with some whiny guy singing about goodnight my love.

And we've barely even fucking started omg.

Finally, we get to the end and all my objects fall quiet and settle in for the night.

I lie in the dark and look up at the ceiling. I imagine there are questions written there, like how did this happen and am I insane and will it stop? What does it mean and why me? Is this really a *superpower* and am I the only one?

Whatever the answers, this is me, Dylan Taylor, human incarnation of the burning dumpster gif, and this is my life. Deal or gtfo. At least it can't get any worse, right?

CHAPTER TWO

Ever since my pillow first said hello to me, my life has turned surreal. It turns out spending all your life reading X-Men comics does not adequately prepare you for mutant reality. I understand there's a possibility I'm hallucinating, so I haven't told anyone. What would I say?

Instead, my new morning routine involves me googling superpowers in general, and my ability in particular. Nothing new ever shows up. The closest thing I've found is psychometry, which is a psychic thing where you get 'readings' from objects like you touch a wallet and know 'oh this person prefers dubs to subs i.e is wrong' or 'the woman who owned this writes Dramione fanfic i.e. is kinda yikes.'

Whereas my ability to speak to objects involves getting trapped in conversations like this one: "Pillow, I will stuff you at the bottom of the hamper for *days* if you cannot shut up when Lou is here. And you know how many disgusting things lurk down there."

"I promise, Dylan," Pillow says softly. "I will not utter a word."

"You said that exact thing last time, and then you started moaning when I was kissing him. He couldn't hear it, but it ruined *my* mood like a dick pic popping up in your Snapchat streaks."

"Moaning isn't talking," Pillow says, which is accurate but unhelpful.

Pear knocks on the door and tells me that Lou is here, which is their not so subtle signal to wear something more than 'just a hoodie.' They're pretty cool about the whole me having a boyfriend thing, new as it is. It surprised them, given that I'd shown no interest previously, but let's be honest, it broke my brain a little bit too. I don't know my sexuality. I've read so much stuff on the internet about it and I just get *more* fucking confused. My god, the hours I spent on AVENwiki. I used to think I was some kind of ace but then this *thing* with Lou started. He was the closest I had to a friend before the kissing part of our relationship started and now it's— Well, it's different. Putting a label on it is complicated.

I've mostly managed to get my school uniform on while I've been musing on grey-aces and demisexuals and the like, but here is Lou tap-tapping at my door like we have a secret knock. I have this brief urge to answer it just in my bra, but we're not there yet, or at least I'm not.

"One second," I say, but it takes me two attempts to do up my buttons. I open my bedroom door to find him waiting there. Lou's dressed in what the school calls the 'alternative uniform,' which is grey trousers and a shirt. His hair is cropped close with the tiniest bit of black fringe that spikes up and I always want to smooth down, just so I can touch him. His skin is bronzy and beautiful, and his eyes are an intoxicating brown shot through with tiny golden bits. I've never seen such a gorgeous boy.

"He's so handsome," Pillow sighs and honestly shut the fuck up, you thirsty-ass cushion, but in her favour she is not entirely wrong. Just looking at him makes me smile. I try to hide it behind my hand, but then I remember he likes my smile so my hand bobs around awkwardly.

"Hello, boyfriend," I say.

He loves it when I call him boyfriend, and he leans in and kisses my cheek, a brush of lips on my skin, speaking a word I can't make out but makes me shiver. I touch his face and turn it slightly so I can reach his lips, but he takes a single step back into the doorway.

Things have been weird since Emma's party. There was an incident where my name came up in this magic app and I kissed Emma. Then it turned into a whole *thing*. I went and told Lou straight away. He was *not* happy, even though it was basically a modern spin the bottle and that's not cheating, right?

The truth is, I kissed her because she's Emma Hall and people like Emma Hall don't usually kiss people like me. It felt shimmery and soft-focus and like an early episode of a Netflix show before everything turns shit. Whatever the reason, it happened and it can't un-happen and now Lou is pissed at me but he's pretending he's not and I'm kind of over it but at the same time am I really allowed to be mad when it's my fault?

"Your parent," he whispers. "They're just in the kitchen."

"They're not a voyeur," I say. "You're allowed to kiss me."

He glances over his shoulder and pecks me on the lips with only the tiniest ghost of an open mouth. Pillow lets out this long, shuddering sigh and then Summers is there, gambolling around our legs. He has sensed affection like it's *his* goddamn superpower and he wants to join in. I reach down to pat him, Lou does too, and I manage to sneak what feels like an illicit kiss over the body of a hyperactively wagging dog.

"We should get to school," Lou says.

I glance at the clock on the wall.

"Be very careful with this boy, Dylan," the clock says. "You don't want him to break your heart." His name is Tempus, according to him, which ok sure fine, give yourself a name if you must, but he seems to think I need a father figure. I definitely do not.

I can't say anything in response because I don't want to be shunned by the two people who tolerate my existence. As I walk past Tempus, I extend a casual middle finger in the clock's direction, hidden behind Lou's back.

"Well I never," Tempus says, so I do it again as I head out the door.

From my house to school is only about fifteen minutes' walk. It usually takes us around thirty, because I am slow and distracted and spend a lot of time searching stuff up on my phone to prove that I'm right in some argument. Today it's Lou's turn to be preoccupied, wobbling along on his bike with his head down. He's probably contemplating the universe, or more likely some shit at home with his disaster parents. I put one headphone in and listen to the new Dreamcatcher EP. It has one super bop that I save to my overstuffed best of K-pop playlist.

"Sorry," Lou says finally, when we get near the school and the lines of girls all converge into one mass. "I'm miles away. Bad boyfriend."

"It's fine." I want to kiss him again, but we're already getting looks. We always get looks. I make the mistake of looking back, and my gaze skids across Tara Pieters, who hates me and has done for many years. She's got shiny hair and shiny lips and eyes that hold little worlds of judgement inside them.

"Oh Dylan," she says. "I just love your hair today. What did you do to it? It makes you look like more of a boy than your, um, your boyfriend does."

I say nothing, but I want to punch her. Why couldn't I have a decent superpower, to encase her in ice or explode her with sparkle lights? Or at the very fucking least, make it so nobody ever notices me. Her emphasis on boyfriend is like claws dragged down my spine. Claws is appropriate, because she's hated me ever since the school costume party years ago. I went as X-23 and got into a fight with her. Even though she was the one who called me an ugly bitch, and said I took after my ugly bitch 'mother,' it was me who got in trouble for stabbing her with my cardboard claws.

Even if I had real claws, I would have learned to keep them sheathed since then. Outside of talking to objects, my superpower is to swallow other people's shit and keep swallowing until I'm just an awful shitty thing dragging around and pretending to be human.

"Ignore her," Lou says softly, and takes my hand. He lifts my fingers to his mouth, all curled in like they're trying to make a fist, and he kisses the tips of them one after the other.

Tara watches with a sneer on her face. "Tragic," she sighs, and walks off.

There are other faces too, a whole unpleasant parade of them. They look at me with all these scribbled and horrible thoughts playing behind their empty expressions. I used to try and appear normal, a blank and anonymous thing, but for some reason nobody believed that. So now I pretend it doesn't matter, and I read online somewhere that if you pretend a thing long enough, it comes true.

"Fuck them," Lou says, his mouth against my ear, but we need to get to class, so instead we get swallowed up by the building.

Brookside Girls' High is a brand-new school, built after the earthquakes a few years back nearly knocked the old one down. It's what they call a smart facility, which means they have lots of electronic screens every-where. The place is an unnerving rabbit warren of windowless rooms and corridors, an experiment with us as the subjects. You can easily get lost, even when you know your way around.

I don't like school, partly because I'm bad at it. Like the stuff itself isn't hard to learn, but having to sit in a room with a droning teacher and a bunch of tedious people you have exactly zero things in common with is a refined form of torture.

If I had to break it down, life at school is twenty percent actual schoolwork, forty percent wishing for a quick and painless death, and twenty percent avoiding contact with assholes. The other twenty percent is having your boyfriend misgendered and deadnamed. Goddamnit humanity, are we not fucking past this?

I correct them, every time. The problem is that Lou's parents won't back him up and there's not enough fuck them in the world to take that anger out of me. They won't let him switch schools either, not that I really want him to. Most of the teachers are fine and correct themselves when they fuck up, but Mrs Alexander in maths is not one of those teachers.

She uses the wrong name three times in a row when she's asking questions. Lou says nothing but I see the tiny flinch—fractional hardening of his lips, skin tightening around his eyes.

"It's Lou," I snarl. "It's he and it's him."

There's a digital marker on the teacher's desk.

"Yes, yes, his name is Lou," it says, in a breathless, high voice. Then it levitates into the air and starts writing on the smartboard. It spells out L-O-U in three foot high letters. The whole time I'm sitting rigid at my desk. I almost freak out and leave because what the fucking fuck is going on? This cannot be me, but at the same time it's obviously me.

So yes, this is the exact plot of Matilda, but it's not Miss Trunchbull, just some middle-aged woman with a bad haircut and an anti-abortion bumper sticker on her Toyota. Lots of people look at me, because they assume I'm responsible, given that I'm usually the one shouting at the teacher about deadnames.

"Oh my God," one girl says from behind me. "Is that supposed to be a magic trick or something? This is the lamest thing I've ever—"

"Dylan Taylor, did you do this?" The teacher is glaring at me like a disgruntled pelican, but it's half-ass because she's got no proof. She must think it's a prank. Nobody can levitate a digital marker in real life, right? I can't believe it myself, even though the marker spoke to me.

"No?" I say, but my voice is so faint I may as well not have spoken.

"Dylan?" The teacher is like a magnifying glass focusing the sunshine glare of the entire room's attention on me. My skin feels hot and tight. Sweat pricks at my temples, and for a horrible second there's a looming blackness waiting for me, but it passes.

I get to my feet, banging my leg hard against the desk, and storm out of class, spitting something about tampons. Lou looks at me like 'why are you like this, Dylan?' As if I'm not doing it on his behalf, but for my own selfish reasons.

I am entirely over every single person on the planet's bullshit, so I go to the only refuge in the school. It's a truly shitty refuge, but beggars can't be choosers.

CHAPTER THREE

I slam my way into the first floor bathroom, making the door bounce off the wall. It's deserted, as far as I can tell. The only thing in there is one of the hand-dryer machines who says, "Oh, I heard there was someone here who could talk to us."

I am not in the fucking mood for *its* shit either, so I punch it with the side of my hand. "Eat glass," I snarl.

It probably hurts me a lot more than it hurts the hand dryer, but you wouldn't know it from the way it whines. "What did I do to deserve this?" and so on. Okay, I feel a tiny bit guilty, but not enough to stop and apologise.

I bang into one of the cubicles, lock it, and perch myself up on the closed toilet. I want to scream or cry. I'm also seriously curious about how I just Matilda'd a whiteboard marker. It's more extreme than anything else I've done with my powers.

I'm trying to wallow, but super loud retching sounds come from the cubicle beside me. There's wet coughing, gross splattering sounds, and finally what sounds a lot like a person sobbing.

"Hello?" I feel like an idiot saying something, but they can ignore me if I'm being a dick.

"Who is it?" The voice sounds weird, like someone's been gargling toxic waste.

"Dylan?" I say it like I'm not even sure. "Dylan Taylor??" Even less sure apparently. "Year Twelve." Finally, something I'm confident in.

"Something really bad has happened," the voice says.

I come out and stand in front of the mirror. "I can get help if you want."

Another cubicle opens, and I realise there is no help to get, because nobody would believe what's happening. Whoever's inside is barely recognisable as human. Her skin hangs off her in folds, like one of those cute wrinkly dogs except just wrinkly. Her limbs are creepy and long, like they've got too many joints. And her face is paper white, scarred and flaking off in chunks.

"I'm hideous," she says miserably.

I swallow, and my heart is thumping. This is like a horror movie. I've wondered before about what I'd do in a situation like this. It turns out I choose the option of squeezing into the stall with her and closing the door. Yeah, I'm definitely dying first.

"You're fine," I say, feeling helpless. "Everyone has bad days. Look at my skin."

She looks at me and begins to laugh hysterically. Except while she's laughing, her body is shifting back to normal—a pretty Pasifika girl with long straight hair that's dark brown and honey blonde all tangled up together. Alyse, that's her name. We have biology together.

Now that she looks normal, I have no idea what to say. It's clear she has some kind of weird ability too, which requires me to say *something* but my brain is jammed. Turns out it's no problem, because she talks first.

"I was taking a selfie for my friend. And I turned off all the filters and was thinking how terrible I looked and then it got worse and worse and—"

"Holy shit," I say. "You're like low self-esteem Mystique." I immediately wish all those words back into my mouth. This is why I choose not to talk to people, because I always say the wrong thing. As if to prove it, my mouth keeps blabbering. "You don't need filters. You're gorgeous. I love your hair. Mine is a total mess. I can never decide what to do with it, but yours is all silky and perfect."

Why am I saying this? Why doesn't she reach out and tear the bottom half of my face off so I have no tongue or jaw or any part required for speech? That would make this situation so much better.

Alyse is still transforming in front of me. I wouldn't believe my eyes if I didn't see it myself. If anything, she's overcorrecting and now she's filter-hot.

"Mystique is a really interesting character," I tell her, because for some reason I'm fucking dead certain she wants to hear about this right now. "Originally they wanted Mystique and Destiny to be Nightcrawler's biological parents, and have him conceived when Mystique was shifted into a male body. But because of the Comics Code Authority, they couldn't do it."

"Um," Alyse says. "What are you—?"

"So they had her fuck a demon mutant instead, because apparently that's way more normal."

"Uh, no offence but what the fuck is going on?" She glares at me like this is my fault.

"I, um, shit. It's like, I don't—it's weird, right?" I lean back against the cubicle wall, wishing I could phase through it like Kitty Pryde.

We stare at each other for a moment. *She* knows this is weird, and I know this is weird but how do you encompass all the weirdness in *words*?

"Please, please don't tell anyone this happened," she says. "Like I appreciate you not freaking out, but this is not okay, and you cannot breathe a fucking word."

Then she literally kisses me on the cheek—leaving me like what the fuck is going on?—and breezes out of the cubicle with a metric shit-ton of confidence. I'm left unphased and feeling strangely guilty. I'm oscillating wildly between wanting to lose the power of speech permanently, and my brain screaming *someone else has a fucking superpower*. I want to run after her and demand she tell me everything, but I've already embarrassed myself enough.

I leave the cubicle and stand in front of the mirror, poking my face. If I straighten my hair and put it into a style then maybe I can look almost presentable, but who can be bothered doing that? My eyes are big, and that's a good thing, I think. Outside of that I'm just the blandest bland in Blandtown, and I wish mirrors had never been invented.

"You know, you're actually rather striking," the hand dryer says with breezy sarcasm.

"Fuck you," I say, because I cannot with its bullshit.

Lou finds me after class. I'm lounging on one of the benches outside the classroom block, watching K-pop videos on my phone.

"Whee-in in a suit," I say, holding out the phone. "That's today's gender. Maybe every day's gender, holy crap."

"What?"

"Mamamoo video."

Lou glances at the screen for like half a second. "Whatever. That thing with the marker. How the hell did you do that?"

"What thing?" I ask, because playing dumb is like my go-to move.

He tries to make a vee with his eyebrows but his scowl game is not fierce, so he takes refuge in heavy sarcasm. "Uh, the one where it wrote my name on the board."

"Magic." I make overly theatrical jazz hands. "I can tip over a water glass and rotate a pencil."

"Don't be annoying," he says, which is fair.

I fish in my bag and throw a mostly empty can of Pringles at him. "See? Magic. That asshole of a teacher was pissing me off."

He looks at me with those beautiful eyes and then gives what sounds like the world's longest sigh. "Dylan, this is my fight."

This is good in that he's moved on from my impossible ability. It's bad in that we've had this argument before. I *get* that it's his life and his thing to deal with, but at the same time Lou is terrible at sticking up for himself. If he had his way his 'fight' would involve him shrinking and shrinking until there was nothing left of him but sad scraps. Someone has to defend him, and it's going to be me because a) fuck other people and b) fuck transphobes especially.

"I know it's your fight." I'm aiming for calm but I'm aware it sounds like somebody trying to scream through gritted teeth. "But fights involve actually fighting. Not—" There are literally a thousand things I could say after this, but all of them are mean. Apologies would take too long.

"I have chosen the path of least resistance," he says, like he is some fucking Zen ninja dude swaying with the breeze. At least they unleash the fury of a trillion fists when they're pushed over the edge, and I can't see Lou doing that.

It's not his fault at all. It's the fucking world and his parents and that awful teacher, but the chambers of my heart aren't big enough to contain all my anger. I clench my teeth, sorting through my brain for words, and come up empty.

"Whatever." I get to my feet, yanking my bag with me, nearly dropping my phone. Got to buy a screen protector, Dylan. "I'll talk to you later."

I leave him sitting on the bench and don't look back.

When we meet at the end of school, neither of us is in the mood to talk. It's the post-school traffic rush, and I skip across the road in front of the oncoming cars. There's a whole bunch parked up waiting for people, and I walk past one with this total asshole inside. I recognise the licence plate. It's BJF something which I always think stands for Bastard Jerk Fucker. He's here like half the time, hooting and shouting at girls. I hate him so much I can't even deal. The shit he says to Lou? I don't want to repeat it, because it's vile bull-shit, but to give you a tiny example he says stuff like 'show us your dick.' Honestly, why has nobody killed him yet?

"Fuck off, you repulsive asshole," I snap at him through the window. He laughs this high-pitched laugh, like it's the funniest fucking thing ever. I wish I was brave enough to smash the wing mirror of his car, but I've seen *Atlanta*.

Lou ignores him and cycles along the footpath beside me, slowly enough that he swerves everywhere. I stare down at my phone, sending gifs to Pear. The one of the kid walking along in the sand with his head down and his arms hanging. The 'I'm Done' one with the guy stepping out the window. The pretty girl with the 'Over It' gun. Pear and I can have a long conversation in gifs. They send me back one of Lorelai Gilmore hugging Rory, and I smile despite myself.

Halfway up the road we come to the shop where we often buy ice creams, except the footpath outside is all torn up. The front window is shattered, and someone's put orange cones all in the path. The guy who owns the dairy is sweeping up glass. He looks pretty slumped and over it himself.

"Hi," I say. I don't know his name but we recognise each other.

"We're closed today."

I pause in the gutter, scraping the toe of my boot through shards of glass. Lou gets off his bike a few meters ahead. I shade my eyes from the sun. Inside the shop, everything's been thrown everywhere. There are piles of food and shattered bottles. It's a mess.

It seems beyond weird that this ice-cream shop also got struck by the same earthquake as number fifty-two on my street, but I'm not whatever kind of scientist knows about earthquakes.

"This sucks." Listen to me, sympathy girl.

"It's the last straw." He's not rude, but his voice is sharp. "Earthquake. Robbery. You name it. I'm done."

"Sorry." I offer an incoherent shrug.

He gives me this grimace, like 'thank you miss for your understatement' and goes back to sweeping. I tip-toe my way through glass and catch up with Lou, who's slouched on his bike like his spine can't hold him up any longer.

When we get back to my house, it's quiet except for Summers who pants and whines and shows his belly. Once the great god of neediness has been appeased, he curls up across my feet. We sit at the kitchen table and do homework and watch YouTube. To be fair, it's mostly me watching Red Velvet's video for Psycho and trying to learn the dance.

Lou is doodling wide-eyed anime boys and pretty anime girls on his pad. The girls all look like idealised versions of me, doe-eyed and floppy-fringed. Is that how he sees me or how he wishes I looked? I watch him work, the gentle strokes of his pencil, the way something beautiful emerges from the mess of lines.

He glances up halfway through sketching hair and sees me transfixed.

"I love that you want to defend me," he says.

"I shouldn't." I look away, because his gaze is impossible to hold. "I know I shouldn't."

"You have my back." He's still drawing, sketching out a body for the Dylan-face, a body that is not mine and wearing clothes I'd never wear. Is that his fantasy or generic anime fantasy? Or am I reading too much into it, like I do into everything? "I like you having my back," he says.

I don't say anything, even though my instinct is to babble.

"When you stick up for me, I feel like—" Another long pause, more lines on the girl's body. What the fuck is she wearing or not-wearing? "I feel like I'm failing." The pencil falls still and his gaze is back on me. "Like I'm not doing my part. Sticking up for— for people like me."

My cheeks feel hot and my eyes feel hot and I want to bury myself in the garden until this conversation is over. I press my lips tightly closed, because if I talk I'll either shout or cry.

"I know that's not fair." His hand touches mine, his fingers nestled into my palm and his thumb stroking the back of my hand. "You defending me is beautiful. But I feel like I don't deserve it. Like why should you put yourself in the firing line because of who I am?"

Finally, I have the words I need.

"Because it's right." My voice is steady and there are no tears. "Even if I wasn't… smitten with you, I would stand up for you." I pull the sleeve of my school blouse up to reveal the tattoo on my wrist—the only one Pear let me get. An X in a circle—the logo for the X-Men. "It's about fighting for those who need protecting, who are hated or feared. And it's about saying fuck people like the Purifiers, because they are the worst."

"Purifiers?" He has this tiny smile that I want to kiss. Sometimes he likes it when I ramble.

"Like this religious organisation that believes mutants and people with differences are evil and must be destroyed." I blush, because as much as Pear has raised me to love the X-Men, I occasionally recognise the need to shut the fuck up about them. "I gave you 'God Loves, Man Kills' to read, remember?"

"I don't like the art," he says, which makes me steal his pencil and throw it across the room. He laughs and gets up to retrieve it. I feel this surge of warmth in my heart that's so strong I want to take him in my arms and kiss him until one or the other of us blacks out.

"Careful," Tempus says from his position on the wall. "Watch your heart, Dylan, my dear. Emotions like that are dangerously powerful."

I want to take the clock off the wall and frisbee him into the other room, but Lou is looking at me with delight in his eyes and I don't want to ruin that, not for anything. I have to treat this carefully because if I break it, there isn't any alternative. It's not like people are lining up to hang out with me.

"Come here," I tell him, and hold out my arms.

CHAPTER FOUR

I get woken up again in the early hours of the morning, except this time it's from anxiety brain. That friendly friend that lurks in my mind just to fuck with me. Summers is asleep on my legs. It's making me sweaty and gross, so I thrash my way out of the blankets to stick my feet out into the cool air. Summers drags himself up to lie right beside my face. I grab my phone to put in a reminder to bathe him.

So, my brain says, you're not the only one with mutant powers.

Fuck off brain, I say, I want to sleep.

My brain is not interested in sleep. Instead, it wants me to think about Alyse. I wish I could remember her last name. Seeing her today was like a Very Special Episode of a kids' show where you learn that even the pretty girl still worries about how she looks. I feel a rush of gratitude for my talking-to-objects ability, because if I had Alyse's I would permanently take the form of a hideous slug. Knowing I'm not the only one with a superpower makes it better and worse. Yay, I'm not alone vs how the hell are real people existing with real superpowers?

I don't even understand my superpower.

"Do objects speak if there's nobody around to listen?" I ask Pillow sleepily.

"We are in hibernation," she says. "I woke up when you spoke to me."

Everything else in the room chimes in too, and they all basically agree.

"It's like we are dormant, waiting to be woken up," the alarm clock says.

"For a signal to connect to us," the Bluetooth speaker adds.

"Meow." Guess who.

"Am I a light in the darkness, Candy?" I ask my candle, who mutters something incoherent.

I have this panicky feeling in my chest at the thought of it. Where were they before that? Where did this awareness come from? I'm involuntarily creating these entities who feel things and have opinions and even make puns for fuck's sake. I don't feel as if I have any control over whether they wake for me.

I ask each of my objects to do something. The alarm clock changes the time. The speaker plays music, except it's still obsessed with nineties guitar shit that sounds both bored and pissed off, so I tell it to stop.

None of the others do much of anything. I try to muster up some anger to see if I can juggle Pillow, but my eyes are droopy, Summers is snoring ever so faintly, and it's hard to feel much of anything.

I wake again much later than usual, because I forgot to tell the alarm clock to set itself back correctly. I crack my eyes to see Pear standing over me, eating toast.

"Fuck off," I groan, because I hate crumbs in the bed.

"You do realise you're late, Dilly my sweet?" There's a gleam in their eyes. It gives them some sick satisfaction when I'm not punctual, because I'm usually the responsible and sensible one. There's a definite Gilmore Girls vibe that we have going on. What it means when I'm up late is that Pear gets to make obscure jokes about deer hitting me, while I ignore them and run around the house swearing. Except this time, they intercept me before I get out the door.

"Is everything still going okay at school?" Their face is intent and serious.

"It's fine." It's not, but what is saying anything else going to do? There's nothing that can be done to fix it. I've endured it this long, and I can probably last the rest of school. Then maybe things will get better? Fuck, I don't know. I'll worry about that later.

"Are you sure?" They really want it to be better, which I get.

"Yes, I'm sure." I trot down the steps and onto the path, tossing a backwards wave over my shoulder.

I'm halfway to school when I get a Snapchat message from Lou to tell me he's sick and won't be at school today. This is fairly common. He doesn't always want to be out in the world. Add to this his parents are…problematic. They try intermittently, but it's super clear to me that they don't really believe he's who he is. It makes me so mad I could smother them with Pillow, but I've promised him not to get all up in their faces about it.

So rather than ranting, I text him back smooch emojis and tell him he's wonderful. They go unread—he's probably sleeping again, or playing some dumb game on his PS4.

I get to school with a bit of time to spare and this urge to find Alyse. It's super awkward, but I want to talk to her about mutants. We've both got powers, which has to mean something. It takes me a few minutes to scrape up the courage. Back when Pear first got worried about my social anxiety or whatever the fuck the counsellor called it, they made me learn these fucking air-quote strategies for interacting with others, but I can't remember a thing.

I eventually find her sitting out by the field with a couple of blonde girls I vaguely recognise.

"Dylan Taylor," Alyse says, in this kind of flirty way that throws me off. She's looking extra pretty again today.

"Hi." I'm suddenly aware of how weirdly I stand compared to normal people. My limbs hang off me like they're badly fitting clothing. I try shifting my weight but that's even weirder. Why do people have to communicate in reality? Gifs or gtfo.

"You're the one who's dating the girl-boy," one of the blondes says, looking up at me through long lashes and stretching her legs out like she's posing for something.

"He's a fucking boy," I snap.

Alyse reaches out and shoves her. "Katie, Jesus. That's rude." For a moment there's this red tinge to her eyes, and her mouth looks blood red and fangy. It's gone in a blink. She gets to her feet and links her arm through mine.

"Thanks for yesterday." She's standing very close and I feel awkward and I don't know how to extricate myself, but I let her tow me off to a safe distance where we can't be overheard. "I mean I know I shouted at you, but what you did for me? In the bathroom? That was very cool."

The inside of my mind is smooth and blank and free of conversation options. "It's, uh, it's, uh, it's fine."

"It's been freaking me out," she says. "Like I've been waking up in the night panicking, so the fact that you were chill about it made me feel so much better. I still don't have any idea what the hell is going on, but you were like a lifesaver, you know?"

"Mutant powers." I say it with way too much intensity, but Alyse doesn't let go of me and run away screaming so I carry on. "I can kind of... sort of, well... I've got my own thing."

Her eyes are enormous orbs in her head and her jaw drops halfway down her chest. Her hair sticks out all around, like a close up anime shock face. It's only there for a moment and then it's gone. I feel a mix of excitement and fear. Her powers aren't just about her looks, they're about her moods too.

"You mean? You can...?" She's still blinking at me.

"Sort of," I say. "Different and... different." Oh very fucking eloquent Dylan, you insufferable blunder. Alyse doesn't seem to notice how embarrassing I am, or is too polite to mention it.

She grabs my arm so tightly it hurts. "That means it's not just me." There's another flash of shock face. "I'm not the only one."

"No." I don't even try to take my arm away, even though my personal space is all crumpled up. "We've both got something going on."

"We should meet up after school, away from all this." She gestures at our surroundings with her free hand. "Talk about it. Trade tips or whatever? Figure out what to do."

I frown at her. "Are you sure?"

"Why not?" She says it so easily, the words spilling out from between her lips as if these transactions are so simple they can be made on a whim.

"Okay," I say, because it's somehow easy.

"I'll meet you after school, by the bus stop out the front." Her eyes are big and brown and there are no worlds of judgement in them.

"Okay," I say again.

"Can we go to your house? My brother's friends will be at mine and they're literally disgusting and I don't want to deal with that."

I agree yet again, and Alyse squeezes my arm like we have a secret—which I guess we actually do—and turns to walk back to her friends. Her ponytail sways with each step. I tell myself I'm not watching, but I am.

After school I'm out near the bus stop for so long that I'm sure Alyse has forgotten. I'm constantly checking the time on my phone and telling myself if she's not there in *two more minutes* I'm going to leave. I'm sure everyone who walks past knows what's happening. Alyse told them all, and now they're laughing at me as I stand here like a patient dog waiting for someone who's never coming. My life is threatening to become that 'hello darkness my old friend' gif when I hear a voice.

"Omigod Dylan, I am so sorry. Ms Bartlett is like an actual dragon and I mean that in the literal sense, even though I know what literally means."

It's Alyse, who is literally sparkling, and I know what literally means. Her hair falls down her back in this glorious brown and golden waterfall. Glittering particles are springing from it, dancing on the breeze. I figure with her mood-ring powers, this means she's happy about the situation, which makes me feel weirdly *connected* with her.

"It's fine." I'm slightly dazed from the enthusiasm. "I don't have anything else to do."

So we go back to my house and we talk the whole way. Like I think I have nothing to say, but then Alyse asks me a question and I find words waiting in my mouth. I even end up talking about Pear with her.

"They gave birth to me, but they're not male *or* female, or maybe they're both. They call it choosing to reject the concept of gender. We have a joke about it, like we'll text each other some random thing." I get out my phone and scroll back through the long trail of messages between me and Pear, who is of course only in my phone as the pear emoji. "Okay, like today's gender is a fox on waterskis. Today's gender is Storm with a mohawk. Today's gender is an ice sculpture in a forest. Today's gender is the precise way Tessa Violet says yikes in 'Bad Ideas.'"

"I like it," Alyse says. "Today's gender is a coin at the bottom of a stream that's deeper than you think it is, so you miss picking it up."

"Wow," I say. "That's actually awesome."

"You can send it to your parent," she says with a grin. "I don't mind."

CHAPTER FIVE

When we get to my house, Summers goes berserk because I'm with someone new.

"He's so cute." Alyse kneels on the floor to give him attention, endearing her to both Summers and me forever. "Look at his little face. What's his name?"

"Summers, for Scott and Alex and Buffy. And Gabriel and Dawn I guess."

"Um, am I supposed to know these people?" Her hands are tangled in his curly ears.

"Cyclops and Havok." My voice is getting geekier, I can hear it. "And Buffy? The vampire slayer? None of this means anything to you, does it?"

"I've never heard of any of them." She returns her attention to the dog.

I wander into the kitchen, find a bag of Doritos, and throw them on the table.

"Wasabi flavour?" Alyse asks.

I crack the bag and she takes one and puts it gingerly into her mouth.

"These are disgusting," she says, as her mouth twists. Her face actually goes green, which I hope is powers-related and not some allergy thing.

"I know," I say, "but I can't stop eating them." I take a big handful and grimace my way through them.

Alyse laughs and takes more herself. "So tell me," she says in between crunching. "You said you can do something like me."

"Like you meaning…?"

She flaps her hands ineffectually, and her whole body becomes watery and indistinct, like she's a painted approximation of a girl. "It's not something I *do*. It's something that happens to me. I don't even want to, but here I am, all melty because I'm anxious."

"And so if you chill it goes away?" I ask, impossibly curious.

"Yeah, like what happened yesterday." Even as we talk, she's resolving back into default Alyse. "You made me feel better and it fixed itself." She narrows her eyes at me. "Are you stalling to avoid talking about you?"

Oh fuck. I've never had to *demonstrate* my power before.

"I can talk to things," I tell her solemnly. I get out my alarm clock and my Bluetooth speaker and I ask them to turn on and do stuff. They obey, but it's not exactly impressive.

Alyse watches me, looking both confused and earnest, like she's really trying to understand.

"So you're something like Siri?" she asks.

I need to show her something better, but I'm way too stressed. My school bag is on the table and I fiddle awkwardly with the strap of it. Tempus is ticking on the wall like a fucking loudmouth. I remember what happened with the marker at school when I was angry, so I start shouting. I obviously haven't had enough embarrassment for one day. "Listen, all you stupid things. Why can't one of you *move*?"

There's utter silence in the house. Alyse looks at me and it's super uncomfortable. I scrape my seat back from the table, and I'm on the verge of fleeing the room. The sun streams in through the window, lighting my face. I'm sweating. Did I put deodorant on this morning?

I take a breath, and the porcelain cat wobbles through from my bedroom, flying through the air in a fast arc.

"Hey," I squawk to it, but it glides over my head and crashes into the wall. It hits hard enough to break, tumbling to the ground in three misshapen pieces.

"Help," it mews pitifully. "Help. Hurts."

I fall to my knees and try to pick it up. "You poor sweet thing," I say, arranging it on the table.

"Ouch. Hurts. So much. Dying."

"I need some glue," I say desperately. "It's really badly hurt."

Alyse is looking at me like I've lost my mind completely.

"It's talking to me," I explain as patiently as I can, because its cries are hard to ignore. "I need to fix it."

I scramble into the kitchen and fumble through our many drawers of junk until I find some glue. I'm too frantic over the cat to worry about what Alyse thinks, but she ends up helping me reassemble the poor thing while it whimpers and sobs. Finally we have it back together and it's very grateful.

"Best Dylan," it says. "Love you, Dylan."

"So that's my lame power," I say awkwardly, as I pat the cat with my fingertips. "I talk to objects and they talk back and sometimes they move around for me."

"It's a bit weird," Alyse says.

"No shit," I say, which isn't funny, but for some reason we're both laughing and can't stop. Once we calm down, we decide to walk to the shops for chips. I ask the front door to lock itself, showing off, and Alyse is all cartoonishly wide-eyed when it does. I feel almost proud of my stupid ability. I also feel like I'm pulling off this other incredible act—I'm talking to someone normal and cool, and I'm not fucking it up.

At the end of our street is a main road. We go hurtling across through a gap in the traffic, and then wander through the park. There are kids kicking a ball around, and two dogs chasing each other in a massive circle while their owners shout ineffectively. All these normal people and we go wandering through, two teenagers with superpowers.

"So how long have you been able to do all that stuff?" She glances sidelong at me.

I pretend to count days, but I know exactly when. "Nine days ago," I tell her. "The day after—"

"Emma Hall's party," she blurts. "It was the same with me."

We stop at the edge of the grass and stare at each other.

"It would be fucking crazy if everyone at the party got superpowers." My brain sprints in circles, but my words are slow. I never go to parties, but Pear made me this time because apparently it would do me good to socialise. "Almost all of Year Twelve was there. I don't think the school would still be standing if we *all* got powers."

"I didn't do much interesting at the party," Alyse says. "Except I kissed Emma Hall. She had this pretty dating app called—"

"FlirtDeck!" I shout. "I kissed her too. I was avoiding people but she found me and showed me my name in the app and then uh—"

There had definitely been some tongue involved, like a surprising amount given she hadn't been drinking anything. I hadn't said this part to Lou, but it had been a pretty good kiss.

We start walking again, cutting through the alleyway that leads down to the main road. It's graffitied with a complex array of overlapping tags. I see something that looks like it says 'new mutants,' but on second glance it says 'new stunts.'

"What else happened at the party?" I ask. "I didn't drink the punch or anything because Pear made me promise to only drink what I brought with me. I kept finding places to hide and sucked at Super Smash Bros. The only interesting thing was kissing Emma."

"I didn't drink the punch or play video games," Alyse says thoughtfully.

"So the common denominator is—"

"Wait, so we think everyone who kissed Emma got a superpower?" Alyse asks me.

I frown. "How does that even work?" It literally makes no sense. Kissing a very pretty Kiwi-Chinese girl at a party is the new radioactive spider bite? What, like her saliva is some kind of mutagenic agent? I mean in comics I would get it because you can handwave literally anything, but surely irl there's chemistry and shit that has to work? I pause outside a cycle shop where some old dude is trying out an e-bike. He almost runs into me and grunts something about phones. I ignore him and look on the App Store, but I can't find anything called FlirtDeck. All the results for flirt are just random dating apps.

"It's crazy," I say. "Maybe we need to talk to Emma."

"And say what?"

"Find out if she kissed anyone else. Find out if those people have superpowers."

"This is really fucking bizarre though." Alyse reaches out and touches my hand, like she wants to check I'm real. Her face is pale and faded, uncertainty making her partly see-through. Nobody else around seems to pay any attention. "All of this is—like me being able to change, and whatever it is that you can do. It's all—"

"I grew up on this," I tell her. "Like I heard X-Men stories the way other kids did fairy tales. But yeah, when it comes to *real life*—"

Alyse laughs. Her fragile self is gone and she's back to normal. "But you're *into* this freaky shit though, right? You were saying something weird about someone called Mystique and demons and I don't know what." Something that looks like mockery sparks in her eyes.

I abruptly want to go home, and for her to go home, and for this to be all over. This was stupid.

"Whatever," I say. "I better go." I turn and start walking away.

"Hey! Dylan!" There are fast footsteps on the concrete and Alyse tugs on my arm.

"What? What do you want?"

"Hey." Her voice is soft. "It's okay. Chill out, dude. I'm freaked out. If I said something dumb, I'm sorry. It's been cool hanging out. I don't understand." She gestures at the world. "Any of this. I'm glad it's not only me."

It's impossible to sort out all the emotions churning in my head, like a million things shouting at me at once. I really want her acceptance to be true, so I just nod.

"Cool." I can't see a sneer on her face anymore. "And we'll talk to Emma tomorrow about the whole kissing thing."

"Okay." I seem to say okay a lot when Alyse is around.

She links her arm through mine again. We buy chips and then walk down to the bus stop, passing the packet back and forth and eating them out of the paper. I give her the very barest overview of the X-Men, and she deliberately gets everyone's name wrong. *Sideclomps* makes me laugh so much, I inhale a chip and have a coughing fit on the side of the road.

While I'm recovering, a car pulls up across from us and the window winds slowly down.

"I thought I taught you to loiter more surreptitiously." It's Pear, in sunglasses and a baseball cap like they're on a stakeout. "What are you up to?"

"Just talking." I'm suddenly an incandescent flame of awkwardness, because two worlds of mine are colliding.

Alyse bounds across the road like a puppy to shake Pear's hand through the car window.

"I'm Alyse," she beams. "I know Dylan from school."

I slouch up behind her. "Yeah." I lean against the car.

"I'm Ness, Dylan's parent," Pear says, with a half-sharp look at me before turning back to Alyse. "I honestly tried to teach this one manners, but it never quite worked."

"That's because I learn more by observation." I take their sunglasses off and put them on my face instead. "Off you go, dearest parent. I'll be home for dinner."

"Yes, Dilly," Pear says, and I close my eyes briefly. I wait for the mortification of my pet name to pass, and hope that Alyse didn't notice. Pear winds up the window and drives away.

"They look badass," Alyse says. "It's hot, or at least hot-adjacent."

"Alyse, that is my parent," I say in this half-shocked voice that reminds me of Pillow.

"I said *hot-adjacent*. I like the androgynous thing. I like lots of things. Like if they were—I don't know—ten years younger…"

"They'd still be too old!" I know Pear had me young, but still.

"I'm only joking." Alyse winks at me. "Dilly."

"Shut up," I say, but I'm smiling. The bus comes along, and I feel this pang. Once this afternoon is over,

I'll be back on the other side of the divide between me and everybody else.

"I had fun," Alyse says. "Thanks for hanging out."

She beams at me and her face is radiant, like angels we have heard on fucking high, and I'm stunned into immobility by it. She gives me a wave of her fingers and bounds up the stairs into the bus.

I watch her go. Somehow I ended up having this wholeass conversation with Alyse and I didn't fuck it up? That can't be right. I try and recall everything I said, to find the bit I did wrong. There's always something. Every friend I ever had as a kid, I did something stupid and wrecked it somehow. It's inevitable I said something that pissed Alyse off, but why can't I *remember* it? God, I'm so fucking pathetic. So desperate and lonely I have to cling to a single conversation as proof of my validity.

I drag myself back home and find Pear banging around in the kitchen.

"What do you want for dinner?" They look tired. I walk into the kitchen and lean against them slightly. Pear's not big on touch, so this is how we do things.

"Don't ask me, because I'll choose pizza."

"Surely we can do better than that." Pear opens and shuts cupboards as if they're magical and a new food option will appear. "Vegetarian nachos?"

I nod, and grab a big X-Men volume from the bookshelf. I page through it idly at the kitchen island. Almost any X-Man's power would be better than mine, even if I had to wear Cyclops' stupid red glasses. It would be hard to have mind reading or mind control powers without ending up a jerk, but I *would* like metal manipulation because a) Magneto was right and b) Toph Beifong, motherfuckers.

"So that's your friend?" Pear asks, interrupting my musing.

"Who? Alyse? Not sure she's a friend. She was hanging out."

"She's new. I haven't met her before, have I?" They say it as if I have a whole host of friends out there hiding from them. It probably makes them feel better to think of me that way, as if I'm not some fundamentally broken thing. "She seems nice. Friendly."

"Yeah," I say, because it's the least amount of words I can possibly use.

"I'm glad to see you with someone else." They frown. "Not that I don't like seeing you with Lou. It's just—it's good to have more people in your life. Isn't it?"

I nod, and look back down at the book. I don't want to talk about this. It's embarrassing being pitied by your own parent.

CHAPTER SIX

Lou is off school again the next day, although we do have a text conversation where he promises he's fine and looking after himself. He's not always good at self-care but nagging him makes *some* difference. He snaps me a photo of his breakfast, so I snap him back one of me doing a kissy face.

Alyse is loitering alone around the main school entrance. When she sees me, she pushes herself off from the wall and zooms over. For a moment, I'm worried she'll walk straight past me, but she stops in front of me with a smile.

"Finally," she says. "I've been waiting. There's no sign of Emma."

I have this super intense urge to be like 'let's go train together and team up and develop our powers and become this awesome paramilitary combat unit,' but I wire my jaw shut. I manage to say nothing embarrassing, and we wander the school grounds looking for Emma. I'm pretty sure I was only invited to her birthday as part of a whole 'everyone can come' type deal, and I don't really know her at all. I'm intimidated by her, tbh, because she's like wicked smart.

We do find her friend Dani Kim who's an even higher-achieving version of Emma. She has major ice queen vibes and is kind of scary. If I was going to be nasty, I'd say she's Azula from *Avatar the Last Airbender* except her firepower is verbal, and hopefully she's less deadly.

"Do you know where Emma is?" Alyse asks, beaming her sunshine smile directly onto Dani who is perfect permafrost snooty and barely reacts.

"Not here."

"Am I supposed to guess every possible location until you tell me?" Alyse is still smiling.

Dani shifts her gaze to me, and I resist the temptation to hide behind Alyse. It's like having a weapon trained on you.

"Did anything weird happen at Emma's party?" I ask in a rush.

Dani lets out a frozen exhale and looks back at Alyse. "She's been off school sick, since Tuesday. She posted to Instagram today, so I doubt she's at death's door." Her lip curls ever so slightly. On a less amazing face it might be a sneer, but she looks like a hot fairytale queen surveying her unimpressive subjects. "Are you happy now, Alyse?"

"It was only a question." Alyse's mood isn't dampened at all. "Normal human interaction."

"Well then I'm so glad I could help a normal human." She looks at me and raises her eyebrow this tiny fraction that's deadly as an anime swordsman. "And you, Dylan."

And before I can even process this or splutter some embarrassing and incoherent response, she stalks off, looking perfect and flawless and oh please Dani, nobody's impressed.

"She," I say, but I can't think of the words that come next. Like even if I could talk to other people, I wouldn't be capable of engaging in any form of conversation with Dani.

"I had a crush on her for a second," Alyse says, with this faint laugh. "But I'm not ready for dating on hard mode."

I find this insight into Alyse fascinating, but I have no idea how to progress the conversation without being rude, so I let it fall. I imagine the only sorts of people Dani Kim would date would be supervillains or extremely fashionable vampires.

"What do we do next?" Alyse asks. "If Emma's not at school."

"I think we have to go to her house," I say. "This isn't something we can do online. We'll probably have to show her what we can do, you know, to prove it." I get that there's a risk with this, but Emma seems chill and besides, there are two of us with superpowers and I don't believe in coincidence. Blame my upbringing with comics.

After school we catch the bus to Emma's house. Alyse has a car but she doesn't technically know how to drive it, and she's not allowed in it when her parents are away. The bus is jammed full of kids from all different schools in some complicated territorial relationship. Our unexpected presence disturbs the balance of power. We get a lot of attention—mostly them calling our school Slutside Girls because teenagers have not evolved since, I don't know, whenever people started being assholes to each other. We mostly ignore them, but Alyse starts changing into something ominous with black eyes and little fangs. I make her stare out the window so nobody can tell, and she puts her noise-cancelling headphones in to block the chatter out.

It leaves me at the mercy of them, which I'm used to. I stare at the dirty floor of the bus and let it all wash over me. If you ignore people long enough, they usually get bored. Underneath the banter, I can hear the bus burbling to itself. It sounds all deep and thoughtful, but whatever it's saying is to the tune of the kids' song about the wheels on the bus. Objects are weird af. Was it always awake or did I wake it up? Are there other people like me, waking up objects all around? More practically, I wonder if I could ask it to open its doors and hurl a couple of the most obnoxious douchebags out onto the road. It's very tempting, but probably too far along the supervillain axis. I bet Magneto would do it. When we reach our stop, the kids all press themselves against the window as the bus pulls away. I give them the finger with both hands.

Emma's house is big and fancy, with a peaked gable that has a massive round window. There are no cars parked outside. The whole street is quiet.

"Fuck it," I say, because I am class personified. I walk up and press the doorbell. We can hear it bonging around inside the house. There's no answer. We stand there and wait, like we're selling something. I press it again, and then try the door, but it's locked.

"I guess she's not here?" I frown.

"Dani said she was."

I make this tiny scornful sound. "Dani doesn't know everything."

"We just leave then, I guess," Alyse says.

We both stare at the door, as if willing it to open. I poke the doorbell again.

"She's inside," the door tells me, as if it's embarrassed. "But she can't hear you because of the things on her ears."

"Emma?"

"I think so? Not the youngest one, but the other small one."

"Well, I'm Dylan. We're good friends of Emma's. We've been here before. Don't you want to let us in?" I run my fingers over the lock. "Please." My voice is husky. I'm grossing myself out, to be honest. "I just want to be inside." Ew, Dylan.

The lock makes a clunk sound and the door swings open with a really faint creak.

"Dylan, did you just flirt your way through a door?" Alyse sounds shocked.

I can't hold back a grin. I don't know if this counts as breaking and entering, but now we're standing inside Emma's house. I don't recognise it at all. Last time I was here, it was full of people. There's a big entrance-way with a door to a massive kitchen. To the left, a wide wooden staircase goes up. An enormous painting—a landscape rendered in scrapes of red and black—is on the wall. It looks like real fancy art, not just the reproduction shit you buy at the mall. On the right, there's a room with an enormous TV. On the couch in front of it, sitting cross-legged with a keyboard balanced in her lap, is Emma. She's wearing a puffy jacket and leggings. Her face is intent. There's all this weird writing on the screen. Some coding stuff, I assume.

"Hello?" I take another step inside and wave.

She must see us out of her peripheral vision, because she gives this massive twitch, and spins around to face us. She pulls her bulky over-ear headphones down and they tangle in her long black hair. Her look of surprise is almost as extreme as Alyse's wide-eyed gape. One hand goes to her chest, as if she's trying to feel her heart rate.

"Dylan? Alyse?" Emma's voice is croaky. "What are you—? Wasn't the door locked?"

"Um, no?" I lie, on reflex. "We heard you were sick and came to check up on you."

"I'm not sick," she says. "There's a coding competition on and I can't do it when my parents are home because they think I waste too much time on screens and—" She breaks off. "Thanks for coming to check on me though?" There's a little frown on her face.

"Except we didn't," Alyse says firmly. "It's not true. We're here about superpowers."

If either of us expected Emma to break down and confess everything, it doesn't happen.

"I don't get it." Her forehead wrinkles. "Is this a joke?"

I have no idea what to say, so I gesture helplessly in response, as if words might come to me if I wave my arms. The awkwardness of the whole situation is gathering steam in my head, like we literally just broke into her house and are standing here like two fu—

Alyse solves the problem by transforming. Obviously she's feeling awkward too, because she shifts into a creepy broken-down thing. Cracks run along the surface of her skin, and one of her arms hangs by a thread. It looks like she's been disassembled and put back together wrong, rickety parts that don't quite connect.

Emma screams and shifts halfway up the back of the couch. The keyboard falls on the floor. Her fingers are splayed on the leather, her body tense and coiled.

"Now *you* show her," Alyse tells me intently. Great, that's fucking awesome. What are my options here?

"Door?" I ask. "Can you please open and shut a few times?"

It's still overexcited and half infatuated with me, and it eagerly bangs back and forward in a violent way that shakes half the house until I beg it to stop.

Alyse spreads her arms wide. "Superpowers," she says.

"But this—this doesn't make any sense." Emma looks at us beseechingly. "Superpowers aren't real."

"Yeah, except there's us to prove you wrong," Alyse says. "The only thing we can figure out is that it happened after we kissed you at the party."

A faint blush colours one golden cheek and Emma drops her head forward, so her hair swings down and obscures her from view.

"Okay, so I kissed both of you," she says. "But that doesn't—"

"Yeah, and the next day we got superpowers," I tell her. "Like we don't *know* if that caused it, but maybe if you kissed anyone else, we can check?"

"Well I kissed Dani, my best friend," Emma says. "Which we both knew was dumb, but she was half drunk and mad about Lina."

Alyse nods sympathetically, but I don't even know who the fuck Lina is.

"Anyway, she doesn't have any powers," Emma insists. "She would have told me. I kissed Bianca Powell too. And there was Lou as well," she ends in a rush.

Something twists inside me. It's not that Lou kissed Emma, because I did too. It's that he said nothing, even when I came stammering to him to confess.

"You mean Lou Patterson?"

"Yes," she says, as if she fears my wrath. "Your Lou."

Alyse's eyes are so enormous in her head it is freaking me the fuck out, because how can her body physically function that way? It at least distracts me from the 'Lou lied to you' parade that my anxiety brain is performing. I force the non-anxious part of my brain back to the problem at hand. How the hell is perfect Emma Hall creating superheroes with kisses? What created her? And how big is our sample pool?

"Where did this app even come from?" I ask.

"It was a dumb idea," Emma says. "I've never even liked anyone, let alone *been* with anyone. When people talk about so-and-so being hot I can never understand why. My Mum had been going on and on about this boy she knew and whether I wanted to go have coffee with him, but I had zero interest."

Alyse flashes me a look. We still can't see Emma's face through her hair. I have no idea where this conversation is going, but I don't want to be rude and rush her.

"I was turning seventeen, and I was worried I'd go my whole life never liking anyone? So I decided to try and kiss some people I'd heard were hot, so I made this dumb app and pretended it was a random thing."

"*You* made the app?" I ask, incredulous. It looked fancy like a real app, and it popped up my name when Emma swiped it. I kissed her, because it was her party and she was cute and the app said so. It was only a kiss. Spin the bottle kisses are like being singled out by fate, and when in my life was someone like Emma Hall going to pay me any kind of attention? And wait, does that mean she heard I was hot?

"It was so stupid," she says. "Like you can't just randomly kiss people and hope it's going to somehow be this romantic moment that will fix your dumb brain that's, I don't know? Blind to hotness or something or—"

"You're probably ace," I say, ignoring the melancholy old-movie heroine version of Alyse I'm looking at, who seems to be highly offended her kiss didn't rock Emma's world. I'd been expecting Emma to be drowning in regret, so bland seems a) predictable and b) kind of a step up for me.

Emma hooks her hair behind her ear, and stares at me like I'm speaking gibberish.

"You know, asexual," I prompt. "Like you're just not interested in sexual relationships with other people. One of my parents is like that."

"Asexual," she says, like I made the word up myself. Honestly, they need to teach this shit in school.

"Google it." Now Emma's attention is on me again. I feel awkward, but I forge ahead anyway even though I'm babbling. "There's like a bunch of different varieties. You might be biromantic like my parent or you might be aromantic which means no romantic feels or—"

She blushes and lets her hair fall back in front of her face.

"I'll Google it," she says.

"So now we have a list," I tell Alyse. "We can check out these other people." Including Lou, my apparent best friend and boyfriend, like what the fuck is going on. Beyond that, I think about what might happen if we all have superpowers. A whole group of us, like really truly X-Men, or more accurately the New Mutants and—

"Dylan," Alyse says meaningfully, and I guess I'm staring off into space. She's been talking with Emma, doing social skills stuff, and I'm rendered into an awkward sketch of a girl. No transformation required for that.

I make stumbling goodbyes and we leave Emma's. Outside, Alyse looks at me with these cartoon eyes with a little tear trembling at the corner of each one.

"I thought the kiss was good," she says.

I have this idea she wants sympathy but my brain is screaming LOU at me like an enormous bass drop. It swallows my mind whole, except a tiny part reminds me that apparently someone thinks I'm hot. Surely that part was a prank.

CHAPTER SEVEN

Alyse and I catch separate buses from Emma's. There aren't as many kids on this bus, mostly just sad commuters who ignore me and stare into their phones. I'm transfixed by my own, staring at a blank message window thinking about how to phrase a hundred variations on 'what the fuck?'

In the end I do the passive-aggressive move of

> Dylan: missing u boyfriend
> Dylan: wanna come over?

He responds in the enthusiastic affirmative. The poor boy has no fucking idea.

I get home and say practically nothing to Pear, who side-eyes me and then goes back to work on their laptop. I consider getting changed into something hot, but it's not really worth it given that I'm not sexy at the best of times. Not that Lou seems to mind. I'm no pretty-pretty girl like Emma fucking Hall, that's for sure.

Ugh, I'm not remotely mad at *Emma*. She kissed a bunch of people on her birthday trying to figure out asexuality. Okay, maybe I personally shouldn't have kissed her, but I told Lou straight away and it didn't *mean* anything. What I can't figure out is—

"Lucifer," I say, as he leans over me with a smile. I didn't even hear him come in. He strokes my hair and kisses my cheek. In any other scenario, I'd be purring like a happy little kitten. Instead, I sit very still and smile mysteriously.

"Dilly," he says, comfortable as can be, scooting onto the bed beside me. He is not picking up signals.

"So handsome," Pillow sighs. I reach behind and shove her back against the wall.

"Missed you," I whisper to Lou, and I lean in and kiss him. He moves back a little, but I open my mouth slightly and let my tongue flick over his lips. There is a plan here, which is to give him one hell of a kiss, then when he breaks it off I'll say 'so, how does that compare to Emma?'

Except I start to get lost in the kiss, especially when he starts kissing me back. His lips feel hot, like he's running a fever. When I place my palm on his cheek, I almost gasp because it's like touching the front of a car that's been running.

My eyes snap open to see why his skin is burning up, and that's when I see him glowing.

"Shit," I squawk. My arms pinwheel and I fall off the bed.

Then Pillow pipes up with "Holy fucking shit, Dylan, your boyfriend's on fire."

I may be a bad influence on her language.

Lou stares at me, horrified. He isn't glowing any more. It turned off when I broke the kiss, like flicking a switch, but there's a scorch mark on my super-fucking-cool duvet with the kittens on it.

"You fucking kissed Emma Hall," I snap. "And now you've got a superpower."

"I'm sorry about the kiss." He slides off the bed and crouches beside me. He takes my hand. It's soft and smooth and regular warm.

"Why didn't you tell me?"

"When you told me you kissed her, I went a bit crazy," he says. "Remember I went offline for the next couple of days?"

I do, but at the same time this is when I was figuring out I could talk to objects. I spent most of that weekend terrified and exhilarated, veering between thinking I was going crazy and feeling like all my dreams of superheroics had come true.

"Sure." I'm still giving him the cold vibes. "I thought you were sick."

"I was upset. You kissed Emma. She's so pretty and I was really mad about it. But it was like I couldn't be mad because I kissed her too. Except I *was* mad, so it seemed easier not to say anything."

I put my face in my hands. Save me from people who think too much.

"You should've told me, Lou." Meaning his god-damn superpower as well, but we've both been keeping *that* secret.

"I know," he whispers. "I'm terrible. I'm the worst boyfriend." He pulls this shit sometimes and it's quite honestly a dick move that I fall for way too often. Except today, beyond all of this stupid 'who kissed Emma' bull-shit, there's a way more major issue.

"No." I don't kiss him, I don't touch him. "You just did a dumb thing. Both of us do dumb things. Like maybe I should've said no to Emma when she asked to kiss me. So I'm sorry for that too, because I should've known it would make you squirrelly."

He takes this big shuddery breath like he's on the verge of tears.

"Let's talk about your superpower instead," I say. "What the fuck is up with that?"

"It's not a *superpower*," he says. "It can't be. Super-powers aren't real. None of this can be real."

"Okay sure." I manage to only half-roll my eyes. "Then can we talk about this totally-not-a-superpower where you glow? Because it's obviously real, whether you like it or not."

He coughs and blushes and stammers. "It started the day after the party. I was in the shower and I was thinking about you and Emma and all this *stuff* and I started to get—"

"Oh shit, you glow and heat up when you're turned on." I start giggling like I'm borderline psychotic. God knows what the poor boy thinks, but it's too disastrous for words. I fight my gurgles to a standstill. "That's why you've been avoiding—"

"If I kissed you properly, I knew it would happen," he says miserably. "But today you were being extra sexy and I thought maybe I could keep it locked down."

It's a tiny bit flattering and still hilarious, but I focus my efforts into what I call scientific experimentation. I straddle Lou, and I kiss him all slow and delicate.

"Dylan Jean Taylor," Pillow says in horrified school-marmish tones. "What do you think you're doing with that boy? You are not that sort of girl!" Um, pretty obviously wrong, Pillow.

His eyes tremble closed, but I keep mine open. I watch in awe as his face suffuses with orange, like one of those old heaters warming up. I put my hands on his cheeks and kiss him harder. Within seconds I have to pull my hands away. I topple backwards off his lap, with zero grace.

"Let's call it a superpower because we don't have a better word." I'm dizzy with it all. "You're a hot glowing boy. And I have something to tell you too."

I feel all the objects in my room reaching out to me. They want to show off what we can do together. I don't have any rage in me, but right now I don't need it. They all slowly levitate off the bed and desk and floor, rotating around me like I'm the centre of their universe. Pillow floats down gently and lands in my lap.

Lou stares. "The whiteboard marker," he says.

"Yeah," I admit. "It looks like the people who kissed Emma got—let's call them *abilities*. Alyse can change her appearance with her mood."

"Alyse?" He gets that little frowny forehead thing going, because he knows exactly who Alyse is, and his brain is putting together the fact that I must have been talking to her to know this and—

"Lou. This is a *big fucking deal*. I'm talking about us all having mutant abilities, not unnecessary jealous bullshit. Can we please for five seconds talk about the fact that we are superheroes?"

"It's not a superhero thing," he says angrily. "It's a sickness thing. I don't want to turn into a torch whenever I get horny. Does Ness know?"

"No," I stare at him in shock. "And you are *not* telling them. They'll—look, I know they're obsessed with the X-Men even more than I am, but—Lou, just don't."

"It's a nightmare," he says. "It really is."

This is not how I wanted this conversation to go. I want to make him understand how potentially cool this is, so we can be excited together. I understand it's a lot to take in, especially when Lou has other dramas.

I grab my phone and text Alyse, who says she's fine to come over. Maybe *she* can convince Lou. He sits on the floor, looking at his knees and picking at the carpet. We sit there for ages, because I've learned there are times to wait together rather than letting all my restless little thoughts off the leash. I can see his nails are bitten all the way down. I want to kiss them, because it's all I can think of to make this better. He's like Wolfsbane in New Mutants, who thinks her power comes from the devil. Except I'm dumb with people and I can't convince him of anything.

"I didn't ask for this." A tear leaks from the corner of his eye.

I move so I'm sitting beside him, shoulder to shoulder. "I know. Everything's different and weird but at least we're together, right? We're a team?"

The thing with Lou and me is the team thing came easy. The two most unpopular kids in the school who bumped into each other accidentally and didn't un-bump. Nobody really likes us, and I've always said that's fine because we don't like other people right back.

Any response Lou might have given is interrupted by a tap at the door. It's Pear who is a) checking that I'm not defiling Lou and b) offering to pick up extra Doritos or chocolate from the supermarket. This time I ask for a sensible Doritos flavour that non-trash humans consume.

When they leave the house, Alyse is on the doorstep ready to knock and Pear ushers her in with their eyebrows spelling out 'ooh, friend' at me. I roll my eyes and shoo them away.

"Hi, Lou," Alyse says with a big smile.

Lou grunts in response. He's hardly over the moon to see Alyse. You'd think he had ice powers. It's so awkward I want to throw up, so instead I get on with the powers demonstration right there in my crappy lounge.

"Right," I say. "Alyse, show us what you can do."

She stands there and blinks at me.

"Like the other day," I prompt. "You were feeling down about how you looked and—"

Her body shifts, like it's being animated from one form to another. The Alyse in front of us looks years older, her cheeks pouching into jowls, her body sagging, eyes sullen. Then she takes a deep breath and forces a smile. There's another shift, and it's Alyse but ever so much more so. Everything is cleaner and brighter and perfectly arranged. An airbrushed, teen-show version of a person. She's almost *too* perfect, and there's this moment where both Lou and I are leaning in slightly towards her. Then she breathes out again and it's regular Alyse.

"Wow," Lou says, which is something of an understatement imo.

"What about when you're pissed off?" I ask. "Today I thought I saw—"

She makes a growling sound, and for the tiniest moment there's a monstrous version of her with claws and teeth and a fiery glow in her eyes. But then she laughs and ruins the illusion.

"I don't get mad much," she says, with this casual shoulder lift. "So what power do you have, Lou?"

Lou stares at me and scowls, like any of this is my fault.

"Just do it once and then she knows." I take Lou by the hand and pull him in for a kiss. He closes his eyes obediently and we start kissing. It's nice but he's not exactly glowing, so I take his hand and put it on my boob. God, Dylan, you slut, I think, and I don't even believe in sluts. What is this, the 90s? It's super effective in that he glows like one of those movie set lights, blindingly bright and hot.

A pulse of energy runs through his hand and I fly backwards into the wall. I'm not even sure my feet touch the ground. I bang my head really hard. Above me, Tempus says something sharp that I can't make out but I'm sure is disapproving. I put my hand to the back of my head and feel the tender spot.

The light pouring from Lou's face goes out abruptly. He looks like he might cry.

I catch my breath and look down. My school blouse has burned away and my bra is singed and smoking. I clap my hand over it and go running into the bedroom. The door slams behind me.

Not only is this the literal most embarrassing thing that's ever happened, but I have to explain this to Pear who will not be happy, not least because school blouses are expensive.

I rummage around on the floor, and pull my No-Face hoodie on and put the hood up.

"I'm sorry." Lou's voice is muffled through the door. "I didn't know this would happen."

"It's not your fault," I shout back. "It's mine. It was dumb."

When I crack the door, both Lou and Alyse are standing there looking awkward.

"I'm fine," I insist. "Obviously Lou's superpower is sponsored by purity rings."

Everyone laughs, but we're all on edge. Even *I'm* scared. For a moment at least, until it's swallowed up by excitement again. These are real mutant powers. I have somehow stumbled into an X-Men comic and it is fucking *wild*.

"I thought I was going crazy," Lou says in a hoarse voice. "I don't know if I feel better or worse now that you can do it too."

"Better," Alyse says. "Way better. Like a million times better."

"But I don't get how Emma gave people superpowers." He blinks at me like a sweet baby owl gif. "Did she do it on purpose?"

I shake my head. "She's freaked out too. We're all freaked out. It's an actual fact we can't ignore, though. Which means we need to figure out—"

"We don't need to do *anything*," Lou says sharply. "It's too much and I need to go home."

"Okay," I say, the meekest little thing. "That's fine."

We say goodbye on the porch. It's awkward because he doesn't want to kiss me again in case he sends me flying into the wall. He peers through the front window to where Alyse is sitting on the couch, but he doesn't say anything.

"Crazy shit," Alyse says, when I shut the door quietly behind me. "Like seriously, the weirdest."

The actual weirdest is having Alyse in my house, sitting on my couch, as if it's normal. I've literally never had another friend here—aside from Lou—since I was really small. Except here's Alyse, and Summers is curled up with his head on her feet and she looks so comfortable. That sense of ease seems like a way better superpower than anything else I can think of.

For the rest of the evening, Alyse and I sit on the couch in my crappy house, and watch all the Lemongrab episodes of *Adventure Time*. His brand of incoherent rage and desperate search for belonging resonate with me in a way that's almost disturbing. Alyse figures out her powers can stretch to making a giant lemony head and she keeps shrieking "One million years dungeon!" I laugh so much that Pillow and my Bluetooth speaker come bobbing through from my room to check I'm not going to die of it.

Later that night, after Alyse leaves, I finally slump into bed. I roll onto my back and hear Pillow groan. This difficulty around not making out with Lou might become a problem. It's not quite a Rogue level disaster, where he could kill me with a kiss, but he could maybe burn me up. What happens when he, you know—? Will he explode like a rocket?

I roll over and grab my phone. I text him a gif of Finn and Flame Princess from *Adventure Time*.

He sends back a string of question marks and then I see the three bubbles before I get the coffee spit-take gif.

I grin up at the ceiling because he gets it, or at least he can joke about it for a second. It feels nice to be understood and at least now there are three of us. I slide out of bed and go over to the window. With my forehead against the chilly glass, I look out into the silent street. I'm a mutant, hiding in plain sight. How many others are out there?

There's an X-Men book called New Mutants about a team of teenage superheroes who are all misfits but end up brought together by their powers. I've read it so many times the book fell apart. Being part of a group of people somewhere between friends and family is something I used to dream of, but it always seemed even less realistic than the mutant powers. In this half-awake time it seems that I'm perched on the edge of it, except it's a void that I can't bring any tangible shape to. A failure of imagination. I can't imagine having a group of friends like that.

I look out into the night, but nothing is there, so I shuffle back to bed.

CHAPTER EIGHT

The next day, I don't feel on the verge of anything. Alyse and Emma have been texting, and apparently Emma doesn't want to talk to Dani about superpowers. She wants us to do it instead. We're talking about a girl who scares her own best friend, and they've picked the world's biggest blunder to speak. We're meeting at the mall, and we're going to ambush Dani. It'll be a disaster.

The mall is crowded like always on Saturdays. Lou and I wait by the bubble tea stall. I'm the tallest, so I'm on tiptoes trying to see over the crowd.

"We should move," Lou says.

"Why?" I can't see any sign of them. I consider climbing up on one of the stools, but the lady in the stall will yell at me.

"It feels racist to pick the bubble tea stand," he says.

"Why would it be racist?" I ask irritably.

"Because bubble tea is Asian and they're Asian."

"Dani's Korean and Emma's half-Chinese." I scowl at him, because now I think he is being racist. "They're completely different. Do you even know where bubble tea is from?"

He grunts. The thing with the bubble tea place is that it's right in the middle of the mall so it makes a good vantage point.

I finally catch sight of Emma and Dani, and Emma waves. I'm edgy because Alyse isn't here to be the bridge between us.

"Ugh, I'm freaking out. Shall we bail?" I ask Lou.

"I didn't want to be here in the first place," he says, which doesn't help.

"Fuck," I say, and some parent walking past glares at me. I'm still trying to decide what to do when Emma turns up right in front of me.

"Hey, Dylan. Hi, Lou." She has a really pretty smile, and it's weird to think that all of us standing here have kissed her. I'm so fucking close to saying this, because I'm an *asshole* but I manage to just say hi instead.

"Hi." Dani does the eyebrow thing again and it's devastating.

I look at the ground and mumble a greeting, while Lou looks at his phone. Such mutants we are.

Emma and Dani are wearing ripped jeans that look artful and expensive, unlike mine which look like Wolverine tried to put them on with his claws out. Their tops have logos I don't recognise. Maybe clothing labels or something? Emma's is fitted, but Dani's is loose and cropped. It slides off one shoulder and reveals a couple of inches of her stomach, showing off a delicate blue pendant hanging from her bellybutton. They both look accidentally glamorous. I kick at the floor in my scuffed shoes and pull my hands up inside the sleeves of Pear's old Sunnydale High hoodie.

"Where's Alyse?" Emma asks.

"She's supposed to be here." I'm honestly a few seconds from fleeing the building, but the others line up for bubble tea and finally Alyse shows up. She hugs everyone except Lou, who's still looking at his phone. Everyone gets bubble tea, except Dani and I get coffee. Then we wander down to find a table. We're surrounded by families who are focused on keeping toddlers quiet and pay no attention to us.

Everyone drinks and looks at me, including Dani who has a smirk sketched on her face. I wrap my fingers around the coffee cup and look at the fern pattern on top.

"Did Emma tell you anything?" I risk a glance up at her.

"She said you were cool," Dani says, although it sounds like she doesn't believe it. She's so fucking suave.

"So then what's your superpower?" Witness me, a blunt instrument. "Your magical ability. The thing you've been able to do ever since Emma kissed you at her party."

This cracks the perfect facade. Dani twitches so hard she knocks over the dregs of Emma's bubble tea. Alyse mops it up as it seeps across the table.

"I don't know what you mean," Dani says, but there's a shift in her tone. She's a normal girl instead of an ice queen, which makes the whole thing unconvincing.

"So it seems like Emma gave us all superpowers," I say. "We don't understand how, but we've got them anyway. Alyse can sort of shapeshift. Lou can do light and heat, under the right circumstances."

"And what about you?" Dani asks me, eyes on mine.

"I talk to objects." I shrug, because I feel like it makes me look badass. Nobody around the table, including my boyfriend, seems the remotest bit impressed. "So either you're a dud," I say, "or you're hiding something."

It feels like we're fencing, and there's the tiniest crack of a smile like I caused a hit. Everyone at the table knows Dani Kim isn't a dud. But she really doesn't like the idea of being a dud, and I know it, and she knows I know it. She rocks on her seat and regards me.

"I can move things with my mind," Dani says, and Emma's mouth drops open.

"Oh my gosh! Why didn't you *say* anything?" Emma shoves her half-playfully.

Except Dani's chair is tipped up and the push nearly overbalances her. She grabs onto the table but still falls sideways, knocking her head against Alyse's. The bubble tea cup skids off the table and across the food court. I feel a strong breeze wash over me.

Both Dani and Alyse are swearing under their breath and rubbing their heads. Alyse has tears in her eyes, but thankfully isn't transforming.

Dani looks furious at everything. "I didn't say anything because this is none of anyone's business," she snaps.

"*You* can move objects," Alyse says to me.

My eyes are fixed on Dani. "No, I ask things to move and they do it if they feel like it or I'm pissed off enough. Dani can move anything, right?"

She makes this little frustrated hiss sound that's kind of cute actually, even though it's clear she's way over me and my questions.

"You're Marvel Girl before she had telepathy," I say. "Unless you've got that too."

She shakes her head. "If I did have telepathy, I'd stop you asking stupid questions." Her lips tighten into a cyborg's smile and her glare sharpens. I drop my gaze awkwardly and see her hands laced in front of her. There's a cluster of bruises around her knuckles.

"The cup moved when you banged into Alyse," I say. "It only works when you're hurt."

Dani has no smile now. "And how is this any of your business, Cyclops?"

I flush bright red at that, because Cyclops is X-Men code for having a stick up your ass. I resist the temptation to pull my hood up and shrink away from her.

"We just thought—" I begin, but my voice dies. "It seemed like a good idea... We're all going through something and—"

"You thought we'd all get together and learn to control our powers." The edge in her voice makes me flinch. All the words dry up in my mouth. Of course Dani wouldn't want to associate with me. It was stupid to come here. Emma should have fucking warned me, but she's too nice.

"I'm—"

"Whatever. This is beyond ridiculous." Dani transfers her attention away. "Emma, you should focus on what you can control, like school. This superpowers thing—whatever it's caused by—it's a freak occurrence and a distraction. It'll mess everything up."

My eyes keep coming back to her hands, lying on the smooth formica surface of the table. "You say that, but you've got all these bruises. You've been practising. Trying to figure out the extent of your powers or whatever."

"Or whatever," she snaps. "Whatever this aberration is, I'm done talking. Emma, let's go."

My heart gallops in my chest. "Fine. Enjoy your mutant powers, Dani."

I get up from the table and start walking away, with Lou and Alyse following. A chair slides out into my path, and I stumble over it. I try to right myself and slip. When I reach out, I grab hold of some poor kid's tray of McDonald's and send it flying to the floor along with me. My head thumps on the dirty floor. I've got tears in my eyes, from the bang on the head and embarrassment and anger. I get to my feet. Everyone is looking at me. Lots of them are laughing. A couple of people look concerned.

I feel useless, humiliation burning a hole in my gut. Even more than that, what I want to do is bounce Dani Kim's smug head off the table. I whirl around, reaching out in my head for any objects that are close enough to listen. I'll show *her* telekinesis. But both Emma and Dani are gone, and the table where we sat is empty.

"Fuck," I hiss, nearly under my breath. A stack of empty trays cascades into a great clattering pile on the floor.

The kid's crying because I've knocked his Happy Meal on the ground. I stammer an apology and Lou drops a crumpled ten dollar bill onto the table, which is weird because who carries cash anymore? He probably stole it from his Mum.

Lou is checking my leg and my head, while Alyse is apologising to the family.

"Wow, Dani Kim," Alyse says, once we've navigated our way out of the chaos of the food court. "What a bitch."

There's a lot I want to say, but I'll probably angry-cry if I open my mouth.

"Let's forget her." Alyse slings an arm around my neck and one around Lou's. He lasts about three seconds before slithering away and glares at me until I do the same. Alyse is unbothered by any of this. "Let's do something fun, like buy superhero costumes!"

I love that she thinks of this detail, even though most costuming decisions in the history of comics are questionable at best. Except then she ruins it by heading to one of the trendy clothing stores.

"They won't have masks there." I'm wandering in the direction of the dollar store instead.

"I'll be doing freaky-face so I won't need a mask." She stands at a shop window, looking at some black playsuit thing.

"You'll need a mask for when you're not freaky-face," I say.

She's still looking at the window display. In the end, I cave and accompany Alyse into the store while Lou waits outside. Alyse ends up buying a playsuit that's very flattering and very expensive.

"It's less inappropriate than most of what Emma Frost wears," I say with a laugh, and search up proof for her.

"I can buy you one if you want," Alyse tells me, which makes me seize up.

"It's two hundred and fifty dollars," I say in a scandalised voice.

"Don't worry about it." She thrusts the shopping bag into my hand and starts skimming her hands up and down the rack. "What size are you?"

The idea of Alyse spending that much money on me makes me uncomfortable. 'We don't accept charity' is a big thing in our house. I don't know how to explain this, so I go flying out of the store with Alyse trailing after me.

"Dylan, it's fine. It was only an offer! I don't mind either way."

"You've seen my house," I say furiously. "Does it look like I've ever bought anything that expensive? And it will look terrible on me because I don't have—" I wave my hand ineffectually at Alyse, and take off even faster, weaving through the crowds.

When we do get to the dollar store, Alyse doesn't mention playsuits, and she's happy to look through the costume rack with me. There aren't a lot of options, especially if I want a full face mask.

I end up with, I shit you not, a Spider-Man knock-off costume that dodges copyright laws or whatever by being neon purple and green and saying "SPIDER HERO" on it. It is possibly the most embarrassing thing in the store but by this point I've decided to lean into it. I'm not going to look cool, so I may as well look spectacularly lame.

Even Alyse's general positivity struggles to encompass it.

"You'd look good in anything, Dylan," she says with impressive loyalty. She buys one of those little half-face masquerade masks with ornate decorations around it. At least she'll look glamorous for the five seconds before she turns into a slavering monster. Honestly, all my dreams are dying in front of me right now. We are even below the levels of early Kitty Pryde costumes.

Lou has found a No-Face mask. *Spirited Away* is our favourite movie so it's sweet and romantic, but then he pairs it with overalls from some old 80s movie about ghosts.

This is the problem with having your dreams come true. Reality is inevitably a terrible disappointment. We're a lame band doing X-Men covers on YouTube, without having read the comics, who only have three subscribers who are all related to us. But still, the fact that I've been shopping for superhero costumes at all is a noteworthy accomplishment in the entirely uninteresting life of Dylan Taylor.

We head out of the mall to the street outside, where we drift in the direction of Krispy Kreme only to find a queue. My craving for donuts and hatred of queues are locked in a titanic struggle, but donuts win the day. We go to line up but there's a commotion from down the street. Some idiot is shouting. I ignore it because the mall is a fucking breeding ground for assholes, but then I hear a scream.

I step out of line and turn my head. I get a shock to see Dani backed up against the window of a bookstore. Some stocky white guy shouts something at her about China and viruses. I'm instantly furious. I don't care about the shit she did in the mall with the chair.

"—inbred conservative fuck," Dani says.

The guy reaches out and shoves her, and she sprawls on the ground. Something liquid slips inside my chest. I walk towards them, not even thinking about whether it's stupid or brave. I'm just mad, like, fuck this guy on so many levels.

"Hey!" I'm shouting like someone that isn't me. "You fuck off and leave her alone."

Dani's on her hands and knees on the ground. Her hair is hanging down and I can't see her face, but I do see her punch the concrete. A sign advertising gelato that's hanging overhead swings down out of its frame, and cracks the guy hard across the shoulder. He staggers, nearly falls, and looks up with a scowl.

I try and talk to the sign, but there's not even the faintest flicker of awareness.

The guy rubs his shoulder. He says something to Dani that I can't hear, and spits on the ground.

"Tell me what to do." The voice comes from a metal bin nearby. It's half full, mostly food wrapping and bottles.

"Get this asshole," I tell it. The bin leaps out of its frame and throws itself over the guy's head. It must hit him hard, because he gives this terrified yelp. I look around for something to hit the bin with, to ring the fucking thing like a bell, except Dani punches the ground again. The bin flies off, dragging the guy with it. He ricochets off a lamp post with a hollow bang and falls down in the street. The traffic's moving slow, but this asshole in a yellow car makes a big production with his horn and then leaps out of his car.

I help Dani up to her feet. She's trembling. Emma's on her other side, pale and quiet.

The shouting guy fights his way out of the bin. He pushes past the yellow car asshole, and storms back towards us.

Alyse intercepts him. "We told you to *fuck off*." Her face is twisted and contorted. Face to face with a monster, he veers off and runs away down the road. I think his head is bleeding, and I feel this savage punch of gladness in my gut.

Other people come up now that the guy's gone, asking if we want to call the cops. Lou reappears. I have no idea where he was hiding, but he stammers something incoherent. The group of us looks around, and then we all start running, like we're the ones who did something wrong. It's only a few blocks before we all pull up panting.

My hands are shaking and I shove them in my pockets, but Dani holds one of hers out. It's sticky with blood and shaking violently.

"Intense," she says, and gives me this half smile. It's not exactly an apology for the shitty thing she did with the chair, but it feels like it.

"Fucking crazy." My voice is croaky like a cartoon character.

"Maybe you're right," she says. "About doing something with our abilities. We just need to be sensible and organised, like properly disciplined."

"Sure." I feel like my smile's so wide it hurts. "It makes sense."

I think she's smiling too, but I can't see it because of the hair swaying in front of her face. Dani freaking Kim is joining the mutants. We could actually be a real gang. It's achievement unlocked in some way I can't even fathom. Hopefully I don't fuck it up.

I'll probably fuck it up.

CHAPTER NINE

There's only one person left on the list of Emma's kisses, and that's Bianca Powell. It's a weird choice, in the same way I was. Who the fuck gave Emma the idea that either of us is hot? At least Bianca is striking. She's six foot tall and pale as an English girl from an old movie. She constantly breaks the school rules with black lipstick and wearing purple eyeshadow in these massive smoky wings. First thing in the morning, she's usually vaping among the trees on the edge of school. I follow the trail of scented smoke and find her leaning against a low stone wall.

She doesn't say anything when she sees me, just exhales another cloud. I'm sure she recognises me, because she and Lou know each other from queer club. I never go, because you have to talk in front of a group.

"Hi," I say. "I'm Dylan."

"I'm aware." It's hard to see her face through the smoke.

There's another pause. I wish I had one of the fancy superpowers that was obvious to demonstrate.

"You kissed Emma Hall at her party," I try.

"So?"

"Everyone else who did wound up being able to do weird shit, like light up or change shape or move things with their mind."

"Wow, super exciting." she says in this fake drawled American accent. "I love that journey for them."

I can feel my cheeks heating up, because I know she's making fun of me, but I can't understand why. Alyse should have done this, not me.

"So you don't have any new abilities or anything like that?" I persist.

Bianca shoves the vape pen in the pocket of her uniform and beckons me closer with one finger. I shuffle forward. Her fingers fumble with the collar of her uniform that she's painstakingly inked with a pattern of shapes that look like some mystical language.

"Um," I say.

At the top of her blouse there's a triangle of pale flesh with a smattering of freckles, poorly concealed with makeup. Her fingers scrabble at her skin and then sink in. She spreads them wide, revealing an odd, shadowy hole inside her chest, full of darkness that shifts and shimmers.

"What the fuck?" I breathe, leaning forward.

A shape materialises from the darkness, a pointed face made of mixed shadows and light. Its mouth yawns wide, revealing something orange flickering inside.

"You don't see me," it hisses.

For a second, the sun dims. The world glitches and comes back extra bright, like a music video. I blink and look around myself. It feels as if I've just woken up. I have no idea where Bianca is, but she's usually here at this time of the morning. There's the faint strawberry scent of vape smoke in the air. I must have just missed her.

I sigh and wander off towards the looming building of the school, keeping my head down to try and avoid any stray looks or words.

Second period is English, and I have it with Emma. She makes an immediate beeline for me. "What you did on Saturday was really cool," she whispers. "Stepping in to help Dani."

"The guy was an asshole and deserved it."

"Yeah, but you still did it." She smiles at me and I feel goofy-stupid, like I suddenly have people who like me. What fresh not-hell is this? Emma slips into the seat beside me and leans in close. Her hair smells amazing.

I search for a metaphor, but all I can think of is really expensive conditioner. This is why I'm such a whiz in English class.

"Couldn't find Bianca this morning," I tell her. "We'll have to look after school."

She shrugs, as if all that's unimportant. "I googled the other thing." Her voice is so faint I can barely hear it. "I think I might be demisexual but haven't found the right person yet." She looks at me, as if I'm the sexuality guru who understands everything. Which is ridiculous, because I don't even know what I'm into aside from Lou.

"Sexuality is complicated," I settle for whispering back. "And fluid. It changes. But it helps to know that you're normal, I think."

She nods, and beams at me. I'm glad for her, but I don't feel remotely normal.

"Oh," she says. "Dani also apologised for the thing with the chair."

I find this hard to believe. "Did she actually say the words 'I'm sorry'?"

"I think she's freaked out about her powers, and that's why she was so rude. Her exact words were 'I shouldn't have done it.' And then she said just because you're emo-hot doesn't mean you get to be so bossy."

"Bossy? Me? Compared to her?" I feel like I'm spluttering. "And what the fuck does emo-hot mean?"

She shrugs. "I'm ace, remember?" Her flash of smile gets lost behind her hair. I find myself staring at my phone, flipping through Snapchat filters, trying to figure out what the fuck emo-hot means right up until the point the teacher confiscates it.

Turns out, it's very hard to concentrate on school when you've got something important going on in your life. There's a reason why teen detectives and vampire slayers have very little screen time set in class. It's beyond tedious. My mind keeps drifting and it's lucky that the teachers don't really care, because I couldn't answer a single question.

Class finally takes a break, and Lou and I manage to find each other. The halls are crowded and we're pressed up against the wall.

"I don't like this," he says to me.

"Don't like what?" We're close enough that our arms touch.

"This powers thing. Abilities, mutants, super stuff, whatever. It's weird and it scares me and—"

"It's an adjustment." I turn my head to look at him.

"But I don't *want* to adjust to it, Dylan. That thing at the mall with you and Dani? It was terrifying. I'm terrified. Don't you want to stop it?"

I clench my teeth really hard until it hurts.

"No, I really *don't* want to stop it." I'm finally special, finally something *other*.

"It's dangerous," Lou says.

I completely ignore him, and so he tries again.

"You don't need this to make you special. You were already special."

"Lou, this is what I've always wanted. Not just the superpowers, but like... being part of the New Mutants, you know." I have so many *feelings* about these stories that they make a painful knot in my throat. All these weird kids coming together to be *part* of something, to be connected and— "Lou, I've talked to you about those dumb kids a thousand times and—"

"I don't need any more problems in my life," he says, his voice sharp. "I have enough trouble. I want to pretend this isn't happening, not add your stupid superhero shit to it."

Ouch. That one hurts. I tip my head back against the wall, except it's more of a slam and it brings tears to my eyes. It makes me furious, because now Lou will think he made me cry and maybe he fucking did, but I don't want him to know that.

I swallow hard around a lump in my throat.

With an enormous crash, the hand dryer from the first floor bathroom comes flying in through the window—entirely under its own steam—and lands in a shower of glass in front of me.

"Dylan," it shouts in this drill-sergeant voice that nobody else can hear. "Who has hurt you and how shall I avenge you, my love?"

I was an asshole to this poor hand dryer, and here it is coming to my defence. I feel like the literal worst person. Everyone else in the corridor stands around in shock. There's glass everywhere, and one girl has a cut on her leg.

"What the fuck?" Some girl sounds like she's hyperventilating. "How did that happen?"

It's a miracle more people weren't hurt. The hand dryer is lying in front of me, humming violently. I can feel its hot breath on my ankles.

Lou looks at me in horror. Other eyes are trained on me too.

I hear a cackle of laughter. I hear my name.

It's all too much, so I swing my bag up to my shoulder and run down the corridor. It's fine having superpowers, but I need to learn to control them. I need my green and purple Spider Hero mask. I need to be *anonymous*.

When I get to the main school entrance, it's still crowded, so I keep going out of the school and down the road. I don't exactly *intend* to go all the way home, but that's where I end up. I'm on the front step, my stomach churning. I know the school might let Pear know I'm absent, so I text them.

Dylan: if school calls, im home sick

The phone rings moments later, as I'm letting myself into the house.

"I'm fine," I say, by way of greeting. "It's a headache."

"Are you sure?" Stupid parent radar. "Nothing happened at school?"

"What would happen at school?" I snap, no doubt proving it.

"Dilly," they say, and then there's a massive pause, a whole gulf of disappointment and frustration and not knowing what to do with their useless daughter.

"I'm fine," I say again. "I'll see you after school."

I hang up and clench my phone so tight it hurts.

"You're lying," Tempus says.

"No shit." I lie down on the couch and put my hands over my face. Maybe I *should* be cured of this stupid power. "Just leave me alone. It's not the time for this shit."

"All this will pass," he tries again. "Time is the wisest counsellor of all."

I laugh. "Time also kills all things," I say. "You mass murderer."

"Rude," Tempus says snippily.

"Tell me the time then," I say, which is mean and I feel guilty immediately, because he starts stammering away. He knows this is his reason for being, but honestly has no clue and is figuring it out from context.

"Is it three?"

"It's one twenty-eight," I tell him. "So you're in the ballpark."

"You're home from school early," he says sullenly.

"Yes, I'm a terrible girl." I bat my eyelashes at him.

"No, you're not at all," he sighs. "You use dreadfully offensive language, but you're quite delightful with it."

When it gets to the time school ends, I change into jeans and a hoodie and head back down. Finding Bianca is still important. Maybe she's not interested, but I have to try. There's a growing possibility these will be my New Mutants. It's very fucking on-brand for me that I can only make friends via some terrible cosmic accident that everyone else is mad about. Maybe one day we'll be a team and can look back on this and laugh.

I find Bianca where I expected to this morning, sitting at the edge of school amongst the trees that runs down along the main road. She's cross legged on the ground, smoke eddying around her head.

"Hi," I say, leaning against a tree near her. "I'm Dylan."

"You can see me now!" She waves one hand in a big arc.

I feel hopelessly lost. "Uh, yeah? I mean, you're sitting right there?"

"You already saw me today and don't remember."

I'm about to explain that of course I didn't see her and then I catch up to the obvious fact. Superpowers.

"You're like ForgetMeNot, real and unreal at the same time?" I frown. "As soon as I'm not looking at you, I forget about you? No, because I remembered you and came to find you and—"

"I have no fucking idea what you're talking about. Just stop babbling and watch." She slips her fingers into her chest and delicately pries it open, revealing a strange void inside her. Three flickering figures of shadow and light crawl out gently, one after the other. They stand in a line, their heads tilting this way and that.

Then they catch sight of me and start scurrying across the leafy ground, moving horror-movie fast.

"Enough," Bianca says, and lets the hole in her chest snap closed. The creatures are sucked back in almost instantly. "You said this morning something about new abilities. I showed you them and they told you not to see me and—"

"I have no memory of it at all," I say quietly. "That's crazy."

"Ya think?" She bugs her eyes at me. "I woke up the night after Emma's party with this awful itch, and when I scratched it these fucking things came out. I assumed I'd finally lost it in some catastrophic way, more than the usual fucking crazy Bianca shit. You know what I'm talking about."

"Know what?" I blink at her.

"Yeah, like you're one of the normies." She laughs. "Anyway, if you're saying I'm not the only one who can do weird shit, that's cool. There are levels to being a freak and I didn't need any more. It's nice to know I'm not the only weirdo, just like faggot club."

"Faggot club," I say faintly.

"Yeah." She snorts. "I'm allowed to say it. Reclaim that shit, bitch. You can say it too."

"I don't—" I flail for words. I don't feel part of any club that's allowed to say anything. "If you're interested in the um, the powers thing. We'll be meeting tomorrow to get to know each other, if you want to join."

"That's what I'm saying. I need my freaks." She waves one hand at me. "Help me up."

I take an awkward step forward and pull her to her feet.

"It's spooky," she says quietly. "I'm glad I'm not alone." Then she puts her vape pen to her lips and envelops me in a sickly cloud of smoke.

CHAPTER TEN

The next day passes so fast it's like one of those shitty star wipe video transitions. The next minute, Alyse is letting me into her giant house, which predictably is a lot fancier than mine. There are three living areas and four toilets. It's only her and her older brother at home. He's playing some shooting game on the Play-Station and completely ignores us.

Alyse gets carrots and celery and hummus from their massive futuristic fridge, puts them on this square white platter, and carries it through into one of the lounges. I pause in the doorway because most of their furniture is white and I feel like I'll dirty it by sitting on it.

"You don't need to be invited in," Alyse says. Here in her home she's more faded, almost see-through in the sunlight spilling in through the massive floor-to-ceiling windows. She puts the platter on a coffee table made of some fancy wood that's been polished to a gleaming shine.

I edge my way into the room. There's a big book-shelf on the wall, filled with carved wooden ornaments and books. One whole section is devoted to books by Iosefa and Tania Sefo. They're all on things to do with parenting and children.

"Your parents?" I ask.

She makes a non-committal noise. "What does your Pear do?"

"Something in like computer security?" I run my fingers along the spines of the books. I don't think they've ever been opened. "We don't exactly talk about their job much, but they help companies with data and stuff?"

"The Sefos do very important work," the coffee table says. "Their insights are phenomenal."

"The table there's a big fan of your parents," I tell Alyse. "It says their insights are—"

"Phenomenal." She grimaces. "I've heard that before. Everyone tells me I must be so lucky to be raised by two geniuses."

"She is extraordinarily fortunate," the table says in thrilled tones. "A truly blessed child."

"Your coffee table is a fucking sycophant." I grin at Alyse. "Want to see what else in the house can talk?"

The ice-maker in the fridge is cool and stand-offish, and the couch is sleepy and dull. The bookcase in the hallway is obnoxiously pompous and full of itself, as well as yet more works by Alyse's parents.

"It's different versions of the same book." She scowls at them. "Nobody ever reads them."

I slide one book out and look at the picture on the back. They're a good looking couple, which makes sense given Alyse and how genetics work.

"Do books talk?" She shoves the book back in with unnecessary force.

"Not that I've ever heard, but I'm still figuring this shit out. They'd probably just read themselves out loud."

We end up in her room, which is amazingly messy, with more clothes than I've owned in my entire life thrown everywhere.

"Floordrobe." Alyse shuffles a path through with her feet. "Still the best organisational system for clothes." She stops in front of the mirror and plucks a single errant strand from her eyebrows. How she can tell they needed it, I have no idea.

"Isn't she beautiful?" The mirror sighs. "I look at her every day and think she's the loveliest girl. Kind, too. Always thinking of others."

"She is kind." I reach out and stroke the outer edge of the mirror with my fingertips. "The mirror here is a big fan of yours." Then I frown. "So you've been aware of her this whole time?"

"It's strange," the mirror says. "Everything up until now has been a dream and in your glow I have finally awoken. I only wish I could speak with Alyse like I can with you."

I lean forward and huff breath onto the mirror, clouding a patch of it. "Try that."

There's a brief pause, and writing begins to appear. It moves fast and I almost pass out making sure there are enough breathy-clouds on the surface to fit it in.

Hello, Alyse. It's so lovely to finally speak with you. You're a brave and beautiful young woman and I'm so proud of how you take care of yourself when your parents aren't around and—

"It's watching me this whole time?" Alyse starts to fade away again, almost invisible.

"I mean sort of, but it likes you. Objects tend to bond pretty hard with their people."

"How can I stare into it every day knowing that it's like, I don't know, it's—"

"Telling you you're awesome and beautiful." I grin. "Shit, I don't know. It sounds tough."

"It's a bit disturbing." She frowns at the mirror.

"Oh gosh, I've ruined everything, haven't I?" The mirror sounds mournful. "I only wanted to say hello."

The doorbell rings and Alyse seizes the opportunity to flee. By the time I finish up with the mirror and get back to the kitchen, everyone else has arrived. Alyse is introducing people, and I pause in the doorway, feeling awkward. It's only when Lou comes to stand beside me that I'm ready to take tentative steps into the room.

"And this is Dylan," Alyse says enthusiastically, even though everyone already knows me.

My eyes dart from face to face. Emma, Alyse, Bianca, Dani. They all look at me expectantly.

"Mutants," I say. "That's, uh, what we are. And we all have, like, powers?" My voice is fading and getting squeakier at the same time, which is just—fucking shoot me now, someone. Everyone looks embarrassed for me. "And I know it's freaky and scary. Powers shouldn't be real. All of this is out of a movie. Except it's actually happening and so—" I flail helplessly.

"Why don't we go around the room and show what we can do?" Alyse says, which is a better rescue than a bullet to the head, but only a temporary measure. I remember I'm the only one that's seen everyone's powers, so this is a good idea.

Alyse starts off by doing her wizened to beautiful transformation.

Dani bends her fingers back enough to make her wince, which sends a glass skidding across the countertop. It stops before it would fall off and shatter. She gives this tiny bow.

Lou lights up a little with exactly zero encouragement from me. I wonder what he's thinking about.

Bianca pries her chest open and the monster-things come stalking out. It freaks me out just as much to see it again. This time they only peer around before retreating. I wonder if they work in response to her commands or urges, and what happens if they stay out for longer. Even Dani is left wide-eyed by this and Lou's practically hiding behind me. Alyse is the only one who has the presence of mind to pat Bianca on the arm gently to reassure her.

We all stand in this loose circle, looking around at each other awkwardly. The fact we all have superpowers is an impossibility, but it's also a) obviously true and b) something we share. So we move past it elegantly as a group, as if it's one small plot twist in our lives rather than a massive cliffhanger.

We don't talk about Emma, and how we got our powers, and nobody asks any awkward questions even though my tongue burns with the need to demand answers. Not talking about Emma unfortunately means it's my turn to demonstrate my ability. I have no idea what to do, so I look at the floor.

Alyse starts talking about the mirror and the cat that broke, and Lou talks over her about the marker in class.

"You hear voices?" Bianca asks. "Like—voices that aren't there? Isn't that—you know?"

I'm flustered, but I march outside and grab the lock from Lou's bike. I close it firmly and place it on the kitchen counter.

"Okay, Locky," I say. "Here we go. You want to be open. Closed blocks you off from experiencing life. You're stopping yourself from being all you can be."

Painful seconds tick by. People shuffle awkwardly. I have sweat in my fucking eyes.

Finally, the lock writhes on the table, scattering chips everywhere. Everyone stares at me open-mouthed.

"That's it," I say encouragingly. "Spin those tumblers. You know the code. The magic word to unlock yourself. Won't it feel amazing once you're free?"

The five tumblers of the lock spin as one, clicking rapidly around and settling into new positions. The lock springs apart, stretching itself out into one long, straight line.

There's a few seconds of silence and everybody cheers, which makes me flush again but not in the usual awkward way. Alyse pours drinks for everyone into glass tumblers that look expensive. I don't even know what the drink is, but I'm exhilarated so I swallow along with everyone else.

Alyse raises her glass. "To—" Her eyes meet mine. "To the mutants."

"To the mutants," everyone echoes, even Dani. We all clink glasses in this tangle of chimes. My heart thumps painfully. I'm standing in this room of people—in this room of *mutants*—and everyone seems happy to be here.

The room gets a lot louder and more boisterous after that. Everyone moves through into one of the lounges.

"You should not be in this room when your parents are out," the sycophant coffee table shouts. "This room is set aside for the Sefo parents to entertain guests, not for the offspring to participate in—"

"Shut up, you smug table," I say, more loudly than I intended. "Fuck off out of here."

"I shall do no such thing, you uncouth brat!" It actually slides across the floor towards me and bangs into my shins. I haven't encountered this from an object before. Usually they love me, which is a nice change from people.

"Ouch, you boring, beige asshole." I flop backwards into a chair and kick out at it with my sock-feet.

Then the coffee table slides all the way across the floor and out the doors, which shut behind it with a bang. I gape at the closed doors, like how the fuck did I do that? Dani is in my peripheral vision, shaking her hand as if it stings.

"You?" I ask.

She flops down on the couch beside me. "Me. You might be able to do fancy detail work like fiddle with lock tumblers, but you can't do big stuff like get rid of that table." She sucks on one of her knuckles, her dark red lips pursed around it. "Except now my hand hurts."

"I don't *do* anything," I insist. My face is close to hers. Her eyes are ridiculously pretty but I can only look at one at a time. "I just ask the lock and it does it. Like—like—" I look around the room for something to demonstrate with, except everything is rotating very, very slowly and I can't find anything helpful. There's a lamp on the side table, but it's sitting there like an inanimate object.

"Nice try, asshole," I sneer at it. "You're not fooling anyone, you douche."

It carries on ignoring me.

"Hold on a second, Dani," I say. "I just need to—"

"Dylan." Lou crashes down on the other side of me, except he ends up mostly in my lap. He kisses me hard until his cheeks pulse orange. We both slide to the floor and by the time we extricate ourselves from each other due to overheating, Dani is gone.

The doors to the lounge are open and the coffee table is muttering to itself in the kitchen.

I get to my feet.

"We should have a competition. Dani! A telekinestris—no, telekinsomething. Fuck. The word. There's a word. Telekineptic?"

Alcohol performs its own star wipe. I don't know if I'm drunk exactly, but things are definitely hazy. Time skids forward. I can't precisely remember the order of events, but I think I may have been shouting about certain X-Men stories.

Now somehow Lou is gone, and I'm standing in a bathroom. It's like a hotel bathroom grew up into a glamorous supermodel. It's vast and clean and everything shines. I'm defiling its beauty being in here, like you'd have to be a nine to even use it. I check my phone and somehow two hours have passed. It makes me shiver and my reflection shivers in sympathetic response.

"If you're going to tell me how I look," I say to the mirror sternly, "you better lie to me."

"I don't need to lie," the mirror says primly. "You're a remarkably attractive girl."

I press my fingertips to its cool surface. "There you go," I whisper. "Very convincing."

It takes a few false starts to navigate my way back down the hallway but I stop near the kitchen when I hear voices.

"I think it's cool," Alyse says.

"She's very intense." I stop dead when I hear Dani.

"Who, Dylan? Yeah, I mean she seems scary at first but like—I think underneath it all she's baby."

"Her power is so weird. I totally don't get it," Dani says.

"Not as weird as Bianca's power. Those creepy things living inside her?"

Dani laughs. "Bianca's is at least poetic. She's manifested her inner demons. It's so incredibly high school, but you can see a metaphor to it."

"Oh god, Dan, please don't start talking about metaphors," Alyse says. I hear the fridge open and close.

"No, but listen. You're someone who wants to get along with everyone. You're a social chameleon, whose personality changes based on who you're around. Your power reflects that."

"Wow." There's a click and hiss as a can pops open. "Should I be offended?"

"No, why? Look at *my* power," Dani says. "I'm a control freak, so I can control things. Except I'm wound so tight it only comes out when I hurt myself."

"Okay, whatever. What I'm hearing is that our powers suck."

"Unimportant. If we follow the metaphor train, then Dylan's power is a manifestation of her avoiding contact with anyone."

"She talks to me," Alyse points out.

"As of five seconds ago when she got superpowers. It's not like I care that Dylan shows no interest in—" There's a pause. "Whatever, my *point* is she's so closed off from people that her powers make objects speak to her as, like, recompense."

"It's sad." Alyse sighs.

"No need to get emo. Like I said, I totally don't care about any of this. It's just interesting is all and—"

Tears sting my eyes. I'm not going to fucking cry over this dumb shit. I can barely breathe with my throat so tight. Something bangs down the hallway, and an answering thump comes from another room. Every *aware* object in the house can feel the tornado of rage and humiliation inside me.

"Well, it makes me feel depressed rather than interested," Alyse says. "Dylan is—"

I don't want to hear what she thinks Dylan is, and I definitely don't want to hear whatever further fucking horrible judgements Dani might have. I need to escape, but the only way out is through the kitchen. I shove my headphones in and walk, stumbling through in a direct line for the exit.

"Dylan," Alyse calls faintly after me. "Shit, fuck. Dylan, wait."

I storm down Alyse's driveway, moving so fast I almost trip. I only vaguely know the direction of home, but I want to put as much distance between me and the others as possible. I hate that I'm crying. I pull my hood up and wish I had my stupid green and purple mask to hide behind. Why am I even mad? Nothing they said was wrong, but it hurts to be pitied. To know you're something less. A mutant among mutants.

I round the corner onto a street I don't recognise. There are houses on one side and a little block of shops up ahead on the other. There's a sign outside one promising chips and burgers, which is honestly what I need after Alyse's fucking hummus. There's someone in a hoodie crouched in front, like they're tying their shoelaces.

I'm heading for the shop when I hear the rumbling, like a massive truck driving past. I've been through enough to recognise another earthquake. It's a pretty intense one and I stumble towards the bus stop near me and cling to the pole. My heart races. I close my eyes and hang on until it stops and my heart returns to something like normal. Whatever residual alcohol feeling was in my system has been stripped out by the adrenaline.

When I open my eyes again, I see the person in the hoodie racing across the road in front of me. They've got a box in their hand, and they leap a fence and disappear from view. A few seconds later I hear the screech of tyres.

People appear at the end of driveways, clustering in little groups and discussing the shake. I detach myself from the bus stop and walk unsteadily down the street. The burgers and chips sign has fallen over, but I don't feel like eating anymore.

There's a car parts store at the far end of the row of shops. The whole front of it is split open from the quake, and a line goes zig-zagging through the car park until it ends in front of me. Where it stops, there are these two messed up holes in the ground. It looks awfully familiar, just like—

I crouch down and place my hands in the two holes. They're too small, but the lines go splintering out from what would be eight fingers and two thumbs.

"Holy fucking goddamn shit," I say.

I get to my feet and the world seems to be as shaky as if the quake hadn't stopped.

There's another mutant out there. One we don't know about. Someone that can cause earthquakes, like the one that happened on my street a few days ago. Someone else kissed Emma, or got powers another way. I remember the person crouched down on the street. Not tying their shoelaces—making the earth move.

"Fuck," I say, and start running towards home. This time I have the brains to use maps to figure out where to go.

By the time I get back, I'm exhausted and my mind is racing far faster than my feet.

I get a shock to see Alyse sitting at the bottom of my steps, looking monochrome and tearstained.

"Dylan," she says. "Where have you been? That conversation with Dani, it was—"

"None of that matters." I dump my bag onto the path. "There's another mutant out there."

CHAPTER ELEVEN

In the morning, I wake to a headache and a string of texts from Lou.

> Lou: sorry for ditching at the party
>
> Lou: you were in a really intense conversation about xmen with bianca and emma
>
> Lou: you didn't even notice when I said goodbye
>
> so

I sigh and try to smother my phone as if it will erase the messages from existence. I only vaguely recall the conversation he's talking about, but I'm pretty sure it was a one-way rant. Nobody's going to want to talk to me ever again. I think about what Dani said, smirking about how I don't talk to people. She is exactly the fucking reason why I don't *want* to talk to people. I should have known she thought she was better than me. Fucking ugh.

The larger problem is that we need to talk to Emma and find out about quake boy. I meet Alyse near school, and we loiter around the drop-off area. We catch Emma nearly the moment she steps out of her shiny silver car. She's with her younger sister, who's practically a clone of her but with hair in a bob rather than falling halfway down her back. The sister goes off with barely a backwards glance, and Emma swings into line with us.

Alyse looks at me, and I look back. We have to do this.

"So we found out that there's another mutant out there," I say. "They've got earthquake powers."

Emma's face falls. I mean, you read that all the time in books, but this is spooky, like bright sunshine swallowed by dark clouds. It's almost as drastic as one of Alyse's transformations. Alyse notices it too, and given that she's much better at this human-to-human stuff than me, she steps up beside Emma and puts an arm around her.

"Did something happen at the party?" It's like she has a secondary mutation of telepathy. In the X-Men, whenever they want to beef up someone's power set or straight up retcon shit, they'll get a secondary mutation. I haven't noticed anything in myself, but that doesn't mean it's not happening to someone else.

Except Emma starts crying, and my train of thought is instantly derailed. We hustle her over to one of the benches, out of the way of most of the other girls, and we stand around her like a little shield in some unspoken code thing, so people can't see she's upset.

"There was a guy," she says. "At the party."

I feel this guilty swoosh in my stomach, because I've always talked with Pear about this, how you look out for each other in these situations. I catch Alyse's eye and there are storm clouds gathering in them.

"He surprised me," Emma says, whispery-soft. "I went upstairs to check if people were anywhere they shouldn't be, and he followed me up. I didn't even invite him."

I make a croaking sound that's meant to be somewhere between a question and sympathy.

"He said he heard I kissed Bianca. I guess she was talking about it. He said it was his turn for a kiss too. I said no, but he pushed me against the wall and did it anyway."

It's lucky nobody is paying attention, because Alyse has shifted into something monstrous with glowing red eyes and upper and lower fangs, her face gaunt and stretched. I'm so furious, clenching my hands into fists, that some cars in the parking lot notice. They start calling out to me and sounding their alarms.

Nobody's watching Emma except us.

"Nothing happened, like nothing terrible." Her words come out in a rush. "He kissed me and he touched me and I pushed his hand away. He touched me again and it hurt and then some people came out of one of the bathrooms. That's when he walked away as if nothing happened."

Alyse tries to master her transformation and fails, so I sit down beside Emma. The cars are still screaming. One of the streetlights down the road explodes with a sharp pop. It's lucky there's nothing else that can sense me in the proximity.

"It's not your fault." My voice is hoarse.

"I know." I can't see her face through her hair.

"Did you report it?" I ask.

"There's nothing to report." Her voice is kinda flat. "I didn't want to talk about it. That's why I didn't tell you, because I hoped it would go away."

"You should still report it, you know, just in case—" I say awkwardly.

"I wanted it over." Her eyes meet mine.

"Sorry." My anger collapses in on itself. I'm the worst. I should be banned from speaking to other humans. Except there are still more questions to ask and I'm too insufferable to keep my fucking mouth shut, so ask them anyway. "I know this sucks and is the last possible thing you want to do, but can you tell us what he looks like?"

Alyse is mostly looking normal, so she sits down beside Emma too.

"It's fine," Emma says. "I'm fine. If this—this guy— is doing bad stuff, then we need to stop him. He was white and had really short blonde hair. His t-shirt had a band name on it. My Chemical Romance. I remember it, even though I kept closing my eyes and hoping it would stop."

A whole bunch of cars open and shut their doors with a massive slam. There are screams. People are starting to freak out. I need to stop being so angry, but I can't. I want the superpower to go back in time and save Emma. I'd throw this asshole down the stairs and break his neck.

I try to find some calm somewhere, lost in the sea of my rage. I hold my breath and count, and the cars begin to settle.

Emma starts worrying about being late to class and finding Dani. She makes Alyse check about twenty times that her face looks fine. I'm very aware that none of our superpowers can make this any better, and I wish I had something more to offer.

At the first morning break, Alyse and I start polling the Year Twelves on who the douchebag in the MCR shirt was. Or rather, Alyse does. I don't end up talking to anyone because they're all either deep in conversation, on their phones, or I'm not even sure if they're in our year. I don't know how to just walk up to someone and say something, so I wander back and forward and hope Alyse can do a better job than me. Five minutes later, I get a text.

> Alyse: jack firestorm
> Alyse: firestone*
> Dylan: who tf is jck fire stone?
> Alyse: ugh

I find her and Lou, and that's when I get a slightly longer description.

"He's a fucking incel," Lou says.

Alyse claims not to know what an incel is, which is ridiculous because she's exactly the sort of girl incels pine after. Lou gets the fun job of explaining it while she frowns deeper and deeper and eventually says, "But we don't owe anyone sex."

"Really?" I say, as dryly as I can, and she laughs and hits me with her bag.

It turns out I *do* know who Jack Firestone is. He's the douchebag who sits in his car and shouts abuse at Lou.

"*That* guy has fucking superpowers?" I shout, way too loud. I toggle my volume down. "How does that prick end up with earthquake powers?"

I don't know why it surprises me so much, given the way he got them. I don't even recall him being at

Emma's party, lurking around like a creep. He gate-crashed and then did *that?* I'm so angry about it all that I can barely concentrate on anything aside from revenge. The whole gang of us, standing around and beating Jack Firestone while he screams and begs forgiveness. I'm aware this is not how you fix anyone, but I don't know that I want to fix him.

I'm too angry to sit in class with assholes and listen to stupid teachers, so I head upstairs to the first floor bathroom in the hope I can hide in one of the cubicles. Except someone's beaten me to it. Two someones, who are clearly arguing, which means I should leave but I don't.

"I'm not the one who cheated." Holy shit, is that Dani?

"Except you *are* the one who was obsessed with someone else." I don't recognise the other voice at all.

"I said she was cute once. One single time."

"Yeah, sure. You brought her up a lot more than that."

"It's not like—" Dani makes a hiss of frustration. "Okay, whatever. I didn't ask you to follow me in here, so why don't you go and find someone else to feed your manipulative bullshit to."

There's a brief moment of silence and another girl storms out of the bathroom. She's short and pretty with this shock of red hair and piercings that are definitely against school rules. I'm directly in her way, and her shoulder hits mine.

"You!" She nearly spits in my face. "Get out of my fucking way."

The fact that this is an unremarkable interaction for me at school is not a good sign, but before I have time to think about that, I see Dani in the doorway, frowning at me.

"Dylan?"

"I was just trying to use the bathroom," I say, like it's an apology.

"Nobody's stopping you." She walks over to the mirror, where she takes makeup out and begins to reapply her dark red lipstick.

I follow her in and lean against the wall by the door.

"I heard about Emma," she says, looking at my reflection in the mirror. "Some asshole at the party? If I'd known, I would have thrown him down the stairs, mutant powers or not."

It makes me smile, because it's so close to what I was thinking.

"I would've done it too," she says, like she thinks my smile means something else.

"I believe you," I tell her.

She sighs and switches to mascara. "Alyse also said you overheard our conversation last night. I'm sorry. Sometimes I can't shut up and I say dumb stuff."

Wow, such apology. I swoon, except only in the sarcastic sense. I wish I was as icy as her, able to freeze everything around me, like I'm fucking Elsa. She saw me blunder out of the house, so she knows it hurt. I don't need to show that again.

"No need." My eyes skitter away from her. "Nothing you said was a lie. I don't like talking to people."

"You shouldn't feel any requirement to talk to anyone you don't want to," she says.

"That's good, because I don't."

I feel the same sensation from the mall, like we're verbally fencing, but I don't even know what we're fighting over. There's a weird expression on her reflected face, and I wish I knew what it meant. It makes me feel flushed and confused, so I push my way into the farthest cubicle from her, where I lock the door and spend the rest of class time watching music videos.

When I leave, the hallways are mostly empty. There are a few people wandering lost and alone. I keep my head down and ignore them, until I round a corner and nearly bump into two vaguely familiar blonde girls.

"Sorry," I mumble, and try to keep walking, except one of them steps into my path and this time I do run into her.

"Excuse you," she says, all exaggerated and slow. She has hold of my bag, and it yanks my shoulder as I attempt to escape.

"Let go." I don't make eye contact. I've learned not to. Some dumbass evolutionary monkey thing, I don't even know.

"Leave it alone," the other girl says. "I don't know what Alyse sees in the ugly dyke anyway. There's such a thing as too much charity."

I flash a glance up and recognise them. They're Alyse's friends. The muscle in my jaw clenches. It's not like I'm even offended by being called a dyke. It's what it says about Lou that makes me furious, like how dare they?

"Pansexual." I spit the word at them.

"You fuck kitchenware?" They both laugh, like they're the first ones in the world to make that stupid fucking joke.

"Pansexual!" There's this stool in a little alcove across from us. It wants to come to my rescue. I know it would come skidding across the floor for me and take out these girls with its metal legs, but it's honestly more trouble than it's worth. Fighting isn't going to change anyone's mind.

"Watch out for Alyse," one girl says with a wink. "She's a slut who'll try to fuck you *and* your boyfriend. And she's not even that good."

"Fuck off," I say irritably. I tug my bag out of the girl's hand and barge my way between them.

"Lock your pots up, everyone," one of them calls after me and I stick my middle finger up without turning around.

I run into Alyse on my way out of school.

"Your so-called friends suck," I say savagely.

"Which friends?" She stays calm and cool.

"I don't know. The blonde ones. The one who called Lou a girl-boy the other day. They were saying shit about you and some shit about me and why are people so fucking *awful?*"

"Her boyfriend hit on me at this party over the weekend. I said no, but she didn't believe nothing happened so then she tried to kiss me, and I said no to that too." There's a little glimmer of frost forming on her skin as she talks. "I try to be friendly with everyone, I really do but—"

"They're not worth it." If I could transform, I'd be molten and fierce.

"It's not that easy." Lines of ice trail down her cheeks, zig-zagging towards her chin.

"No." I sigh. "It really isn't."

Jack isn't in his usual spot after school. I'm not sure what I'd do to him if he was. There's a baseball bat in the garage at home that's sentient, and I'd love to watch it smack him in the face a time or two.

Lou and his bike wobble home with me, up to the point our paths diverge.

"Sorry about ditching early at the party last night," he says.

I embody the entirety of the shrug emoji in all its forms.

"I don't want to lose you." Finally we're getting down to the bottom of it. He thinks I'm going to join the powers club and I won't have room for him anymore.

"I'm right here." I watch him as he shuffles with his bike. "I don't want to go anywhere. It's powers *and* you, not instead of. I want a team with us both on it."

He nods. There's a whole minute of silence, not like I'm timing it or anything.

"I was thinking about Spider-Man." He pauses. "Is he a mutant?"

"No, Spider-Man is different," I say, but I'm smiling because it's kind of cute.

"But anyway, there's that Spider-Man thing about powers and responsibility." Oh god, he's flailing, and that's even cuter.

"With great power there must also come great responsibility." I can't not say it.

"Yeah, that one. So I get it, I think. Like in your head, you have to do this, right? Because you've got these powers and so you have to use them for good."

I have never actually thought this logical progression out in my head but he's right, which makes me stop on the side of the road. I yank him halfway off his bike and kiss him so thoroughly he almost burns my lips.

"That is exactly right," I say fiercely. "Thank you for understanding."

"So you could say I'm dating Spider-Man," he says, which makes me laugh.

"You could pick literally almost any X-Man, boyfriend. It's the most important thing that's ever happened to me." I try to say it with gravitas, because it's a fucking movie trailer moment if ever there was one. I sound like my regular dumbass self but he grins at me and I feel like we've swung back into orbit together again. It's nice. I don't want to lose my only friend in the middle of all this.

CHAPTER TWELVE

We're meeting at my house for the Jack hunt. Emma can't come because she's got family obligations, and Bianca says it sounds boring, which is fair. Dani says she'll be there, and thinking of her being in my house makes me start obsessing about what emo-hot is. I don't know why I care about what Dani thinks of me. No, I don't care. I *shouldn't* care. I still find myself putting eyeliner on, which I haven't worn since I was like fourteen, and then I straighten my hair so I can swoosh it across my forehead. I'm squinting at the mirror, trying to figure out if it looks any good, when Lou turns up.

"Do you have makeup on?" He says it in this odd voice, like he's both annoyed and laughing at me.

"Panda eyes," I shout, and charge him, batting my enormous eyes. He runs to the other end of the room. I don't even notice when Alyse and Dani turn up, because I'm too busy chasing Lou around the room pretending to be a panda. I tell you, I am a fucking catch. Dani is staring at me and I wish I had a map to her face, because I cannot figure it out. This whole eyeliner situation is her fault in the first place.

We're supposed to be stalking Jack online, but it turns out we're pretty bad at it. All we know is he's a douchebag and he hangs outside a girls' school. His Facebook page is mostly just his friends talking about where to buy weed, and his Instagram hasn't been updated in months.

"How do people find anyone?" Lou slouches on my bed beside me.

"The cops can look up anything," I say. "There's a database or something."

"This is a waste of time," Dani says. "I'm texting Emma." The only space left on the bed is beside me, and she slots herself in there as if it's entirely normal to be this close to me. Our thighs are literally touching.

"She's out for dinner." Alyse is lying on her front on the floor of my bedroom, kicking her legs and watching dance tutorial videos. Hardly research. "You need patience, Dani. You too, Dilly."

Oh God, why did Pear call me Dilly in front of her? Also, I'm the least patient person I know. I can't even wait for YouTube ads to load without throwing my phone across the bed. I'm half-zoned out, reading some Twitter thread ranking K-dramas, when I feel Lou leaning across me.

"Can you not sit so close to my girlfriend?"

"Oh, I'm so sorry," Dani says. "I didn't realise Dylan was unable to control herself around me."

I'm blushing. I know I'm blushing but how do you stop? Her face is right beside mine, and she's looking at the side of my head, so she can totally see the hot pink of my cheek.

"Just give her some space," Lou says, even though she's right at the end of the bed.

"Dylan, if you turn your face to the right, will you be overcome with desire and unable to stop from kissing me? Because I never knew you felt that way." Dani's lips are right there and if I turned my head, I actually would have my lips almost against hers. My heart is thumping. I slide myself between them and off the bed. I almost land on Alyse, who is watching with an amused look.

"Stop it," I say to Lou more than Dani, whose eyebrow arch is an unsolvable mystery.

"Boys," Dani says. "Always so obsessed with sex." She gives me her half-smile and looks back down to her phone.

Lou is giving me the dead-eye stare. I don't want to talk about it, so I sit with Alyse and keep my back to them both, while we practice all the hand movements for an Itzy dance.

Dani's phone dings a bunch.

"Ha," she says. "Clever girl is hiding in the bathroom at this restaurant. She's got Jack's address, his parents' addresses, and a bunch of shady looking earthquakes."

"What?" I perch on the edge of the bed, so I'm not remotely touching Dani. "How did she—?"

"Emma's regular-person power is computer shit," Dani says. "You know she made that FlirtDeck app, but she does all kinds of stuff. Apparently his parents live just down the road from here? At number—"

"Holy shit. Fifty-two," I say.

This gets even Lou's attention. "It was the first earthquake he did, as far as we know."

I nod. "So you get earthquake powers and the first thing you do—"

"—is fuck over your parents."

It's hard to argue with. Lou can understand it for sure. His parents deserve a quake or two.

Dani's still scrolling through her phone. "She's crunched all the raw data on these quakes and apparently there's a pattern which identifies his. He's quaked a dairy, a car parts store, a liquor store, and a house which she can't figure out—" The phone dings again. "Oh wait, Emma says it's his ex-girlfriend's house."

"What a dick," Alyse says with a sigh.

"She's figuring all this out in the bathroom at a restaurant?" I ask incredulously.

"Regular-person powers can be handy too, Mirage," Dani says, which confuses me because Mirage is one of the leaders of the New Mutants, but I can't figure out how Dani knows that. "It looks like this dude is just a dumbass robber."

"With fucking earthquake powers." I try to keep my voice steady. "Like who knows what he could do next. You're the one who said we should do this properly."

"Ugh." Dani shoves her phone into the back pocket of her jeans. "Fine then. What should we do? Get proof it's really him, right? Spy on him?"

"It's a start," I say.

"Okay, whatever, let's call it a plan." Dani slides herself off the bed and stretches.

I watch her for a second, then glance away. I have to treat it like staring at the sun.

"I need to go study or my life will fall apart even worse," she says. "We'll meet up tomorrow?"

"Sure." I think I'm playing it cool, but both Dani and Alyse are watching me with near identical little smiles that make me think I'm kidding myself. I walk to the front door to say goodbye to them, but Lou doesn't join me.

When I get back to my room, I find him slumped on the bed. His head is almost touching Pillow, who's humming in anticipation. I think Pillow has a little crush. She's so soft.

I collapse down onto the bed beside him. I know he's mad at me from the way he breathes, and I know *why* he's mad at me, but I don't want to talk about it, because it's stupid.

"Sleepy," I say, but he doesn't get the hint.

"You like Alyse, don't you?"

"I'm not into Alyse." I have no idea where this is coming from. Save me from jealous boys omg.

"What about Dani?" This is where I knew he was heading.

"What? No? What are you even talking about?"

"You think she's hot," he says.

That's an opening I can scoff at. "What, you don't think Dani Kim is hot?"

"There's something going on between you," he says.

"Jesus fucking *Christ*." I slide off the bed, pace to the wall. I can sense all the objects in the room holding their breath, like they want to weigh in on this discussion. "There's nothing going on. Even if I did like Dani, which I don't, there is no way she'd want to be with someone like me."

"I think you like girls," Lou says.

My alarm clock flies off the desk and lands on the carpet. The beanbag rustles in the corner.

"I don't want to talk about this." I rub my eyes, trying to blot out everything. "I'm attracted to *you*. This is the stupidest fight ever."

"It's not stupid to me," he says quietly.

I make the dumb mistake of looking at his eyes and they're filled with tears. I feel instantly sorry for him, like I want to make everything better. And at the exact same time I'm fucking furious, like incandescent with rage, because how the fuck do you make someone trust you? If I had telepathy, I could slam my brain into his and show him everything that makes him special.

Except he's not done. "I'm not a girl, Dilly."

I try and take a deep breath. I try to count to ten. I try to visualise a beach with water lapping over my toes.

"This is in your head, Lou," I say. "I know you're a boy."

"I listen to your words," he says, "but I keep feeling this way."

He makes it sound like some failure on my part. I can't convince him. I'm so shit at loving someone that they can't even feel it. I'm such a failure at humanity that my feelings dead-end inside me and don't connect. As an undertow to that feeling of worthlessness, there's anger too.

"Sorry I'm such a shit girlfriend." The beanbag in the corner of the room explodes, showering us with little white pellets.

"Dylan, wait," Lou says, but I'm already storming out of my bedroom.

Pear isn't there, which is good. They're probably at Sarah's, who is their platonic maybe sort of girlfriend in a relationship of mutual pining and cuddles. They're asexual and far better at any of this stuff than I can ever imagine being.

"It's bullshit," I say, to anything in the house that will listen.

Tempus rattles on the wall. His hands spin in frantic circles.

"Dilly, love, please—" He shoots off the wall like a discus and goes flying into the kitchen. There's a massive crash. "Oh dear, that hurts. Dylan, can you please stop being so *emotional?* It's hard to control myself when you're—" Another crash, this one definitely with something breaking.

I run through into the kitchen and see Tempus flailing around like a blowfly in the middle of a pile of dirty dishes. I wrestle him out and hold him to my chest.

"It's okay," I whisper. "Everything's okay."

Lou stands in the kitchen doorway. His face is pale. There are still tears on his cheeks.

"Please can you stop doubting me?" I beg. "I love you." It feels like a desperation play, even though it's true.

Desperate or not, it works.

"Really?" His face lights up.

"Yes, you idiot." I'm crying too, for some reason. "That's why I get so upset when you talk like that, because—"

Then he's holding me really tight, with Tempus groaning in between us, which is killing the mood for me. Lou kisses my cheek, my lips, my other cheek.

"I love you too." His voice is low and urgent. "You really—?"

I manage to pull Tempus out from in between us and shove him on the bench. "Yes, for fuck's sake. I love you." I put my hands either side of his head and look into his eyes. "My handsome boy." And I kiss him as soft as I can, even though all kinds of emotions are confusingly bouncing around in my head.

After he goes home, I still want to scream or punch things or both. I go for a walk because otherwise I have to talk to all my objects about this rancid stew of feelings churning in my gut. I'm stomping down the road, my thoughts chewing over Lou, when I run across a familiar figure perched on the back of a bus stop bench.

"Dani," I say.

She's head down on her phone but she glances up at me. "Oh, hey Dylan. I missed the bus."

Everything about her seems distracted and faraway.

"You ok?" I nudge the end of the bench with one foot.

"Me? Uh, yeah." She scowls at her phone. "My ex. Won't stop texting. Saying the dumbest shit."

"Annoying." I don't know what else to say.

"You saw her today," Dani says, as if I'm too dumb to put that together on my own. "Sorry about tonight, with you and Lou. I was being a dick. Letting this inter-fere." She waves her phone at me.

"You were fine." I've got a weird almost-smile on my face.

The bus approaches, all lit up, and Dani raises her arm in signal. It comes to a halt and the doors hiss open.

"I'm so emo-hot you probably couldn't resist," I say as some mysterious parting jab.

She jerks her head up and looks at me, and the arch of her eyebrow literally slashes me right through the heart. Maybe I don't know what literally means.

"Emma has a big mouth," is all she says in response as she jogs up the stairs.

The doors hiss closed and the bus pulls away.

I watch after it, poking my lips like they have a life of their own. Why did I say such a fucking stupid thing? People are impossible and I am the worst example. I stare after the disappearing lights and wish my super-power was being mute. Then I wander home and go to bed. I try not to think about anything at all.

CHAPTER THIRTEEN

The next day, four of us are waiting to catch the bus to Alyse's house, where we're supposed to be planning the next move on Jack. It's me, Dani, Alyse and Bianca, leaning against the front fence of a house, talking idly about what a douchebag Jack is.

The only other person waiting is a woman in a hijab. A bus approaches, but it isn't ours. I glance over as the woman flags it down. It wheezes to a stop, but the door doesn't open. The woman stands patiently waiting, but the bus edges forward.

"What the fuck?" I nudge Alyse and gesture towards the idling bus.

The big vehicle burbles to itself as the driver puts it in gear and starts driving away. The woman lifts her arm, trying to flag it down all over again, but the indicator says it's going back out into traffic, and the doors are firmly closed.

"Is he not letting her on?" Bianca asks.

I feel a surge of anger. First of all, fuck you. Second of all, no fucking way.

"Open up," I snap at the bus. There's a lurching connection between us. Both sets of doors open with a pneumatic hiss, and the bus murmurs apology or fealty.

The woman takes a couple of steps towards it, but the driver hits the button to close the doors. I do a full-on fist of rage and tell the bus we'll have a big problem if the doors don't stay open.

Bianca moves up the steps and stomps inside, like a vampire queen lurching forward to feast.

Alyse follows, shifted into something intimidating. She's a half-feral warrior with whipcord muscles and catlike eyes. It looks as if she could crush the bus like an aluminium can.

Dani and I walk up beside the woman and I give an encouraging gesture. She nods and climbs up into the bus behind Bianca and Alyse, who've paid and are standing in the aisle beside an empty seat.

"I'm paying for three," I say, shoving my bus card towards the driver. I take my phone out and swipe the camera open. "Unless there's a problem."

He mutters something, but he processes my card and we escort the woman down the aisle.

"Thank you." She takes her seat and balances a voluminous handbag on her lap.

"It's cool," I say, because honestly, it's the least we can fucking do.

She tries to give me bus money, which I say no to, but then I take it because it's awkward and I'd want to pay my own bus fare too.

The four of us stay in the aisle. Bianca and Alyse are drawing a lot of looks.

The bus isn't going remotely in the direction of Alyse's house, but we're committed now. There's some muttering from further down the bus. Two hollow-cheeked dudes in skinny jeans and stained t-shirts that look like walking advertisements for 'don't do meth, kids' are having this intense conversation with a group of teenagers from the boys' school near us.

There's a squawk of laughter from one boy, who stands up out of his seat and lifts up a can of energy drink to throw. He hurls it in our direction, but it slings around like a boomerang and flies back towards him. It smacks him in the cheek and his head flicks back, hitting the window. Everyone's shocked and can't understand what happened, but then his friends all start cackling like the fucking hyenas from the Lion King.

There's only one explanation, and she's standing beside me. I give Dani a version of her own eyebrow arch back. She opens her hand and shows me where she's scraped her fingernails across the inside of her palm, leaving red welts and tiny trails of blood. My heart skips a beat or two.

"Are you okay?" I ask her, my voice low.

"It's just a scratch." Her mouth curves and she looks away from me.

In all the commotion, I don't notice the hijabi woman getting off the bus. I see her through the window, walking down the street with her bag slung over her shoulder. At the last minute, just before the doors close, the two meth-head looking dudes get off too.

"Fuck," I say. "Do you think those guys—"

"Call the police," Dani says. "We can't do anything about this now. We're in school uniform."

"I don't care," Bianca says. "I'll set my monsters on them."

"They'll see your face. Let me do it." I rummage in my school bag, a flash of green and purple in my hand. I shove my bag at Alyse, who takes it without any questions.

"Dylan, this is a terrible idea." Dani puts her hand on my shoulder.

"Call the police." I grin at her and ask the bus very kindly to open the doors again. It's barely moving, because after-school traffic is a fucking nightmare, so when they open I just trot down the steps.

I pull my stupid Spider Hero mask over my face and duck between parked cars. I can see the two assholes and the hijabi woman too, turning a corner just ahead of me. I'm not used to running, but I go after them anyway. I can still hear Dani's voice in my head. This may indeed be a terrible idea, but at the same time, what am I supposed to do? Just stand there and watch? Hope the cops turn up in time and won't be assholes? I've got fucking superpowers.

The woman looks over her shoulder and sees the two men following her. One of them calls out something after her.

"You leave me alone." She takes her phone out of her bag and presses it to her ear. "I'm calling the police."

"Might take a while," one guy says. "How long you think?"

"Hey, assholes," I shout, my voice muffled by the mask. They ignore me, so I put on as much speed as my unaccustomed legs can handle.

"Fucking racist assholes," I shout as loud as I can.

My amazingly detailed plan works. The two dudes turn to face me. They do this weird double take. It's the middle of the afternoon and here's this girl in school uniform with a stupid mask on. You can almost see the cartoon speech bubbles floating over their heads.

Hey look. Now all their attention is on me. Great fucking job, superhero. The dudes are about five houses away from me. I wonder how fast they can run.

"Who the fuck are you, little girl?" They start walking towards me.

I hate that people like this exist, who'll follow a woman home to scare her. I want the place where I was born to be safe for anyone. At the edges of my awareness, I feel objects stirring. There's a sofa in the house near me, and a swingset in a front yard.

And closer, far closer, in the front pocket of one of the dudes still advancing while I stand here like an idiot—

He pulls the knife out of his pocket. With a fluid motion, it unfolds into a gleaming blade.

"Ohfuckohfuckohfuck," the knife says, high and sharp and urgent. "Listen, I really don't want to hurt you. I'm so sorry, but they keep making me do it. I hate the taste of blood, but this guy is awful and keeps feeding me."

"Don't let him." I know I should be running instead of slowly backing away, but the knife is scared and sad. Why are people such assholes? "Stop him. Make it so he can't use you again."

A door opens nearby. "What are you two doing?" An old dude stands on the steps of a nearby house with his phone out. "You get out of here or I'll call the police."

"Fuck off, old man, and get back inside." The guy is scary close now, and the knife is straight up screaming.

I take a few quick steps backward.

"Please," I beg the knife. "Don't let him hurt me."

The knife twitches and swings outwards. It carves a jagged line down the other guy's arm, and then stabs itself into its owner's thigh. "How do you like that, you motherfucker?" The knife howls. "You'll never do that again, will you? I'll live out my days in an evidence locker!"

The other dude has realised that a) his arm is sluicing blood and b) that his meth-head buddy just stabbed himself in the thigh and he's scream-swearing over and over. The old guy on the porch has his phone to his ear.

The woman from the bus stares at me. She knows what I look like. This could be really bad.

Instead, she smiles and nods. She puts her phone back in her bag.

I give her this stupid-ass wave and she mirrors it back at me.

Fuck me. My work here must be done.

I turn and go haring off down the road, running faster than I ever have in my life. When I get to the main road, I'm breathless. I take off my mask before anyone else sees me in it, and shove it into the pocket of my uniform.

I check my phone to find I've missed a flood of messages from the others, who are waiting a couple of stops up ahead. I'm shaky but manage to tap out a response telling them I'm fine.

When I catch up to them, I'm still panting. At the sound of a faint police siren, I drag everyone across to the other side of the road without any explanation. We hop the first bus going in the other direction. As soon as we take our seats, a police car speeds past with lights flashing.

"What did you do?" Alyse asks me.

I shake my head. "Nothing."

Dani gives me an extremely sceptical look.

"You're the one that called the cops." I tilt my head back and tell them the whole story. The more I talk, the more Dani's expression goes from concerned to cold-ass murder-droid.

"You could have been killed," she says. "Do you understand that, Dylan?"

"If it wasn't the knife, I would have been able to talk something else into helping me." I meet her gaze. "There was a sofa and a swingset."

"It's reckless." I feel her judgement like a tangible thing pressing down on my chest. "I thought we talked about this."

"So you would have just let them walk after her and stab her?" My voice is low, but I want to scream.

"We have a system in place to protect people from things like that," she says.

"The system doesn't always fucking work," I mutter.

"That doesn't mean you solve the problems on your own in a stupid mask."

"If she hadn't gone, I would have." Bianca leans over the back of the seat and pats my shoulder. "But you're right, Dylan, they would have seen my face."

"Two reckless people doesn't make it right," Dani snaps.

"I'd do it again," I tell her. My voice shakes, but I feel steady.

She tenses, and I find myself staring at her face. "This isn't going to work, you running after people with knives." Her eyes meet mine. They're ridiculously beautiful—like hazel, I guess, but there's not really a word that can explain it—but I know what they're saying, and what her lips are about to say too. "I won't run around risking my life. This whole mutant idea of yours is dangerous. It puts everything at risk. I can't do it."

"Fine." I clench my jaw really hard because I'm worried I'll start to cry, and I couldn't bear to do it in front of Dani of all people. "Quit then."

"I am."

How can she be so fucking resolute? The ice queen, back in her frozen tower, looking down at me. I stare out the window at the rows of cars heading for their destinations.

At the next stop, we all get off.

Three of us get on a bus in the direction of Alyse's house, and Dani gets on a different one.

"I'm not quitting," Alyse says, when we take our seats at the very back.

"Neither am I." I don't think I'm capable of it.

"Looks like you'll both have to put up with me too," Bianca says.

"However will we possibly survive?" Alyse grins at both of us, but my brain keeps bouncing off the idea of Dani leaving. I held this group together for how long? Barely a few days? It's already falling apart because people can't stand to be around the train wreck that is me. Dani's only the first. Before long I'll be alone again.

The bus tries to murmur something reassuring, but I can't understand the words.

The next day at school, Emma finds me. I actually scurry in the other direction, but she corners me near the cafeteria.

"I'm sorry about Dani."

"You're not in charge of her." I still feel the horrible twinge of ineptitude. "I doubt anyone can tell Dani what to do."

Her hair sways as she shakes her head no. "Dani's intense," she tells me, and I manage not to roll my eyes. "She's going to be a doctor, ever since I can remember. She's driven and disciplined and not really about chasing guys with knives."

"A doctor," I say. "Of course. What are you going to be?"

"Well, I want to code obviously. I can do way better stuff than FlirtDeck, but who knows? Maybe I'll end up being a lawyer, like Mum. If I can stand the cliché. What about you?"

"I don't know." This is a question I consciously avoid. "I'll figure it out."

"Sure." A look of melancholy settles over her face. It makes me worried, as if I've seen her shift into some protective mode like a hedgehog.

"Are you okay?" I ask in a rush. I don't usually say this sort of thing, but it feels important.

"Yes," she says. "I guess. It can be—a lot some-times."

"The superpower thing? Or the uh, the…" I feel like an idiot dancing around this, but I don't want to say his name to her.

"No." She looks up at me. "Neither of those. It's… life in general. Family and schoolwork and you know."

I don't really know, and I feel immediately guilty for that. "If there's anything I can do," I say incoherently. It feels useless.

"I want to help," she says. "With the team. Like the other day, looking up the stuff about Jack. That was useful, right?"

"It was amazing."

Her face breaks into a smile. "There are other things I can do to help, I swear."

Maybe I'm not the only one who really wants this to work. I watch as Emma reaches up and gathers her hair into a ponytail, hands moving deftly as she loops a hair tie around it, pulling it through like a silken rope. It's mesmerising, like watching a snake. She lets it fall and the end of it drapes over her shoulder. There's nowhere for her to hide.

"Mutants together," she says, which is not a real catchphrase, but I feel it so hard it makes me abruptly tongue-tied. I attempt to bump fists with her and it doesn't work on either end, but we're still smiling.

CHAPTER FOURTEEN

After the whole bus incident and Dani quitting, we need a team meeting to regroup. Alyse and I are hanging out by the lockers at school, even though we should be in class.

"My parents are home, so we can't use my house," Alyse says with a full-body shudder. "If I turn up with a bunch of teenage miscreants, they'll try and analyse us all."

"What's a miscreant?" I ask.

"One of you." She nudges me. "And Bianca, holy shit. Bianca is like a cartoon version of a miscreant. They'd peel her open and check for so many issues. And Lou—let's just not."

"We can postpone and you can hang out with them instead, if you want?"

For a moment, she does a weird transformation and in place of Alyse is a neatly folded paper girl, demure and buttoned down, with careful writing printed all over her.

"No." She leans in so her mouth is close to my ear. "I'd much rather spend time with the miscreants."

Once I've confirmed that Pear is actually going to be out of the house this evening, Alyse texts everyone else to let them know it's on at my place. She even texts Dani, which does not go well. Turns out it's not easy to shove a seven foot tall girl with sabre-tooth fangs and claw-hands the size of shovels into a supply closet, but I manage to do it. I'm just glad nobody else is around to see her change.

"It's like you've never been left on seen before," I shout through the door.

There's a crash from inside. I hope there's nothing important in there.

"Seen," the Alyse-monster roars.

I lean against the door and try to look normal, which I am not naturally talented at. Finally, Alyse calms and I let her out. She's normal size and her eyes are only glowing a tiny bit red. Her school uniform looks like it's been distressed, but it's not quite Hulk levels. Her phone is a little bit crushed around the edges too, which she's not happy about.

"Bitch," she says.

"Don't you fucking start again," I warn her in a pathetic attempt at stern, which makes her laugh enough to dissolve the last of the red glare from her eyes.

With that out of the way, now I can start panicking about the fact that everyone is coming to my lame house, and that my lame self is going to have to talk. I hide in the bathroom again and sit there with my head between my knees until something stabilises inside me. I am ditching way too much class since this shit started, but it honestly doesn't feel important. Rather than go to the last one of the day, I leave early and hope the teacher doesn't notice I'm gone.

Back at home, I change into the jeans that Pear says are more rip than denim, and put on my Totoro hoodie, which is my most voluminous of all hoodies. Then I sit in my bathroom and try to decide whether I need to crap or throw up. I don't do either, but I feel desperately in need of both. I listen to Stray Kids to try and hype myself up, but even that doesn't work.

"You're the world's worst idiot," I tell my reflection, which looks various kinds of ghastly. Maybe I need to go full panda eyes. "They'll all bail like Dani because you're a reckless fucking disaster with trash superpowers." I pull faces and try to look like something approximately human. There's a knock on the door which makes me jump, because nobody's meant to be in the house.

"Hello?" I squeak.

"It's me," Lou says. "Are you talking to yourself again?"

"Yes, but I won't even listen to me." I tear myself away from the terrified girl in the mirror and open the door.

Lou is waiting in skinny jeans and a Bakugo t-shirt. He's looking pretty hot, so at least one of us isn't going to send everyone fleeing.

"Calm down." He's got slight frown wrinkles. "Dylan, this is your thing. You'll be amazing."

I shrink into my hood and pull the drawstrings tight so only my eyes are visible.

"Do you think this will inspire confidence in the troops?" I ask.

"If you be yourself, that's all you need to do."

"Excuse me, I just filled my entire hood with vomit, thank you very much." I loosen the hood enough for him to kiss my cheek, but the doorbell goes frantic and I almost dash into the bathroom again.

Lou drags me over to the front door, and we open it to find Alyse and Emma on the porch. They're each holding a supermarket bag full of snacks.

"Oh shit, I forgot to cater," I say.

"You're host and you're leader. You don't need to cater." Alyse brushes past me, and Emma waits for me to step aside and gesture her in. I have a hysterical thought that I've just invited a very cute vampire into my house and have to clamp down on nervous laughter.

"Hi." I feel shy and aware of how small and shit my house is. "This is where I live. With my parent. They're not home so it's all good." I feel this intense awkwardness, but Emma's very gracious and has manners and shit.

Summers comes exploding out of my bedroom like a furry rocket and capers around us all. Emma is unnerved by his manic energy, but Alyse wrangles him under control. Once she finds his ear spot, he becomes a fur puddle.

The coffee table is now piled with chips and cakes and drinks. I'm amazed Alyse didn't bring more carrots and hummus, but maybe she's realised I'm a chocolate and cake person. Lou perches on the edge of the couch and busies himself with opening packets and organising things.

When I turn back around, Bianca is on the doorstep, wearing a flowing black dress with this massive vee down the front, presumably to give her easy access to her inner demons as well as to show off other things.

"Greetings, mortal," she says, and envelops me in a hug. She smells of a weird mix of berry-scented vape smoke and old-lady peppermints, and her hug is really fucking tight. I'm on the verge of thrashing out of her grip when she releases me and looks deep into my eyes. "How *are* you, little Dylan?"

"Nervous," I say, because the weirdness of the situation has destroyed my filter.

"So am I," she says, holding me by the shoulders and shaking me slightly. "I was already half pissed when I turned up at the other one and now I'm sober and realising I'm in a room with cool girls."

Being lumped in with cool girls makes me let out this terrifying whinny of laughter.

"Well, aside from you," she says.

"Obviously. It's only Alyse and Emma and they're, like—" I glance over at the two of them, sitting side by side on the couch, with Summers in Alyse's lap and Emma tentatively reaching out to pat him. I don't think of them as fundamentally different from me anymore. "They're actually cool, not cool girls."

Her purple-black lips twist in a grimace. "Let's hope so, otherwise I'll have to set my babies on you all." She pats her chest and wanders over to take the seat next to Lou, who actually greets her with some enthusiasm.

Everyone's sitting on my crappy couch while I stand awkwardly. Gradually attention turns to me. Alyse nods at me encouragingly. Who the fuck does she think she is, my other parent?

"Hey everyone," I say, and flap a hoodie arm at them. "We all know each other so we can skip that bit.

We also know about our bad guy mutant, Jack Firestone, who's a total prick that makes earthquakes. He's busted up his Dad's house and his ex-girlfriend's and he's robbed a few places."

Emma pulls up a photo on her phone and shows it around to everyone. "He's twenty two, so why he likes to hang out in front of a school yelling at teenage girls is a mystery to me."

I don't think it's a mystery to anyone else, but nobody wants to burst her bubble.

"Here's a thought," Bianca says, gesturing at Emma. "Why don't we get this one to kiss a bunch more people and make more of us?"

Emma freezes up and her eyes go all big.

"Number one," I say, "Emma doesn't have to kiss anyone she doesn't want to. Number two, I don't know if you've noticed, but some of these powers are unpleasant. Telekinesis triggered by pain? Transformations tied to self-esteem and mood? Whatever the fuck is going on with you?" I gesture vaguely at her chest. "Even if Emma said yes, there's no way to know what people are getting themselves into."

"I'm sorry," Emma whispers. She covers her face and topples over into Alyse, who doesn't seem to mind at all.

"You didn't do it on purpose. It's like our weird origin story. The movies tell it over and over, but the real important stuff comes next. What do we do with our powers?"

It wasn't actually a rhetorical question but everyone's looking at me like it was, and it drags on until the point where I'm either a) super fucking dumb, or b) have some amazing plan that is going to blow everyone's mind.

It's a) of course. It's definitely a).

"I think we should stop this guy," I say. "He's an asshole who doesn't deserve powers. He stole them, and he's using them to rob people and be a prick. So I think we need to like web him up and leave him for the cops. I know that's Spider-Man and we're the X-Men, but like—"

Everyone's smiling at me like it was b) after all and internally I'm screaming 'this is not a fucking plan' but at the same time I can't say that, because then the bubble bursts and I'm stupid Dylan Taylor again.

"So yeah," I say. "We're going to prove it's him, and we're going to catch him in the act. But that means going into the field." I'm light-headed but I'm still talking. "So if you don't have a mask, you need one, and we'll need codenames too. We can't be shouting out real names because then people might know who we are. We need something short and catchy."

"Like the Sideclomps," Alyse says wisely, and I try not to crack up.

"Yes, like *Cyclops*, but they should fit our powers." This is a very specific fantasy of mine, happening right now, and I want to freeze every single moment of it.

"Me first," Bianca says. "Monster Girl. Or Demon Girl!"

I close my eyes and let out this faint, tortured moan because oh my fucking god people, do you not have any sense of *style*?

"Snappier," I say. "One word if possible."

"Demon," she says.

"It's not very hero-y," I say, which is not a word but it totally should be.

Bianca sighs at me because I'm shooting every idea down but come on, this needs to at least sound halfway cool when we're done.

"Wraith," Lou suggests, which I admit is actually pretty good.

"Oh, yes, Wraith! I like it!" Bianca leans over and high-fives him.

Bianca then immediately suggests Fleshlight for Lou. "Because he's like a sex toy that lights up," she cackles.

Lou looks mortified so I push on to spare him embarrassment, and the group discards Lighter and Flasher to finally settle on Glowstick.

Emma gets the codename Goddess, which makes sense because she created us. She gets this beatific glow which is very on-brand and very cute.

Alyse ends up with Moodring, which is my choice, although I'm immediately unhappy with it once everyone agrees on it so easily.

Then it's my turn. I'm excited to see what they choose but trying to play it down completely.

"Chatterbox," Lou suggests, "because she talks to objects and they talk back."

I wait for the group to argue and suggest something infinitely cooler, but they all think it's an amazing name. Great. I've waited years and years to join the X-Men and get a fucking codename, and I get stuck with *Chatterbox*. I feel like I'm going to be like Kitty Pryde who keeps changing codenames because they *all fucking suck* and then being just Dylan Taylor for my whole life. I almost open my mouth and demand a better one, but I don't want people to think I'm rude and ungrateful.

"And what do we call ourselves?" Alyse asks. "Like we need a team name, right?"

There's a stack of X-Men trades on the table from where I was potentially hoping to draw inspiration for various things from—like my fucking codename. Lou's been flipping through them idly.

"New Mutants," Lou says. "That's what we are, right?" It's a tiny bit annoying because I've been trying to get him to read that book, particularly the Demon Bear Saga, since we first got together and finally now he looks at it.

"More like Cute Mutants," Alyse says, and this is met with applause.

I don't even know where to start. Democracy has failed again. We're the Cute Mutants, and I'm Chatterbox. It's not the worst, but it's hardly badass.

"Wraith, Glowstick, Goddess, Moodring and Chatterbox," Alyse says, pointing around the room.

Everyone laughs, and right then, right there we actually feel like a team. It's insane—the whole situation is surreal—and yet here we are. Dylan Taylor is finally on a superteam. It feels momentous and at the same time, it's just a bunch of teenagers sitting in a house.

Pear comes home shortly after to find a mess all over the lounge and all these randos sitting around talking. They give me this weird look like 'who are you and what have you done with my child.' They've got their girlfriend Sarah and her three kids with them, as well as Sarah's dog. The house becomes a whirlwind of bodies and voices and leaping animals. Rather than risk any awkward explanations, I manage to drag the Cute

Mutants out of the house.

"Right, so everyone needs costumes if you don't have them," I say. "Which mostly means you, Wraith."

Everyone stares at me, like they don't know who I'm talking to.

"Bianca," I say heavily. "Codename Wraith?"

"Oh, fuck, yeah." She laughs. "Is this not a good enough costume?" She gestures at the dress, which I mean, okay, if we were a team of vampires intent on sexually harassing the world into submission, maybe.

"You at least need a mask," I say faintly, because I have to accept the hand I've been dealt.

"I can start surveillance tomorrow," Emma says, her hands in her pockets but her eyes all lit up. "We just need a place, because Mum and Dad would not approve."

"Mine leave at like four in the morning for a flight to Aussie," Alyse says. "So come to my place whenever."

"It sounds like a plan," I say as decisively as I can, which is still janky as fuck but okay.

Everyone hugs each other as we leave. I don't hug people, but I hug *these* people. I'm trying not to be tense and also trying to sense if they hate the forced proximity to me. I'm still so overwhelmed with everything that I can't really tell.

When I go back into the house, both Pear and Sarah are looking at me.

"What was that?" Pear says with a vaguely believable casual air.

I walk over to the coffee table and start collecting up the leftovers.

"Kids from school," I say. "They're making us do clubs this year."

"I've never seen you have more than one person over at a time." They regard me with suspicion. Generally I tell Pear everything, but this isn't only my secret— it's everyone's. Pear is the one who brought me up on X-Men. Those comics saved their life as a teenager. Yet I feel like if I confronted them with a whole bunch of kids with real powers in real life, the romance would die instantly. We'd be at the doctor getting poked and prodded, rather than going to Xavier's School for Gifted Youngsters. So I say nothing and put my headphones on and tidy the lounge until Pear turns their attention elsewhere.

CHAPTER FIFTEEN

Emma turns up at Alyse's house the next morning just after me, which is stupid early. I'm yawning in a t-shirt and literal pyjama pants and clinging to coffee like it's the only thing keeping me alive. Emma is bright-eyed and excitable and has her cousin with her, a lanky Chinese guy who immediately starts unloading a whole bunch of gear from his car. We all help him, ferrying it to the table in the dining room.

"This is Wei," Emma says. "He stores all my gear for me."

"Illegal gear." He dumps a box with drones in it onto the table.

"It's not all illegal." Emma opens a bulky laptop that has gadgets plugged into the USB ports. She waggles the power cord at Alyse, who connects it up. "Some of it is stuff that I don't want to explain to my parents."

"Supervillain in training," Wei says.

I stare at Emma behind his back and make a lip-zipping motion but she doesn't see me.

"Not *villain*," she says. "I'm like the voice in the heroes' ears."

Wei laughs and spins a drone's rotors with his finger. "Don't say anything else. I don't want to be in the position of having to lie to Auntie Jing."

As soon as he's gone, Emma has three laptops set up on the table. One's showing a map of Jack's earthquake sites, another has a top-down map view around Jack's house, and one is currently blank. She's fiddling with a drone that has a real estate company logo on it.

"Did you steal this?" I ask, more incredulous than I've ever been.

"No!" She pushes my hand away, but there's a faint blush in her cheeks. "People think it's taking property footage if they see it."

"Omigod, you're so properly devious." I'm impressed and delighted.

"Stop it," she says quietly, but she's smiling wider than I've ever seen her. The third laptop screen flickers to life, showing the interior of Alyse's house. I carry the drone outside and fling it into the air like it's a little bird I'm setting free.

The drone wobbles and rights itself with a whir. It ascends to float away over the line of beautiful houses.

"—totally illegal," Emma is saying as I come back into the house. "It's got crazy range and the camera in it is stupid good. If it got caught and traced back to me, it would be very bad."

"What have you used it for before now?" Alyse asks.

She shrugs. "Nothing, really. I just wanted to see if I could do it."

Alyse catches my eye.

"Supervillain," we say in unison.

Emma grins and ignores us, because she's concentrating on piloting the drone. It's cool to see the city underneath it, and the way she tracks the progress on the other laptop, moving the map around the city.

"An eye in the sky," I say. "Like a fucking Goddess."

Finally, the drone floats down to perch on the roof of the house opposite Jack's.

"Motion detector," Emma says cheerfully. "It'll ping me when there's movement."

It's cool to see her like this, confident and in control. It's her element, and it makes me wonder what mine is or if I even have one. She seems entirely happy fiddling with her computers, so Alyse and I drift through to the lounge and end up watching Food Wars. Every so often, Emma gives us an update that nothing's happening, although she seems quite content.

I text Lou, but he's non-committal about coming round and in the end he doesn't show.

"Are you guys okay?" Alyse asks me.

"I honestly don't know." It gives me the beginnings of a headache thinking about it.

"Well good luck with it. I had enough of boys, and now I've had enough of girls," Alyse says. "I'm single until I find someone legitimately irresistible and hopefully uncomplicated."

"Seventeen is far too young to be so jaded," I say in my best impression of Pear. "And good luck finding someone uncomplicated."

She laughs. "Insanely hot would do as a backup. No, I'm kidding. I just want to find someone nice. Like kind, you know. Is Lou kind?"

I look at the credits on the TV because looking at Alyse and talking about this makes everything too real and in sharp focus.

"I don't know if kind is the word. But it's like… I care for him, you know? I want him to find a way to be happy in the world. Like he deserves it, he's been through so much shit and if I could look at him and know he was going to be ok then I could breathe easier."

I dare a glance at her, and she looks like some mythical creature, green and gold and willowy and sad and I think the word is ethereal? It's trippy and gorgeous, and I get a lump in my throat looking at her.

"I think you're the kind one, Dylan," she says from golden lips.

I get this lurch in my chest when she says it, because I'm not sure what she means and I don't need my life being this complicated, thank you very much.

"Oh God," she says. "No, sorry. I'm not hitting on you." The willowy creature is gone and in its place is the scuffed and faded embarrassment Alyse. "I honestly don't want a relationship right now. But being friends with you is exactly what I need."

This makes me feel even more heart-fluttery because, aside from Lou, I don't have friends. Not people that are willing to call me a friend anyway and that I like and think are cool.

"Good," I say, and I'm blinking about a thousand times per minute because I'm pretty sure tears are imminent, but Alyse flits away to the kitchen and returns with lemonade and we drink it as if nothing happened.

We're halfway through an episode when Emma shrieks from the other room. Apparently Jack is on the move. On the laptop screen, we watch him cross to his assholemobile and get inside. The drone floats into the air.

"It'll be hard to track his car because it's just a boring black," Emma says. "We should've tagged it, or had someone tailing him."

"Who is this mysterious hacker girl we invited to your house?" I say to Alyse over Emma's head.

"I have no idea," Alyse says. "I don't recognise her. I think she's some kind of evil genius."

Emma gives both of us the finger, one with each hand, and we mock stagger as if we've been shot.

"All I mean is I might lose him, so don't bitch at me if we do." She grins up at me. "We'll do it better tomorrow."

In the end, we don't lose him. Emma's drone tails him to a computer warehouse store over by the airport. It's still an hour or so before it's due to open. Jack stops in the middle of the car park. We see him get out of his car, and walk to the front of the building. He crouches down. A few seconds later the building shakes, as if the entire image is being jolted.

Jack goes inside, and Emma floats the drone lower, switching cameras so we can see a shot of the ruined front of the building. It's pretty fucked up. One of the doors is shattered and the right side of the building leans precariously.

"Can you record this?" I ask.

"I've been recording this whole time," Emma says, as if I'm incredibly stupid, which ok, fair point. "It's all evidence, right? Illegally-obtained, but still."

She's on the verge of floating it inside when Jack comes out with a pile of boxes in his hands. He's wearing a balaclava. Emma sends the drone soaring skywards.

"Shit," she says. "I'm running low on battery, even with the extra pack. Gonna have to park baby somewhere safe. We have enough footage, right?"

"Are you kidding? This is amazing!"

We're all grinning at each other, like we've accomplished something incredible. Except we have to go pick up the drone from where Emma parked it behind a dumpster at the edge of the industrial park. At least Alyse orders us an Uber rather than having to take the bus.

Last thing of the day, we all convene in the group chat to organise what's next. It's adorable because everyone has changed their display names to their codenames. Alyse was first of course.

Moodring: cute mutants group chat what what
Moodring: code names only bitches

Goddess: Okay so we really need some close-up footage if possible.

Goddess: Which means someone will need to get up close to him.

Goddess: I've got a hidden camera setup that might work.

Moodring: of course u do u villain lol

Chatterbox: wraith seems like ur dontseeme trick might work best

Chatterbox: u ok to stalk tomo?

Wraith: on it

Chatterbox: after schools find

Chatterbox: fine

Wraith: i said im on it chatty

Wraith: gonna ditch

Chatterbox: u dont have to

Wraith: no but i want to 🐨

Moodring: he has a car tho. do u drive?

Wraith: no but my gf does and she'll take me

Wraith: she doesnt have uni tmrw

Moodring: ur gf is at uni?

Wraith: ya shes 21. we can use her car its all good

Wraith: she knows my secret & shes cool

Within thirty seconds a side chat has popped up between everyone else to exclaim that omg Bianca has a 21 year old girlfriend and discuss whether a four year age gap is creepy, and if so what level of creepy it reaches. I mute the notifications and go back to the other chat.

> Chatterbox: thanks wraith
>
> Chatterbox: keep the group updated

The next morning, my phone buzzes on the way to school.

> Wraith: um slight early problem
>
> Wraith: i tested dontseeme on shell and um
>
> Wraith: lets say now shes mad im not here yet lol
>
> Chatterbox: who the fukc is shell?

Wraith sends us a video of a petite blonde with big circle-glasses. She's on the phone, leaving what sounds like a very pissed off voice message.

"—I could have done many other things today, but for some stupid reason I promised you that I'd help you with some stupid fucking errand—"

Wraith: i dunno how long it takes to wear off
lmaooooo

By the time I'm at school and in class, Wraith is still blathering on. Her girlfriend still hasn't found her. The teacher is actually focused on us for once, so I have to look attentive and engaged. Alyse is the only one with a smart watch who can get texts on her wrist, but she's not in this class. I'm trying to balance my phone surreptitiously on my knee without the teacher noticing.

Wraith: alg were on the way

We get a photo of an angry blonde and then one of Wraith with her chest open and one of the little demons reaching for the camera, surrounded by about fifty cry-laughing emojis.

Wraith: lil fuckers are feisty today
Wraith: guess thats what happens when ur girl has
a tantrum lol

I don't see that much to lol about, but Wraith is fucking weird at the best of times, and that's coming from me.

Wraith: at his house now
Wraith: let the stake out begin!

It's really annoying having to actually *be at school* when there's important shit to deal with. I find it hard enough to pay attention in class at the best of times, but today I am next-level scatterbrained like it's my secondary mutation. All of which makes it worse when I get to chemistry class and I'm paired with an ultimate high-achiever.

"Dylan, what did I just say?" Dani is looking at me with a) those eyes that honestly look like some real-life Snapchat filter has made them into something extraordinarily complex and beautiful and b) extreme fucking disdain.

"I don't know," I sigh, flopping down on the desk so my fringe swooshes in my eyes. Lou finds this endearing. I don't think Dani does, although she does flick my hair off my face. Her fingertips are warm on my skin.

"Listen." Her tone has the exact same snippiness it does when she's telling me what a mutant disaster I am.

"I actually want to get credits for this, so can you please focus?"

"I don't care about credits," I tell her.

"Well I do." She frowns. "What are you going to do after high school?"

"I have no idea."

"But you have to know." This seems to exasperate her beyond reason, which is dumb. It's not her life. Her life will be fine. She'll be successful and rich and whatever else it is that people want.

"I'll figure it out."

"Stop shrugging." Dani sighs. "I don't know how you can do that. Just… I don't know, assume the future will work out."

"It's reckless too, is it? Maybe I'll be a superhero and you'll be in your fancy doctor clinic saving lives. Some supervillain will attack and I'll come in and save the day."

There's a tiny smile on her face. There must be a translation, but I still don't have the guidebook. "Who's going to pay you to be a superhero?"

"In comics they always find a chill billionaire. The problem is irl billionaires are giant problematic trashholes. I'll have to do it for free."

She shakes her head, like a dismissal. "Well unfortunately for you, I still need credits. So I'll do the thing, and you take notes."

It's fascinating to watch her. Everything is so precise and organised. It's like she doesn't doubt herself for a second, and I wonder what that's like. She murmurs things to herself as she works and I find myself with my head resting on my hand, watching her lips and her deft movements. I wish I were as good as her at anything.

I manage to write some notes, which she reads at the end of class and deems adequate, which I'm pretty sure is like bouncing up and down and saying squee in Dani-speak. I realise I haven't even looked at my phone. I fumble for it, but there are no notifications.

I'm on the way to history, feeling like I'm swimming upstream in the corridor against a bunch of sharp-eyed, sharp-chinned girls with aggressive hairstyles, when my phone starts vibrating like crazy. I duck off into an alcove.

Wraith: hey look its ya boi
Wraith: except hes not ya boi he is the actual worst obvi
Wraith: actually for a skinny white dude he's kinda dummy thicc
Glowstick: so are u wraith
Wraith: excuse the fuck u
Moodring: omg wait
Moodring: i know ur stealthy wraith babe but watch out he doesn't hear the clap of ur ass cheeks

Chatterbox: omg brb literally dying

Glowstick: haha my chest hurts i think i swallowed wrong

Wraith: i will end all u birches i fucking swear

Wraith: argh bitches**** fuck u phobe

Wraith: phone FUCK

Wraith: point being u dicks wish u had an ass like me

Wraith: ok wait hold up fucknuts is moving

I stay in the alcove rather than going to class. There's a bench seat and I curl up with my phone, staring down at it like I can will time to move faster.

Wraith: um fuck

Wraith: so we pulled up at this liquor store on fitzgrld ave

Wraith: and omg it's middle of the day so hardly anyone there

Wraith: he just fucking kneels down in the carpark

Wraith: RUMBLE RUMBLE

Wraith: fucks the place up!!!!!!

Chatterbox: when was this?

Wraith: right now!

Glowstick: take pictures

Wraith: YES LOUIS YOU DUMB FUCK I KNOW WHY IM HERE

Glowstick: jesus calm down

Chatterbox: fucking codenames WRAITH

There's another long pause and *finally* Goddess sends through the footage that was streamed from Bianca's camera to her server. It's pretty damning, in that you can clearly see Jack's car licence plate. Someone fitting Jack's description crouches down with a balaclava on, and the whole store shakes violently. Then balaclava dude makes a few trips inside the bottle store, coming out with black sacks and taking them to his car. The camera abruptly jerks in closer, then tilts and sways. It looks like it's been dropped, but it finally resettles.

In the next piece of footage you can clearly see Jack Firestone, unmasked and looking around wildly.

Wraith: he couldn't see me

Wraith: snatched that shit off his head and he went buckwild

Moodring: holy shit

Goddess: Good work, Wraith! The footage is perfect.

Wraith: im ur girl snatching ur wigs

Goddess: So it's definitely him, which means we need to intercept him on his next attack.

Moodring: so this is two in two days

Moodring: will he do one tomorrow?

Goddess: We don't really have enough data to extrapolate a timeline.

Goddess: It's too erratic.

Goddess: It might be tomorrow, it might be a week.

Moodring: so we have to tail him every day for a week?

Wraith: i dont mind

Chatterbox: no, none of this matters

Chatterbox: just go to his house

Chatterbox: we've got the footage

Chatterbox: we tie him up and leave him with it for the cops

Goddess: You're right. That's all we need.

Glowstick: are u sure?

Moodring: omg im nervous chatty

Chatterbox: we have the proof what else do we need?

I remember the way Dani looked at me when she called me reckless. I really hope this isn't a mistake, but I don't know what else to do. Standing by and hoping someone else will solve the problems is how the world ended up so fucked. I refuse to be one of those people. We're going to go out there, and we're going to stop Jack Firestone.

In my head I've started calling him Tremor.

CHAPTER SIXTEEN

start the mission by throwing up. I try not to take it as a fucking omen. Witness Dylan Taylor aka Chatterbox, mutant superhero and ultimate trash fire. We're meant to have left at this point. Instead I'm in the bathroom, curled over the toilet and retching. Lou holds back my hair, not that it needs it. The door is open and I keep asking him to shut it, because I know the others are watching. What kind of look is it to have the field leader throwing up? Not only this, but my skin is breaking out and I've got my period. They don't show this in comics *or* the movies.

I've got my Spider Hero costume on, except the mask is discarded on the floor. I'm pretty sure I didn't get anything on it. That would be the last straw, honestly. I think I'd quit.

When I'm finally done throwing up, I get to my feet. The mask seems unpuked on.

Emma's at the table with a row of energy drinks and laptops. On one screen is the view of Jack Firestone's house. His car is outside, which probably means he's home.

I want to throw up again.

I want to descend from the sky like Magneto and rip his world apart.

"Are you okay?" Alyse asks me. Her eyes are wide, and her mouth is dragging downwards like that horror movie mask. I guess my cheerful fucking manner is contagious.

I go to the garage and find the baseball bat. He was one of the first sentient objects I discovered when I got my powers, but he was edgy and paranoid, like he had some dark secrets in his past.

Now he seems happy to see me.

"Ooh, friend!" His excitement tails away, like he's picking up a vibe from me. "What are you going to do with me?" His voice is suddenly small and worried.

"You'll be a threat," I assure him. "Nothing else. Implied violence only."

I swing him in my hand experimentally. He's got a satisfying weight, and I imagine smacking Jack Firestone in the face while Emma looks on. It's not very heroic, but it makes me feel better.

"Cute Mutants assemble," Alyse says, when we're all back in the lounge together. It's not the right battle cry, but it'll do. Better than 'hope you survive the experience,' which is probably more accurate.

We end up catching the bus to Tremor's house. Yes, it's embarrassing. Me in my Spider Hero costume, Alyse in some stylish pantsuit with a masquerade mask, Lou in No-Face mask and overalls, and Bianca in a black flowing dress with a demon mask. The bus driver makes a joke about what a weird fancy dress party we must be going to. I ignore her. The thing about bus travel is that we're only a half step removed from the usual evening bus crowd. We get a lot of looks, but nobody wants to say anything.

We make it to the stop down the street from Jack's and spill out. The evening's warm. Night has almost completely fallen and there's only a faint smudge of pale yellow in the west. The streetlights are on. There's nobody around and everything's quiet aside from the pulsing of music from Tremor's house. I bet he's the one all the neighbours hate.

I double-check the address. The lawns are slightly unkempt, but someone's looking after them. Is it Jack? Is he a lawns guy? Or is there a landlord who does it? Could there be someone else in the house? It's too late to worry about this, but my brain is flailing in three distinct directions.

Fuck it. Time for action.

I run up the concrete steps and knock on the door. Lou and Alyse flank me—fuck, no, Glowstick and Moodring. This is a field situation. Wraith stands at the bottom of the steps. Her fingers move restlessly over her chest. I pull my mask all the way down. There's a cloudy glass pane in the door and I can see someone approaching.

The door opens, and I'm face to face with Tremor.

Up close, he looks totally anonymous. A random dude. Pale skin, thin lips, a heavy brow that's a few hairs from being mono. His hair is blonde and shaved so his scalp shows through. I feel a familiar rush of anger, for all the asshole things he's said to Lou. I hold the bat behind my back.

Tremor's eyes aren't all the way focused. "Who the fuck are you?"

"We know what you've been doing," I say.

He steps forward. "Whatever. Take your stupid-ass mask and fuck off."

Even though this wasn't entirely the plan, Alyse takes off her little masquerade mask and changes. It's legitimately scary—her face becomes this mouldering skull with little bits of flesh peeling off it. Her jaw creaks open and something oily moves inside. An insect with too many legs scuttles out of the hole where her eye should be. She lurches forward towards Tremor.

He looks at her with a panicked expression. Except instead of staying scared, Tremor lunges forward and punches Alyse in the face.

She staggers backwards, one hand at her mouth, making these terrible whimpering noises like a hurt dog.

I'm so shocked by this that my brain hasn't really caught up. I've never been hit in my life. This isn't something that happens in my world. I understand fight, flight and freeze but I thought he'd pick one of the other two.

"You can't punch someone," I say in this shocked voice that sounds like Pear.

Of course then he hits *me*. His fist impacts below my eye socket and it *hurts*, like it really fucking hurts. My head swims and everything throbs. I drop the bat. I catch onto the side of the house, slip and fall into the little garden that runs along the front.

While I'm falling, Wraith pries open her chest. The little figures that live inside her scuttle out. The problem is they don't go after Tremor at all. Instead, they turn on Wraith, clamping onto her face. I can't see her properly through the shadows of them. She thrashes about on the ground and I blink tears away.

My stupid mask is twisted and half-obscuring my vision, but I crawl over where Wraith seems to be choking on something.

Glowstick steps forward. I have no idea what he's planning, but nothing happens. I can't honestly blame him. Could anyone get turned on at that moment? Instead he leaps down off the steps and starts moving back towards the street. I can't see his expression behind the mask. He looks like No-Face.

I grab hold of Bianca's hands and force them closed. The figures disappear back inside her chest. Her breathing is shallow and her eyes are still closed.

"You fucking bastard." I get to my feet and adjust my mask again. "You don't get to just hit people."

"Oh wow, looks like I just did, you dumb bitch." Tremor takes another step towards Alyse, who cowers away. She's tiny now, almost like a child, and he does a double-take, like he wouldn't hit a kid.

"We've got proof of what you're doing." My voice is screechy like Lemongrab, full of all that impotent rage. I pull the USB stick with the evidence out of my pocket, hold it out in a fist. "We'll take it to the cops and they'll put you away."

Once I say 'cops,' he ignores Alyse, who scrambles down the steps and away from him. All his attention is now fixed on me. Good job, Chatterbox.

"Bitch." He's on the top step breathing hard. "You're going to narc on me?" He holds his hand out towards me.

I look up from the bottom of the steps. Wraith is beside me, while Moodring cowers on the lawn and Glowstick backs away at the edge of the property.

Where's my fucking bat gone? I can't see it. Something's wrong.

Something's really fucking wrong.

My head swims and the ground lurches. My heart beats frantically, like it wants to burst out of my chest. My limbs shake. I try to talk, but my teeth are chattering too hard, and that's when I realise.

Tremor is quaking me. He's making an earthquake happen inside my body.

My vision blurs. I don't even know if I'm standing or lying down. Someone's screaming. It might be me.

I'm going to die.

I'm one hundred percent convinced of it.

This is how my shitty life ends. Lying on the ground in a knockoff Spider-Man costume. Murdered by mutant powers. It's the end. There's no revolving door of death for me. I won't—

Everything stops.

No, not the world. The pain, the trembling.

Lou and Alyse are beside me. I think they're both crying.

"I'm fine," I try to say, but I bite my tongue.

They pull me into a sitting position and then up to my feet. Tremor's sprawled at the top of the steps, feet dangling off the end. His head lies just inside the doorframe. The baseball bat rolls down the steps and over to my feet.

"Couldn't let you die," he says. "There's no way I could let you die."

I grab the bat and cradle him to my chest.

"You're the best bat," I say in a slurred voice.

Bianca is on her knees, looking dazed.

"We need to get out of here," Lou says urgently.

There's nothing in me that argues. We've failed spectacularly. The only reason I'm alive is the intervention of a sentient baseball bat, who overcame his fear of violence because he didn't want to see me dead.

We make a pitiful group as we limp away down Jack's street. With every step, I worry that he'll regain consciousness and come after me. I'm trembling. My heart's still not beating right. We make it to the bus stop without any sign of him. For a second I wonder if the bat killed him. I'm sure he's fine, the fucking asshole.

My stomach lurches as I peel the mask off.

"Oh god, Dylan," Alyse says. "Your face."

I use my phone to check the damage. There's blood and swelling. It's going to bruise.

"You're no better." My teeth are still chattering, but I think it's from something else now.

One side of Alyse's mouth is grazed and her lips are puffed. Blood spills from the inside.

"Pear's going to kill me," I groan, looking at my face in my camera. "I can't let them see this. How am I going to hide it?"

"Mine wouldn't even notice." Alyse is still diminished. Pale and fragile and dusty, like something you'd find left under the bed for months. "They're both away and even if they weren't..." She shrugs. There are tears in her eyes.

"That doesn't—"

"Such a cliché, aren't I?" I've never heard her sound like this. Her swollen lip curls.

"It's still shit," I say. "Pear will care. But they'll ask a lot of questions that we might not want to answer. I don't know which is better."

"Yours," Alyse says, and I avert my eyes.

"Well, we can't go back to mine," Lou says. "Not only will they notice, they'll ban me from seeing all of you. Getting into fights?" He stands with his hands in the pockets of his overalls. His mask is still on, and his body looks poised for flight, like he wants to run through the evening streets until we're a distant memory.

Bianca looks off into the distance. I watch her. She barely blinks.

"Let's go to yours," I say to Alyse.

My phone has a message.

> 🕊: I'm at Sarah's. You're welcome to stay. We'd like to see you.
>
> Dylan: ill be at alyses
>
> Dylan: you met her the other day remember

There's quite the pause before they text back.

🥄: hmm ok. Stay safe love. Please call me before bed. Anytime is fine.

Fuck, of course they have questions. I feel crampy and my vision swims.

A bus comes looming up out of the dark, and Bianca lifts her hand to signal.

"This is me," she says.

I reach up and touch her arm. "Come with us."

She turns her eyes on me and blinks.

"You can go home later." After a failure, the leader needs to look out for the team. I feel the tension of her arm against mine, but she finally lets it fall. The lighted windows of the bus go humming past.

Nobody says anything. Our bus comes a few minutes later. This driver barely blinks at the state of us. Alyse hides her face behind her hand awkwardly, but I don't even think he'd care. The bus is almost empty. We take the row of seats at the back and sit in a stupidly-costumed line.

What a disaster.

I lean my head back. I wish my mask was still on so I could cry without anyone seeing me.

"We messed up," Lou says quietly.

"I'm sorry." It sounds like Alyse is crying but I can't see any tears. "I'm so sorry."

"It's not your fault." I close my eyes. "It's mine. I was worried we weren't prepared, but I tried to do it anyway. We'll be ready next time."

I feel Lou's whole body tense against me. "Next time?"

I roll my head slightly to the side. His mask is off and he's frowning.

"We'll talk about it tomorrow," I say. "With everyone. We'll debrief." It's such a stupid grown-up business word that it makes me laugh. It makes my chest hurt. I don't remember ever being in so much pain. I'll need to get tougher.

When we reach Alyse's, the house is dark. She lets herself in with a key. The sound of ambient music and shooting comes from deeper in the house. She flicks on all the lights in the kitchen.

"The bathroom's third door on the left down the hallway if anyone wants to clean up," she says. "If it feels like a long journey, you're not lost, just keep going."

"God, yes," Lou says. He disappears down the hallway gratefully. Bianca looks dazed but follows him.

Alyse looks at me. "Ice," she says.

"For you too." I follow her into the kitchen, which is vast and gleaming like the inside of a supervillain's laboratory. She opens a drawer, finds some towels, and takes them over to the fridge, where she pushes a button and it grinds out big chunky ice cubes. She fills the towels and hands one to me.

"Your face," she says and touches her fingers gently just below where it hurts.

"Does it look awful?" I ask.

She winces. "It looks sore."

I put the ice on my face. Tears involuntarily spring to my eyes, and I turn away.

"I need to lie down," Alyse says, except instead of finding somewhere comfortable, she clambers up onto the kitchen countertop and lies there like a body on a slab. The lights overhead are bright.

My skin feels sticky and my chest still hurts.

"Is the ice in the right place?" Her voice is muffled against the towel.

I step over to her and adjust it minutely. Her hands fall away, and I'm left holding the ice against her face.

"Yours isn't," she says, and moves the ice up a little bit. The pain gets worse. "Let me do it." She moves it up even further, and my head swims. I've obviously been avoiding the worst of it.

"Ouch," I say.

"I can't believe he punched us," Alyse says.

This weird cough-laugh thing escapes my throat. We stand there, holding ice against each other, like a sculpture of two broken things trying to connect.

"Dylan Taylor." Alyse's eyes are on me. It's a look I don't remotely have the energy to parse.

"What?"

"You said your name to me the day we met. Like it was a question." She smiles. "Ouch, gentle. I knew who you were, like I knew you from around. I always thought you were a mystery girl. And the more I know you, the more mysterious I think you are."

"I'm about as mysterious as…" I can't think of anything.

She moves the ice and I barely feel it. I think I'm going numb.

"…a blanket," I finish, because I can't think of anything lame enough.

She laughs, and she's so beautiful. Like I know she's shifting, but the weight of my regard renders her into something that would take anyone's breath away. I wonder what it would be like to kiss her. Like just out of curiosity. What would she turn into? This whole situation is weird. How am I standing here with Alyse, a couple of steps away from being actual friends?

"That feels better." Lou's in the doorway to the kitchen. He walks over and takes the ice away from

Alyse. He stands really close and holds it against my face. I shut my eyes briefly, and lean into him. I've still got my other arm stretched out, holding the ice to Alyse's face.

"I'm sorry," Bianca says, drifting towards us.

"What happened?" I try to meet her eyes.

"I couldn't bear for anyone else to feel what I feel." She goes very quiet and still.

I'm exhausted. I wish I could fix everything. Fix anything at all.

"That's terrible," is all I can say. "You don't have to do this anymore. It's not fair."

"I thought we were going to die." Her voice is high and strangled.

"It's okay. We're all alive, and we'll talk about more tomorrow," I tell Bianca, then I turn to Lou. "Does my voice sound normal?"

He shrugs and nods, so I call. I hate voice calls, but they insist sometimes.

"Hey, Pear," I say, like everything is fine.

"Dilly." Their voice is rough and warm and comfortable. It instantly makes me feel better. There's an urge to tell them what happened, but I quash it hard. That way lies madness and interrogation and unspecified consequences.

We talk briefly and it's like hearing my voice calms them too. They trust me. I've never given them much of a reason not to. I'm aware I'm breaking that, but I also feel like it's time. Mutations come in lots of different ways.

After I hang up, we all move into the lounge. Alyse and I hold ice on each other until we go numb. We all fall asleep in the same room—the four of us, survivors of our first catastrophe.

CHAPTER SEVENTEEN

I sleep surprisingly well, but wake up with the sun. Nobody closed the curtains, so it streams into the room. Usually I sleep terribly anywhere aside from my own bed. I wonder if Pillow missed me. Lou lies near me, his face loose and peaceful. I kiss him on the forehead and wander through to the bathroom.

The door is open and Alyse is regarding herself in the mirror. She's warped and sagging, her face covered in thousands of little scars.

"Morning," I say.

She sees me in the reflection and blushes. "I'm feeling pretty crappy after last night."

"None of it was your fault," I say, but she shrugs. "Your transformation was amazing. He lashed out because he was scared. You did too good a job."

"Really?" Her reflected eyes meet mine.

"Totally," I say. "You freaked me out completely." I step up to the mirror beside her and poke the blossoming shadow of my bruise. It makes me wince.

Alyse's reflection blurs as she returns to her normal self. "Come here and let me fix your face."

We stand facing each other. Her skin is darker than mine, so I can't use her concealer, but I find a small tub at the bottom of my bag. She stands very close and her face is intent. Her lips do this little pursing thing every time she touches me. When I turn back to the mirror, there's only the ghost of the bruise, like it's almost healed already. I dab some more over my forehead, to hide the worst of my skin.

"It's not that bad," Alyse says. "You should've seen mine before Mum put me on medication." She runs her fingertips over her own smooth face.

I look at our two reflections in the mirror. One of us is perfect and vibrant, while the other is a shadow of a girl. It makes sense, because I've never wanted people to see or understand me. It seems easier that way, so when people reject the projection of Dylan, they're not rejecting the real me. Except I'm still in here, inside this tangle, and I don't know how to get out.

There are so many things I want to say to Alyse. Forgive me, like me, take pity on me, don't give up on me even though I'm useless. Except if I say any of them, then my pride is gone, and it's the last thing I have.

"Are you okay?" Her eyes are whirlpools of sympathy that I can't let myself drown in.

"I'm fine."

We get to school barely in time, and Emma rushes over, pale and worried. Dani is beside her and won't even look in my direction. I guess if she does, the instinct to say 'I told you so' will be too overwhelming.

"I saw the footage," Emma looks from Alyse to me and back again. "It looked really bad."

"It *was* bad." My voice shakes, and I clench my fist as if that will centre me. "We'll talk about it properly later."

Everyone drifts away, even Alyse. I don't even see Lou. He's scared after last night. This was never anything he wanted, and now he's gone too. My real superpower is making people disappear.

Except when I turn around to head for class, Dani is still there. I don't know what she wants, and I'm too exhausted to even try decrypting her facial expressions.

"Are you okay?" Her voice is low.

"I'm fine." Bitterness floods through my response. "Just reckless, I guess."

"Did he hurt you?" She almost touches my face where the bruise is under the makeup. Her fingers hover, but I flinch away.

"It's fine. We'll do better next time."

I'm sure she wants to tell me all the things I've done wrong, but she doesn't.

"You need to look after yourself," is all she says, and then walks away. It's somehow worse. I'm so pitiful she can't even gloat. I'm a failure all around, a crappy leader with a crappy superpower. Reading comics didn't prepare me enough. I haven't learned to inspire people or manage my powers or anything useful. In the comics, people fuck up but they always regroup. The difference, as far as I can tell, is that people like them. In real life, they chose a dumbass leader and who'd stick around for me?

After school, we go back to Alyse's. I almost don't show, because I don't see the point. Why watch a slow-motion replay of your failure? Except Alyse waits outside school when the day limps to a close, ready to drag me off to my trial.

Emma has the drone footage on her laptop and asks if we want to see it. Every other fucking asshole in the stupid Cute Mutants says yes. It happened mostly the way I remember, except it's surreal to watch me drop and twitch around. I was down for longer than I thought. It's impressive when Batty leaps up off the ground to catch Tremor one hell of a whack across the jaw. He never even saw it coming.

"Give that bat a kiss," Alyse says with a laugh.

"There's nothing to laugh about," Lou snaps. "Dylan nearly died. We could have all died. We were playing stupid superhero games, but it's serious."

"He was supposed to be a robber." Bianca's quiet for her, leaning against the wall on the far side of the room. She rubs her chest as if she's soothing her demons. "Stealing shit from a liquor store doesn't make you deadly. Who hasn't shoplifted a bottle of vodka before?"

Um, me, but I don't bother saying it.

"We're obviously finished," Lou says. "Take the footage and give it to the cops. Game over."

"As long as Emma won't get in trouble for getting the footage in the first place," I say.

Emma's eyes flicker between us. "It should be fine. I'll be anonymous."

I feel like I'm collapsing. It's hard to breathe. Everyone is posed awkwardly, separate figures instead of a group. If this was a comic book page, they'd show the lines drawn jagged between us.

"This guy hurt us," I say. "He hurt Emma."

Lou moves restlessly. Nobody else says anything. Of course they don't care. Why would they care? They didn't grow up with this dream.

"He hit us like we were nothing." I target my words at Alyse. "He's a bully. We're not people to him, we're bitches."

"You know I'm in." Alyse is a gleaming statue of a warrior. I'd follow her into battle, but it looks like I'm the only one.

"I *was* in," Bianca says.

I turn towards her like I want to attack.

"Honest, I was, but that was all kinds of fucked up. Dylan, you're fucking mental." Bianca won't even look at me. "Like I get people have stupid obsessions, but you should stick to superhero tattoos instead of trying to live it out."

My hand goes to the X-Men logo on my wrist. My fingernails dig into my skin.

"Good luck with your demons," I say flatly. "I hope you enjoy playing with them on your own. We're supposed to *help* each other, to make each other better, to look out for each other, but I guess you want—"

"What I want is for you to get over your drama and fuck off," she says, exhausted by me.

"Don't you realise you could have died, Dylan?" Lou's breathing hard.

"Except she didn't." It's Alyse, with arms crossed and her skin gleaming. "We survived and got out of there. It's not like you were any help."

Lou flinches away from her. "It's not my fault," he says. "My powers—"

"You didn't have control of them, fine. But it was Dylan's power that saved us, and all you can do is tear her down about it, and tell her she's not good enough."

"That's not what I'm doing!" Lou's voice comes out high and whiny.

Bianca straight up walks out of the room at this point. She's done with us. Emma goes too, obviously happy for the opportunity to get the fuck out. This is all falling apart.

"I'm sick of you being a jealous asshole," Alyse says, her face demonic. "You're the one that's wrecking this group, because you can't fucking handle the fact that you don't have exclusive rights to Dylan anymore."

"She doesn't love you," Lou says sullenly. "She told me."

I have no idea where this came from, but Alyse reacts immediately. The demon is gone and in its place is this shrunken, shadowed thing that tears off down the hallway.

"You," I snap at Lou. "Shut the fuck up and go home. We'll talk later."

Then I stalk after Alyse.

It takes me three attempts to locate her room. I find her brother on the way, curled up in a gaming chair wearing nothing but baggy shorts and Beats head-phones. He doesn't even notice I've accidentally barged into his room.

When I do find Alyse, she's on her bed among all her clothes, curled in a ball. Her skin is stretched tight and her bones are crumbling underneath. It looks like she's deathly ill or about to be blown away after a Thanos snap.

"Hey." I sit down on the bed beside her. My hand flops stupidly between us, not brave enough to touch her. "Are you okay?"

"You two really talk about me behind my back?" Her voice is muffled in her pillow.

"Not really. The only conversation is Lou accusing me of being in love with you, and me saying you're my friend."

"I don't want you to be in love with me."

"No, I didn't think so." I have half a smile on my face.

"I thought you were both sitting there and saying horrible things about me. People have done that before. I couldn't face it from you." She begins to fade again, but I poke her in the side with my index finger.

"I would never," I tell her, completely honestly. "You're the sunshine one, like the trope, you know, because I am obviously the grumpy one. And I'm not professing my love for you or whatever, but having a sunshine person in my life is definitely cool."

She beams at me, and she's gorgeous. And I'm definitely not in love with Alyse, but I'm still vaguely curious about what it would be like to kiss her and how that would work with her powers. For scientific experimentation purposes only, obviously. Luckily I'm enough in control of my own brain that I don't do it, because it would make all this even worse.

"I'm really sorry it's over, Dilly." The beauty is fading, replaced by the waterlogged outline of sad Alyse. "I know the Cute Mutants meant a lot to you."

I'm so glad I don't have her powers, because I'd be a whirlwind of damp confetti, falling into the black hole that lurks at the heart of me.

"I'm sorry too." My voice is hoarse, and I flee the sympathy in Alyse's eyes.

When I make my way back, I find Lou waiting, all on his own. I barely look at him and head for the front door.

"I'm sorry," Lou calls after me. "I really am, Dylan. It's just—"

I'm halfway down the driveway when the door slams. Lou jogs past me. He stands in my way, so I walk around him.

"I don't want to talk to you." My emotions are smeared and jagged. I don't want to feel any of them.

"Look, it's just really scary. We can't run around like that pretending we're—"

"So that's all it is." I feel a rush of scorn so hot I think it'll scald me from the inside. "It's not that you're jealous of the fact I have other friends now."

His mouth twitches, like I've slapped him, and then he goes on the attack again. "What did you go off and do in Alyse's room?" He folds his arms and looks at me like he's unleashed some deadly strike.

"I talked to my *friend* and made her feel better after you were a dick."

He opens and closes his mouth a bunch of times, like he's frantically writing shitty dialogue in his head and discarding it.

"How is it you've surrounded yourself with hot girls in your pet little superhero team?" He asks it helplessly, like I've orchestrated all of this and he's the fool at its center. I don't have anything left to give him aside from the sullen remnants of the fire that burns at my heart.

"Then I guess you're extra glad you destroyed *our* team, aren't you?"

He stops dead when I say that, and I stalk off down the road. I refuse to look back. I won't let him see me cry. I wish I could hate him, but I can't. This disaster can be laid at my feet.

I'm almost pathetically relieved to get home and find Pear is there. They're on the couch reading some old sci-fi paperback with their glasses on. I slump on the couch beside them, almost touching.

"Dilly." The way they say my name has been a magic charm since childhood. It still works, but I wonder if it will ever wear off. "I feel like we've been missing each other lately."

"Busy bees," I say. "No Sarah tonight?"

"I love her," Pear says absently, "but sometimes it's exhausting."

"Ha." I nudge them with my elbow. "You love her."

"You're a remarkably immature child." They smile and touch my hair. I lean back against them.

"I had a fight with Lou." I recap the worst of it. It's hard to skirt the edges of my new mutancy, but I manage to. I talk about how he thinks I'm in love with Alyse and how his jealousy is insanely annoying and how he thinks I like girls, when as far as I'm concerned, I like *people*.

Pear grunts. They don't really get Lou's obsession with gender, even though they should because they've spent their own life trying to carve a space outside of it.

"In an ideal world, none of it should matter," Pear says eventually.

"It does to Lou," I point out.

"We're out of my territory," Pear says. "Sarah being a woman doesn't really mean anything to me. It's not anything about her looks that makes me like her." Which is ridiculous, because I know Sarah's in her thirties and a Mum and everything, but she is seriously good looking. "She's the kindest person I've ever met, and her smile lights up the world and that's what I love."

"So fucking sappy," I say, and I laugh because it's sweet and I adore it. Pear wasn't happy for a really long time, and it's not like they're a ray of sunshine now, but it's a lot better and a lot easier.

"So what should I do about Lou?" I ask.

"Do you love him?"

I nod. I think so. Love doesn't make any sense, but the knot of emotion I feel is complicated enough to be love, isn't it?

"And you're attracted to him?"

"Definitely," I say. That's not the problem.

"And he's kind to you."

I start picking at the band of their smartwatch. When did they get a smartwatch?

"Yes," I say eventually, but it's too close to the conversation I had with Alyse. Kindness is a hard thing to figure out. Sometimes people are kind when you don't expect it, like Dani checking in with me after my failure, when I was sure she'd dismiss me with the full power of weaponised snootiness. I remember her hand, tentatively reaching out to touch my face.

I want to tell Pear everything. About my powers, about everyone else. About my failure. Yet even though we're so close, there's a point we hit the parent/child divide. They still see me as a kid, and they care so much I can't see the edges of it. If I slit my heart down the middle and spill out all my loneliness and self-loathing, they'll buckle under the weight of it. They'll blame themself for what I've become and won't see they're a lifeline. I have to climb out myself, which I'm trying to do.

"I'm fine," I say and they brush their hand over my cheek. Their fingertips touch my bruise and I don't even flinch away. "It's just… tiring."

"Bed, then," they say gently. "Maybe things will look better in the morning."

I stumble through to my room, where Pillow and the others are both happy and concerned to see me.

"What happened to your face?"

"I banged it," I say.

"I hope it wasn't your silly superpowers game," Pillow says in a disapproving voice.

"Just clumsy."

It takes me a long time to fall asleep because my brain keeps cataloguing my failures and presenting them to me for inspection. Worst girlfriend, worst mutant, worst leader. Pillow mumbles underneath me that she thinks I'm delightful. I appreciate the effort, but really, she's only a pillow.

CHAPTER EIGHTEEN

I wake up bleary on Saturday morning, and the world looks no better. My alarm clock behaved itself, and didn't wake me up early even though it's still obsessed with catching worms. I open the curtains. A lady two doors down is out on the verge, fiddling with a lawn-mower. The douche across the road is in his garden, poking around among the weeds. It's the weekend and people are busy. Everyone's got shit to do. Except me, who now has nothing but a wide open future. I'm a lone mutant with no dream to follow and no team to support me.

Pear taps at the door.

"Lou's on the doorstep," they say. I feel a swoopy feeling in my chest. The odds of this being good news are super fucking low.

"Tell him I'll be right out." I spend five minutes staring at the mess on the floor. Why do I have no nice clothes? Oh, right, because I don't care about this shit, except for an occasional panicked moment when I do.

I put on truly shabby sweatpants and one of Pear's old t-shirts with a very faded band logo on it. I'm trying to make a statement about how few fucks I give.

Lou is on the couch when I come out. His eyes dart to me and then away again. Skittish, or else repulsed by my terrible outfit.

"I'm making pancakes," Pear says, and I want to message them the gif of the mind blown dude with the fireworks popping around his head. Unfortunately I can't psychically communicate with gifs, which would be my most useful day-to-day superpower. The reason for the shock is that cooking is not a typical Pear thing, like ever. The Gilmore similarities run deep. So this is some weird thing in aid of what? Fixing our relationship via food? Does that work?

"Cool," is all I say.

"Cool. Cool cool cool cool cool. No doubt no doubt no doubt," Pear says, shuffling around the kitchen with AirPods in a dance that's no dance I ever saw in my life. Lou and I catch each other's eye with a tiny smile, bonded by the weirdness and embarrassment of parents. I wander up to the breakfast island.

"Smells good," I say.

They don't hear me, so I wave. They pull one little white earbud out and lay it down on the bench. "Go talk," they say with a meaningful look.

I grimace and turn back to the couch. Lou's got his hands folded in his lap. He's watching me. I sit. There's enough room between us to hold hands, but neither of us makes a move.

"Hi," I say. My throat hurts. "I didn't think you wanted to see me."

"I usually come on a Saturday."

"We don't usually have a fight on Friday night." There I go, pressing the issue like an idiot. We can't even talk about the superhero thing, not with Pear right there.

"I was tired," he says. "Worried. Stressed. Upset." All those feeling words. I almost get heart-eyes, but the words are all about *him* and *his* feelings.

I close my eyes, because it's all too much. I'm not built for all of this. People are too difficult.

"I don't like being me," Lou says quietly.

All the careful hardness inside me melts in a flood. There are tears in my eyes. I pull him in close, and kiss his head. "I like you," I tell him. "I like you *so much*."

He lies against me, and he's warm, and I feel a rush of desire. I'm glad my superpower isn't glowing at certain precise moments. I notice there's no glow and no heat coming from him. The knowledge of it nags at my brain.

Pear bangs a plate down. Lou flees the obvious awkwardness of my embrace and goes to eat.

After breakfast, we walk down to the park and sit on the swings. I kick off and let momentum carry me back and forth in an arc.

"I'm not going to apologise for the hero thing," Lou says.

I close my eyes and tip my head back to feel the sun on my face.

"It was the right decision," he tells me earnestly.

I don't know how he sounds so fucking sure of himself.

"Dylan, are you listening to me?"

Everything about me right now can be summed up as ¯_(ツ)_/¯.

"I *am* sorry about Alyse though," he says. "You were right and I was a dick."

"Really?" I face him, trying to read the expression on his face as we pass each other in the air.

"Yeah, Alyse has been cool the whole time. It's just that I get scared and… I don't get what was so bad about how things were before all this?"

I try to smooth the frown off my face. "There was nothing *wrong* with how things were. But there's room in my heart for more than just you."

"You want to date more than one person at once?" Lou's voice is scoured clean of emotion.

"*Jesus.*" I fling myself off the swing at its apogee and land awkwardly on the grass. I whirl to face him. "Not everything is about dating! It's the team! Don't you get it? I want the team. Mirage, Cannonball, Karma, Sunspot and Wolfsbane. Cypher, Magik, Magma and Warlock. The New Mutants."

"But that's just a story, Dylan."

"It's not a fucking story." I'm crying and I don't care. "We were so close to having it, but I dropped it and it broke, and then you wouldn't even let me pick it up." The sun is warm on the back of my neck and my cheeks are wet. "I had room in my heart for you *and* the team." Every vowel shudders on the way out.

Lou steps forward and puts his arms around me. I know that he doesn't understand, but I cling to him because what else do I have?

"I'm sorry," he says again, and now he's apologised, it seems like it's all he can say, his mouth pressed against my hair.

School is even more hellish than usual. I try to avoid everyone. I know it's rude and I'm an asshole, but it hurts to see the Cute Mutants, and there's nobody else I want to interact with. Definitely not fucking Tara Pieters and Alyse's bigot friend Katie, who I find standing by my locker before school.

My teeth ache from clenching, from locking words inside my jaw. I can't even be bothered talking to them, so I veer away. The book in my locker can wait. It's not like I'm excelling in class.

"Dylan," one of them calls after me. "Dylan, wait."

I don't wait. There's no point. It'll only end in trouble.

One of them grabs me by the shoulder. I'm so fucking close to lashing out. All that stops me is the flash-memory of Tremor punching Alyse in the face. I've never actually punched someone, as often as I've imagined it.

I'm face to face with Tara. Her lips are stretched in a smile.

"I'm sorry to hear about you and Alyse."

"Fuck off, Tara. I don't want any of that."

"No, it's really sad." She mock pouts at me. "All of Dyke Club has broken up, it looks like. Such a tight little group and now you're sad and alone."

"Shh," Katie says. "The first rule of Dyke Club is you don't talk about Dyke Club."

"Why do you do this?" I can't hold this stupid facade up any longer. "What's the fucking point? Does it turn you on to be assholes to people for no reason?"

"We're trying to be nice," Tara says, although I can see she's trying not to laugh.

"Don't you remember we warned you about Alyse?" Katie says. "You were so rude and now you've figured it all out yourself."

"Oh stop." Tara smiles even wider, like the fucking Joker. "There's no point talking about it. Dylan's never played well with others. I remember when she turned up at school, this ugly little boy, and—"

I haven't thought about this in years, but it comes back in a rush. Tara was the leader then too, convincing all the girls not to play with me because I looked like a boy. The boys wouldn't play with me because they said I *was* a girl, then Tara convinced them all to call me 'it'. I remember drifting around the playground alone, trying to pretend I was going to find somewhere I belonged. At the end of the day, I went home crying. Once they managed to interpret my tears and awkward silences, Pear sat me down and told me very seriously that one day the world would accept people who were different.

Here we are today, and sure, things are more chill overall, but there are still Taras in this world.

"Oh look how sad." She smirks. "It's going to cry."

Something uncoils within me. I hear the row of lockers beside me draw in their breath sharply. There's so much rage in me it boils over. I couldn't hold it back even if I wanted to. There's a high pitched screaming noise that only I can hear. All the locker doors fly open at once with a sudden sharp movement.

One hits Tara directly in the face and another catches Katie a glancing blow to the temple. Tara screams and stumbles backwards to fall on her ass. One side of her face is a mask of blood. Her whole cheek is wet with it. People rush over, and someone kneels beside her.

"What the fuck did you do?" Katie screams at me, hand to her head.

"I didn't touch her." I'm an oasis of calm.

People are swarming, buffeting me from all sides. I feel numb and sated at the same time. All the rage in my heart has drained away. It doesn't take long for teachers to appear, a group of them calling for order and demanding stories.

"The locker doors flew open," I tell them. "They did it on their own."

A couple of people back me up, but Katie swears it was my doing somehow, and when Tara can talk sense, she blames me too. In the end, the deputy principal sends me home because she doesn't know what else to do.

"You were involved somehow," she says grimly. "Everyone agrees, and I don't need to call an ambulance for you."

Such is fucking justice.

My sentence ends up being a week of 'stand down.' It doesn't bother me at all. I sit at home and sleep a lot. When I'm awake, I re-read lots of old X-Men comics and catch up on the new ones too. I want to live on an island in the ocean with all the other mutants. I want my team back.

Lou, Emma, and Alyse all ping texts into my private void. I text back enough so they don't freak out but not enough to feel like I'm grabbing onto their stupid lifelines. I don't know why they bother. I wish I was a cyborg that could disconnect from everything and shut down.

Occasionally I read the news, looking for stories about quakes. I want to text Emma about it, to see what her data shows, but surely she'll tell me if there's something to share. There's a handful of similar quake-robberies. The cops have finally started to put it together that they're linked, but the name Jack Firestone is never mentioned. I wonder if Emma ever sent them the footage. If she did, they didn't care.

Eventually, I have to go back to school. On the first day back, I'm in biology along with Bianca, Alyse and Dani. Some shitty almost-team reunion that nobody wants to be at. The teacher's out at a meeting and we're supposed to do self-directed learning, which means everyone's hanging around talking or on their phones. I'm paying attention to nobody, doodling names on my pad. I'm barely aware of what's going on until Bianca sneaks up and swipes the pad out from under me.

"Fuck off," I say tiredly.

"Mohawk Storm," she reads. "Magik with a k and like love hearts beside it. Who is Magik and why do you love them so much and is Lou super jealous?" She sing-songs the last word.

"Shut up and give it back, Wraith," I say, feeling a little punch of rage in my chest.

"Not Wraith anymore, am I?" She carries on reading. "Dazzler, Mirage, Boom-Boom."

"Bianca, can you not?" I hold out my hand, but she ignores me.

"What the fuck even is this?" She waves the pad at me.

"It's a baller X-Men roster," Dani says and I frown at her, like how does she know this?

"Jubilee with stars beside it, and then it says Emma or Jean with a bunch of question marks."

"Emma Frost for sure." Dani smiles. Of course she'd pick her. Someone beautiful and capable of being vicious, who has a perfect diamond form.

"Fucking hell, Bianca." I'm out of my seat, but she dances away with a grin on her face.

"And then it says Chatterbox," she says.

"Who's Chatterbox?" Dani asks. "That's too niche even for me."

Alyse has her hand over her mouth and her eyes are sad. Bianca looks deflated and she drops the pad on the desk, like she realises it went too far. Maybe in her head it was a joke but once it was out of her mouth it wasn't. I get that. I do it all the time. But here and now I can't breathe.

"Oh," Dani looks from Alyse to me and back again. "Oh, shit."

I leave my bag and walk out the door. Maybe I'm crying, maybe I'm not. I head up to the first floor bathroom and barricade myself in a stall. I wish I could dissolve and flush myself away, out into the ocean where I'd be a polluted mess killing everything that lives there. Not much different to my actual life. I try and dredge up a spark of rage at fucking Wraith—no, Bianca—for doing this, but the flame won't catch. I sit there and hug my knees and play some mindless tapping game on my phone.

I don't come out until the end of the lesson, and I'm heading home when I see Lou and Alyse in some deep conversation. I naturally assume it's about my terrible freak out. That's the last thing in the world I want to deal with, so I duck into one of the tiny storage rooms where they keep spare computers or whatever. We're not supposed to be in here, but I don't care.

It's pitch dark inside and I lean back against this rack of stuff and say 'fuck' very quietly.

"Dylan?" Obviously the way I say fuck is very distinctive, but I know that voice too.

"Dani? What the hell are you doing in here?"

"Counting computers," she says. I can't see her, but it sounds like she's really close to me.

"In the dark?" I ask, and then feel stupid because of course she's hiding here, like me. "What happened?"

"Stupid ex." She sighs, and maybe there are tears in it. "She says I did something I didn't, and now people are—"

"Being fucking assholes." I feel this is a pretty solid guess, people being what they inevitably are. Dani makes a choking sound that I hope is like a combined laugh/sob and not actual choking.

"My mother would find your language appalling," she says.

"With all due fucking respect, fuck your mother," I say, feeling reckless and angry and stupid all at the same time.

For some reason, this makes her laugh. I can't see her face in the darkness, but I like hearing that.

"Fuck her," Dani says, her voice low and thrilled, as if she's saying it for the first time. "And fuck Lina too."

"Especially fuck Lina," I say. "She's honestly too dumb to fucking live."

"I don't even know why I went out with her." Dani sighs again. "Like she's cute and queer and—"

"Those sound like two perfectly good reasons."

"She's also fucking nuts. I need to vet people before I fall for them. Or stop settling for other people because the ones I really like aren't remotely interested."

I don't say anything.

"I should take my own advice," Dani says. "Don't be reckless. Do the sensible thing. Plan. Fall in love with the right girl, but love doesn't work like that does it?" She makes an incoherent noise, like she's venting all her frustrations in a single sound, and then falls silent.

We stand together in this tiny space and say nothing. I think about how Dani's always so disapproving of everything I do. The silence starts to get weird, so of course I make it weirder.

"Why do you hate me?" I ask.

"What?" I hear her body shift. Her tone is hard to read.

"Is hate too strong a word?"

"Dylan," she says, and pauses for what feels like a month. "I promise you I do not remotely hate you."

I don't know what she means by this, and I don't get a chance to ask because she pushes past me and leaves. The light from outside is fluorescent and bright and now the storage room is empty of her.

Out in the corridors, nobody is around. I head home before I run into anyone else.

The next day, I tell Pear my cramps are terrible and I can't get up. They make me a hot water bottle and give me headache pills and call the school. I stay home and do nothing. I ignore any messages I get.

The next day, I do the same thing. I don't know how long I can keep this going for, but I'm willing to go for a fucking record. Except after school, my phone won't stop chirping. When I give in and check it, I see an astonishing string of emojis and gifs from Alyse. I scowl at it until she sends a long series of Chris Evans laughing gifs and I finally crack.

> Chatterbox: ok hello alyse
> Moodring: oh look the beast awakes from slumber
> Chatterbox: im tired what do u want
> Moodring: enough sulking dilly
> Moodring: come to my house at six
> Chatterbox: i dont know
> Moodring: please
> Moodring: can u please please come

I stare at the messages. It's probably some stupid attempt to cheer me up, but it makes me smile all the same.

"You should go, Dylan," Pillow sighs. "As much as I love having you here all day, it'll be good for you to go out and see your friends. You miss them, don't you?"

She's right. I miss them desperately. So badly I don't know if I can face them. But my fingers are moving on my phone of their own accord.

> Chatterbox: ok fine
> Chatterbox: ill see u then
> Moodring: omg finally
> Moodring: im so excited 😬

I'm worried about what this is, but it's Alyse, so it could be anything.

CHAPTER NINETEEN

Alyse answers her front door looking like a Disney princess. Her eyes are enormous and her hair is a foaming torrent around her face. She looks like the word 'delight' has come to life in futuristic neon.

"I'm so excited. Come come come." Alyse takes my hand and tows me into one of the lounges. Emma is there, smiling almost as wide. She's practically dancing and her hair is pulled back in a ponytail.

"Tell her, Emma," Alyse says, and then when Emma doesn't move at light speed, she blurts it out herself. "We got you something—*us* something."

Emma rummages in a bag at her feet and pulls out some folded black clothes. She shakes them out so they hang down. There's a black sports bra with a Cute Mutants logo on the front in yellow writing. It's an adjustment of the latest New Mutants logo that's in this angular digital font rather than the old fashioned one, but it's a perfect choice and makes me nearly swoon to see it. She flips the bra over, and it says Chatterbox on the back.

Then she shows me some yoga pants which have Cute Mutants on the ass and Chatterbox written down one leg.

"This… I don't get it." I *do* get it. I'm not completely fucking stupid, but I want someone to spell it out before I jump to conclusions like an idiot.

"You were obviously upset," Alyse says. "About the Cute Mutants. I thought you didn't want to do it anymore, because you wouldn't talk about it, and were pretending it didn't happen."

I can't stop gaping at her. I never considered how it would look from the outside, to see my stupid Dylan facade with barely a crack in it, even though inside I'm blackened wreckage.

"Then with the thing in class the other day. Dani said you were making yourself part of the X-Men or something, I didn't really understand that bit."

God, this is so fucking embarrassing.

"So I talked to everyone," Alyse forges on. "And we all agreed that we'd do it again."

"Even Lou?"

Emma grins at me. "Alyse guilted him into rejoining. I don't know how. Anyway, he's trying his costume on right now. We got him a little sporty jacket in case the bra thing makes him feel weird." I'm still dazed by all this information and my expression must not be encouraging, because her smile fades. "I did the logo in Photoshop. Is it right?"

"It's—" I have to clear my throat, because the words are stuck behind something. "It's amazing. Like honestly, it's the coolest fucking thing."

Emma lights up again and her eyes go to Alyse, who is an incandescent candle of beauty. Of course everyone rallies around her. We're moths to her flame, except you don't burn from being near her, you transform in her aura. Even I become a little less awkward and worthless just by proximity. In this sprawling and beautiful house, she is a melancholy ghost wandering its corridors, but with us she becomes the sun we orbit.

"Thank you," I say, my voice all whispery again. "It means—" I gesture in incoherence, because if I dare unpack the jumble of feelings inside me, it will shatter my fragile shell.

"I think that means she likes it," Alyse says to Emma. She steps forward and hugs me, and my face is in her hair. I inhale the tangy-fruit smell of it and it tickles my nose. Emma puts her arms around us, and we stand together in Alyse's beautiful lounge. With every beat of my heart, I think that this is what a team feels like. I'm desperate to never fuck it up again.

When we finally disentangle, Lou is in the doorway watching us. The outfit looks good on him, like he's from some cyberpunk bike gang. It's got the Cute Mutants logo on the front and when I make him spin around, it says Glowstick on the back. I get tears in my eyes again, because I am apparently the sappiest fucking person that ever lived.

"It looks good," I whisper. "Really good. It suits you."

He nods and his hands go to the hem of the jacket. He tugs it down, because there's an inch of smooth brown belly showing the curve of his waist down to his hips and he hates it. All I see is Lou, my perfect mutant, and I wish he could see himself how I see him.

"I'm a Cute Mutant after all," he says.

"Really?" I take one of his hands and hold it tight.

"We've always been a team. That's what you said."

"We *are*," I say emphatically, and seal it with a kiss.

"Also Alyse is like very hard to say no to," he says, with a slight eye roll. "I don't know if you've noticed."

"You talked to Alyse?" God, I wish I'd had fucking tickets to that.

"There was some shouting," he admits.

"From who?" My eyes must be taking up half my face.

"Both of us, but in the end it was good."

I look over Lou's shoulder to where Alyse is standing with Emma, her hand over her mouth while she laughs. Being able to talk to people really is a superpower.

"She's not so terrible," I say, and Lou laughs.

"So I'm sorry for—"

"You're here now, which is the best apology." I kiss him again, because I'm feeling awkward and it's a nice shortcut for all the words that are hard to find. I don't want to prod deeper and find out he's only doing this for me. I want him to feel part of the whole group.

Even Wraith is here, although she ducks away when she sees me. I was such an asshole when the team fell apart, and I haven't made the slightest move towards an apology. I want to do it, but I don't know how to start.

"Okay." Alyse claps her hands and everyone turns towards her. "I'm so glad everyone could be here. The Cute Mutants are back together again." She beams, so bright we have to avert our eyes. "Except Glowstick is the only one properly dressed, so it's uniform time."

Everyone scurries off to different rooms to change. I end up in a bedroom on the other side of the house. The bed's a lot nicer than mine, but I don't know if anyone's ever slept in it. There's not much else here except a dresser with a fancy lamp.

I close the heavy drapes and start to undress.

"Oh, it's the sensitive girl," a soft, breathy voice says.

I freeze, but almost immediately realise it's the bed.

"I heard about you via the grapevine. Coffee table was talking to the lamp in the hallway, who passed it on via the mirror in the girl's bedroom. The coffee table thought you were frightful, but everyone else said you were lovely."

I finish getting dressed. There's no mirror, so I sit down on the edge of the bed and pat the bedspread gently.

"It's nice to meet you," I say.

"Can you lie down on me? It's been quite some time." The bed sounds lonely. I haven't been doing this long, but it seems like objects often are. They're made and they're bought and they're often left alone, parked away in rooms. We discard them after a handful of uses. I have this horrible nightmare of going to the dump and hearing all the objects calling out to me, thousands upon thousands of voices.

I swivel around and lay spreadeagled across the bed. It murmurs happily like it just wants a cuddle.

"How often do people stay with you?" I ask.

"Hard to know," it says. "Time is difficult, isn't it? Each time you open your eyes the years have flown by. You're just a little thing, but don't close your eyes for too long, or everything might change underneath you."

There's a tap at the door.

"You okay in there?" It's Alyse.

I open the door, and she looks me up and down.

"Chatterbox," she says with a lazy smile. "You look amazing."

I look at the floor. I know I don't look amazing and she's only being nice, but I can understand the urge to transform into something beautiful when you're noticed.

"The outfits are great," I say. Alyse looks like some Amazonian warrior in her Cute Mutants uniform. I have no idea how much is genuine and how much is Moodring.

We go into the kitchen, where Emma leans against the counter. In her uniform, she looks petite and impossibly perfect. I feel like a lump beside her. Except she grins so wide and claps her hands when she sees us, and none of that matters.

"I've been working on an app," she says to me. "If we all put it on our phones, I can track everyone from my laptop, communicate with you all by voice. It'll make it way easier to coordinate things in the field." She blushes and brings out her phone. The app has this pretty pastel colour scheme. She brings up the map view and I can see two glowing dots close together. "Me and Alyse are the only ones who have it installed." When she taps one of the dots, it pops up some icons and she taps one that looks like a phone.

"Hey," she whispers.

Across the room, Alyse's head jerks up and she smiles at Emma. I see her lips move, but I don't hear what she says. Whatever it is, Emma smiles in response.

"I can have multiple calls and switch between them and can link up whoever to communicate. It even does video feeds which stream back so we can record from multiple sources. We can plug in extra GPS trackers as well if we want to follow anyone and—" She cuts herself off and looks at me nervously.

"This is amazing," I say. "Every superhero team needs a genius to provide cool tech stuff. Can you put the app on my phone? Everyone else's too."

Emma hustles across the room to her laptop. She sits down, tapping away.

I glance across to Alyse, who's watching her too. There is definitely something appealing about someone who's good at what they do. I remember Dani in science class, the mix of certainty and expertise. Except given the rosy-tinged glow surrounding Alyse and the willowy, swaying form she's adopting, I wonder if there's more than admiration going on.

"Dylan." Bianca is standing behind me. I turn to face her, but she won't meet my eyes. She looks so fucking *long* in the new outfit, like she towers above me. Why is everyone so goddamn intimidating? I wish Batty was here. Maybe he could save me from awkward conversations.

"Hey," I say. "Look, I need to say that—"

"I'm really really sorry about everything," she blurts. "I was such a dick with your X-Men list."

"No, *I'm* sorry." My chest feels tight. "The thing I said about your demons. I'm the worst asshole."

"I told you I couldn't bear for someone else to feel what I feel, but that wasn't true." Her gaze finally flashes to mine, mascara streaked around her eyes. "They just—they hate me. If it's a choice between even a terrible incel prick and me, they'll hurt me. Because I'm just a shitty person with a shitty superpower and— Jesus fucking Christ, Dylan, why are you smiling?"

"I'm not smiling," I say, even though I am. "It's— I feel like that too."

"No you don't." She frowns at me.

"Who fucked all this up?" I'm talking way too loud, and I know everyone's looking at me. "It was my idea to confront Tremor. I was the one who had no real plan. I was the one who nearly died. I was the one who freaked out at you. I was—"

"Okay, fine." She reaches out and shoves my shoulder. "We both suck. Are you happy now?"

"Maybe we should call ourselves the Shitty Mutants," I say. "Or the Trash Mutants."

"Sadly, we have Alyse and Emma," Bianca says. "And I can't even call them trash mutants ironically."

"I was right about one thing," I say. "We need to help each other and make each other better. We need to train." My heart's skipping in waltz time.

"Like the X-Men," Alyse says from behind me.

"Like the Cute Mutants," I correct.

She smiles at me and my heart speeds up further. I look around the room.

Glowstick, Wraith, Goddess, Moodring and Chatterbox.

We're together again. I really, really, really can't fuck this up.

CHAPTER TWENTY

There's a reason TV shows and movies have training montages. It's because training is long, boring, and difficult. I know this in my head. It's a logical thing that everyone knows, but when you get up and do it every day, training is a real pain in the ass.

Running. Yoga. Self-defence classes. YouTube is our teacher. YouTube and Bianca, because once upon a time, she used to be very 'into' sports. This mostly means she shouts at us. It is not even a little bit fun, except it's not actually the worst thing either. She's genuinely the bossiest person I have ever met when she's in training mode, but she does make you feel good when you manage to finally do twenty pressups in a row. Then she ruins it by talking about how many more you'll be doing tomorrow like stfu Bianca.

The funny thing is how much Lou is into it. Our relationship has mostly been one of lying around, sometimes making out, often watching pointless shit on YouTube and occasionally wandering to the mall at a snail's pace. Now he's doing kickboxing classes and working out all the time. It makes me a little uncomfortable at first, to know I'm not the only one mutating.

The five of us become a unit. People see us differently. Emma makes us bracelet things that have a little metal CM charm attached. We wear them all the time.

The earthquakes don't stop just because we're training. There's another one at a jewellery store. The cops make oblique hints in the news articles we read online. The word *unusual* is used multiple times and there are earthquake scientists quoted. They're even more vague. Emma swears she sent the footage, but it's probably sitting in a spam folder somewhere. This is why we need goddamn vigilantes.

Everyone looks to me to make a decision. It's an easy one.

"We've been training for a week. Most of us can barely run to the corner and back. We're not ready."

Nobody argues with me, and we get back to training. It's painful. I can barely walk some mornings but

I keep at it anyway. I've never had anything I want this much before. We're all getting faster and stronger. It's still horrible but it's also kind of cool.

We learn to block punches, to take someone down with simple holds, to go for the crotch and the eyes. I can do Cobra pose and Happy Baby pose and even Intense Side Stretch Pose. I wish my superpower was training montages.

The other thing we need to train is our powers. We have to be able to rely on them when it comes to a fight. I figure it's easiest to work with people one on one. I start with Alyse, because she's probably the best with her power out of all of us. She's too distracted by external things, so we have to cut those down. I blindfold her and she uses her fancy noise-cancelling headphones. Then I play different types of music. Happy, scary, tense. When she focuses on them, she shifts, guided by nothing else but her mind and the sound. We spend hours flipping through her phone and choosing songs. She sits on the floor in her Cute Mutants outfit, flowing through various forms.

A vampire with bleeding eyes and fangs like a sabre-toothed tiger.

A vaporous, rotting skull atop a body that gleams with scales, her arms sinuous and strangling.

A twisted ragged doll-like thing with black button eyes and limbs that flap in impossible breezes. We're both scared by the movie *Coraline* that we saw as kids.

Things get even more bizarre.

Her face becomes a tumbled pile of grave dirt. Hands reach out of it and insects thrash busily among the soil. I scoot backwards along the floor.

Worst of all, her as a corpse, her skin waxy, her eyes sunken. I can barely look at her like this. My chest hurts. It's like a horrible vision of the future, and I close my eyes.

She takes her headphones out and pulls the blindfold off her face. She shifts back and she's Alyse again, the Alyse that she is when it's us together.

"Was I that scary?" She sees that I'm halfway across the room from her and the look of delight on her face makes me laugh, even though my heart still races. I bring her phone back over and we sit side-by-side and make playlists for different transformations. Being with her is easy, and I feel like we're gaining control. She tells me I'm amazing. Some days I believe it. I want to tell her she's my best friend, but I'm scared I'll ruin it.

Working with Lou is the most uncomfortable. I can make him glow. Even though things are still unsettled between us, I can do that much. Except we can't exactly stop and make out during a fight. If we were trapped in a dark cave, then sure, he could light the way out. If he gets really turned on, he gets hot enough to melt stuff, but again that seems more useful for escape-type situations too. I'm stuck until we get into an extremely uncomfortable conversation about edging. The upshot is that if Lou can fantasise about something and control himself from doing anything about it for a period of time, he can release a lot of light or heat in one go, like a flash grenade. The first time he does this, he blinds me so badly I can only see blobs of colour for half an hour. I have to wear sunglasses after that, and eventually he gets so powerful I have to wrap a towel around my head. The first time I warn the others of what he can do, they don't believe me and stand around laughing.

When he lights up they all scream. He watches them scatter, and he looks sad.

"You don't have to do this." I nudge his shoulder.

"It's so important to you," he says. "And I don't want to be left behind."

The others are flapping their hands and squealing about flashing lights.

"You asshole, Glowstick," Bianca shouts, but she looks happy.

"I'm part of the team," Lou says.

"You *are*," I say, as emphatically as I can, like leaning my whole body into the word. Sometimes I still feel like the rest of us are all joined tightly together and he's floating off on a kite string on his own. I'm frantically trying to pull him in, but I don't know the words that can make him feel the way I want him to feel. This could all be in my head. The main thing is he's here and he's trying. Maybe I really *can* bridge my old world and my new world.

"I love you," I offer, because it's the best thing I have.

"Ditto," he says, his lips soft on my skin.

I can't solve Bianca. I wish I could. We spend hours sitting crosslegged, knee to knee. Mostly we just talk.

Sometimes we play music for each other. We have entirely different tastes and make fun of each other for it, but sometimes we find a song we both like. Funnily enough, it's usually Pear's old music like New Order or Blondie. Bianca tells me I'm good at listening, but it's mostly that I shut up. She has a lot of questions too.

"Why don't you ever go to Queer Club?" She prods my knee with one finger.

"You have to talk in a circle. Lou told me." There's a long pause. "Plus I feel weird trying to claim queer, like—"

"Dylan," Bianca says. "You're in a relationship with a—"

"Boy," I say firmly.

"Yes, I know, I know, Jesus Christ. But like, you're pan, right?"

"Maybe. I don't really worry about labels. Like I don't feel like I'm really a girl, but I don't know what I am instead. My body doesn't feel right, and if I could be an alien or a ray of light, I probably would. But I don't know. I feel like I'm just me."

Bianca rolls her eyes. "Speaking as a defiant queer, we need all the help we can get. Bring all the weirdos into our big tent. Have a party."

"I'm shit at parties," I say with a grin.

"Maybe you just haven't been to the right ones."

I shrug, and she gives me a wicked grin. "By the way, you're definitely pan. I've seen the way you look at Alyse and Dani."

"You can't define me! Besides, I don't look at them."
I know I'm blushing.

She pats my leg. "It's ok. You can admit it to me. I'm your emotional support himbo."

"Himbo," I snort, and dissolve into helpless giggles as she strikes muscle poses, and holy shit, with all the working out we're doing she is getting crazy buff. We should've given her the codename Scorpia.

"It's Dani, though," she says. "I watched your face when I said the names."

"It was a twitch." I fight to stay deadpan.

"You're allowed to be attracted to other people. You can even be poly if you want."

I fix her with a stern glare. "You've met Lou, right?"

She bursts out laughing. "Lou likes sharing as much as Shell. God, you should hear what she says about you lot. She calls you my work wife cult."

I laugh, but there's an edge to it. "Does she make you happy?"

"I don't know," she says. "Does Lou?"

We're quiet for a minute after that, and then we change the subject.

I never ask her to use her power. I don't want those things to feed on her, and I don't want them to feed on me either. We just talk.

"I've been practising," she tells me one day when we're out in the garden at Alyse's house. The lawn is smooth and green. They have people that come in and make it this perfect. "On the nights where Shell is sulking about whatever and it's just me alone with my little demons."

"Bianca." I sigh. "I never asked you to."

"I know. But I want to be part of the team." She pushes her knee against mine. "The fact you never demanded it makes me want to do it more."

"Because you're stubborn?" I ask.

"You treat me like I'm not a piece of shit."

"I feel like that's a pretty low bar to clear," I say, and that makes her laugh.

"You'd be surprised. Anyway, watch." She pulls down the top of her bra. Her fingers scrabble at her chest. There's that disturbing visual of watching her fingers sink under her skin. The darkness inside ripples, and three creatures come stalking out on shadow legs. Their little heads tilt left and right. Their mouths yawn open.

"No, no," Bianca says. "Behave. Run over there and see what's happening." She points to the far end of the garden, where the swimming pool fence is. The creatures go skittering off, fast and jerky. When they reach their destination, they turn back quizzically.

"Come on then," she whispers. The creatures blur back towards her and she lets the opening in her chest close up again.

I stare at her. "That's amazing!"

"I learned my pain is real but it doesn't own me. I don't have to always be that person." Her eyes meet mine. They seem calm. "You showed me that."

And then there's Chatterbox. I train myself relentlessly. I'm not getting enough sleep between everything that's going on, but when I do it's deep and dreamless and Pillow keeps me safe. I'm trying to understand objects.

I walk down our street at midnight, a gaggle of recycling bins following, tipped up on their wheels and their lids dangling. I feel the cool air on my skin, my bare feet on the damp grass, and listen as they murmur among themselves about what they hold inside, and about me too. They find me fascinating. To them I appear as a blur of light, a gossamer girl trailing glowing streamers from her hands.

I detour through the mall car park on the way home from school. I run between the rows of cars.

"Unlock," I say, and I hear the rapid *ka-chunk* of cars opening to me.

"Lock," I command and they return to their previous state.

I blip their alarms and silence them. I turn their stereos on, and make them rumble so the bass bleeds static. I flash their lights and screech their wipers over dry windscreens.

Here is the secret, and it's an ugly one. Cars are made to serve. It makes me uncomfortable how eager they are to do the bidding of humans. Tools in general are easier to get a response from. Things made to be used. All I need is a small amount of anger and when I speak, they hear me.

I cultivate my rage. There are a lot of things to be angry about.

The other thing I learn is about volume. I don't need it. They can hear a whisper across a crowded room. I feel like if I could learn the secret of it, they could hear me thinking. They're so receptive. They're made to be servants, but they see me almost like a prophet. It makes me feel uncomfortable, but powerful too.

I feel like I'm changing too fast, like my brain can't fit everything I'm learning. Sometimes I lie there at night after I've been out in the dark speaking with objects, and I feel like my skin is superheated and my brain can't fit all my thoughts in. It's Pillow that pulls me together. She's very soothing and patient.

Pillow also seems to get smarter the more we talk, like there's something symbiotic happening. It gives me an idea and I start bringing the baseball bat to bed with me too. He's tentative at first, but soon joins in our conversations. I feel guilty, like I'm using him, but I want him to bond with me. He already saved me once.

I paint him up purple and green to match my costume. I write *Smash the Patriarchy* on him because sorry Harley, but 'good night' isn't badass enough for us. I tell Pillow and Batty the things we want to do. I spill my dreams and the mundane shit we've done in training. They hear about Tremor and what he did. I feel a little cruel that I'm expanding their minds only to fill them with the bad things in the world.

One day I find myself lined up in the cafeteria next to Dani. She's been orbiting us on the periphery because Emma drifts between her and the mutants. It's clear she still wants nothing to do with the reckless lot of us.

"I hear you're all trained up," she says.

"I remember someone telling us we should do things properly." I keep my tone cool, try to stay as fucking chill as her.

"I didn't mean this." She gestures to the charm bracelet on my wrist, and I close my hand around it. "What some of you can do—It's serious, Dylan, and you treat it like you're still playing games with your little superhero club."

My eyes meet hers. "Oh, I'm entirely serious. We all are." My heart is thumping like I've been training. I don't want to interrogate this feeling because I'm honestly scared of what it means and I'm not ready to follow that thread. "Your power is amazing and our team could be even stronger with you. We could be—"

"She made her decision." Lou comes up behind me, his hand grazing my waist.

Dani's gaze shifts to a point over my shoulder and her lip curls. "Oh yes, I'm well aware that you don't want me on your team."

I turn against Lou's hand, glance at the line of his jaw. "What are you talking about?"

"Lou was very clear there was no need for me. Not that I wanted to join."

I frown at Dani, transfer it to Lou.

"Lou, what the fuck?"

"She made her decision." His eyes are fixed on Dani, like they're having an argument of their own that I'm left out of.

"It's not like a permanent decision for the rest of time," I protest, trying to insinuate myself between them. "Dani, you can always join."

"There's no way," she says. "You're all as crazy as each other, no matter how much you pretend. And by the way, Lou, that thing we talked about? There's no way in hell you could stop me."

She turns and walks out of the cafeteria, and I watch her the whole way.

"What *thing* is she talking about?" I ask, once I can't see her anymore.

"Nothing," Lou says, and leans away from me.

I try to get it out of him, but he won't budge. There's no point talking to Dani about it. I wish there was some way I could change her mind, but she doesn't want to be part of the team. I'm grateful that everyone else wants to do this with me, but there's a part of me that keeps replaying her walking away.

Later that day, there's a bigger quake. It's at Eastgate mall on the other side of town. It's right at the end of the day, so everything was mostly empty, but a couple of people got injured when a display in the supermarket collapsed on them.

The pictures in the news don't look good. The front of the mall has crumpled in and the neon sign on top has come crashing down into a splintered wreck. There's an ambulance there, and official figures standing around.

"We should be doing something," Alyse says.

"Don't worry." I'm staring at the TV. "We'll do something when we're ready." I'm scanning the crowd shots, wondering if Tremor's there somewhere, watching the chaos.

"Aren't we ready now?" It's Bianca, sitting on the edge of the couch, drumming her fingers rapidly against the leather. She gets to her feet and paces the room. "You're not freaking out because of what happened last time are you? Because we're a lot better now."

"I know." I look around the room at everyone. "We're so much better. We're nearly ready. But we need to do this right. This has to be the endgame. We're going to stop Jack and deliver him to the cops in a way they can't ignore."

Everyone nods. They trust me, which is still a disorienting feeling. I think I'm the same person I always was, but maybe I'm not, and I'm too close to recognise it.

CHAPTER TWENTY-ONE

The decision hits me out of the blue. It's three days after the quake at the mall. I wake up one day semi-well-rested and my brain is like *well fuck it, let's go.*

"Yes, dear, sounds utterly splendid," Pillow murmurs and I wonder if she read my thoughts or if I accidentally said it out loud.

There's a plan in my head that seems solid. I poke at it with my drowsy brain. I know life is unpredictable, but I've got contingencies in there and everything. It's slightly more advanced than knocking on his door and asking him politely to stop. I chat with Pillow and Batty about it, and then text the gist to the group.

> Wraith: omg look guys chatty's all grown up
> Wraith: jk that sounds amazeballs
> Goddess: Chatterbox this is amazing!
> Goddess: I'll be your eye in the sky!
> Goddess: 🥳🥳🥳
> Glowstick: sounds good babe

Moodring: ok sure i know im the one with the
biggest mouth
Moodring: but wow this is scary good
Moodring: and scary scary too
Moodring: we can do this guys!!!

I sit on the bed with my phone on my lap. I try not to think about the one million things that can go wrong, and instead think about the fact I've got a team and a plan. I lie back down, look up at the ceiling, and don't even try to hold back my smile.

"Yes, you're very clever," Pillow sighs contentedly.

We meet at the mall and eat burgers and tacos and sprawl over two tables. Alyse has her giant iPad. We bring up maps and notes and poke around with greasy fingers. We all talk over each other, but everyone defers to me. It's dizzying. We refine the plan. We memorise the plan. We spill taco fillings all over the plan.

When we leave the mall, everyone knows what they need to do.

Pear is at Sarah's, so we get ready at my house. It's not at all the same mood as last time. I don't have my period. My skin's semi-sort-of-ok. I don't feel any urge to throw up. If I could transform like Alyse, I'd be a warrior made of steel and bone. Everyone else seems infected with the same mood.

We play the theme song to the anime *Yuri on Ice* on repeat. When that chorus hits, we feel fucking invincible. We turn it up and dance around the living room. It's the dumbest thing ever, but I honestly feel like a superhero.

The song ends and Emma sits down at her laptop, immediately bringing up the drone feed which shows the car still parked outside his house. We've all got her app on our phones and headphones in so Emma can speak to us.

"Let's fucking do this," I say.

The main group heads off to the bus stop, while I get on my bike and head through the streets. I'm wearing baggy sweatpants and a hoodie, with my costume on underneath. Luckily the autumn weather is cooler. I cycle slowly through the streets of suburbia, swerving in big arcs along the quiet streets. They're deserted aside from a few dog-walkers. People pay no particular attention to me, aside from the low-level wariness around teenagers on the loose. They have no idea.

By the time I reach Tremor's house it's full dark. My tyres hiss on the smooth asphalt. I detour into the park a few doors down from his house, where I take off my hoodie and pants and shove them to the bottom of my backpack. I pull my mask down over my head. Visibility's fine. I'm going to need it.

Chatterbox, garish Spider Hero costume and all, reporting for superhero duty.

I cruise my bike down and stop opposite his house, legs dangling down to the ground. The curtains are open and the lights are on. Patterns from the TV are cast on the wall.

"I'm in position," I say to Emma.

"I can see you." Her voice is calm in my ear. Reassuring. "You're good to go."

I climb off my bike and let it fall to the ground. I pull Batty off the frame and heft him in my hand. Tremor's car is pulled up onto the side of the road so the tyres are on the verge. I fumble in my backpack for one of Emma's gadgets—a little GPS tracker in a key hider. I crouch down and attach it to the car just above the front wheel.

"Done," I tell Emma. "Does it show up?"

"Perfect. Tremor's now wired in."

I take a deep breath. "Hey, buddy," I say to the car. "I'm really sorry about what's going to happen."

"What *is* going to happen?" His voice is a low rumble. It's wary but excited too.

"It'll hurt a little bit, but not too bad. Mostly just a loud noise."

"Is it for an adventure?" God, save me from fast cars.

"Something like that," I say. "Scream for me, kitten." It's embarrassing, but cars enjoy being talked to like characters in the noir movies we studied at school. I stand under the harsh LED glow of the streetlight. It makes me lurid. I fancy I look like an aberration, something that doesn't belong. A dangerous girl, let off the leash.

The car raises his voice, a harsh electronic siren.

The door to Tremor's house bangs open. He stands on the front steps, peering across the road at me.

"Oh fuck," Batty says, as I swing him back and smash him into the tail light of the car. "Ouch, that hurt."

"Hush, you big baby," I tell him.

The alarm splinters into static and resumes.

Tremor thumps down the stairs, arms out and swaggering. "Hey, you're that little spider! Back again for more, you dumb whore? You want to tattle to the pigs? I'll fucking kill you!"

Tremor extends his hand and points it at me, but this time I'm ready. I run to my bike and straddle it, then kick off hard. I pedal as fast as I can, cranking through the gears. A grinding sound comes from behind me. I turn and watch a crack zig-zag towards me, the earth tearing open. I swerve wildly to avoid the tail end.

"Fucking bitch!" Tremor runs across the road to his car and the alarm blips off. His door slams. The ignition catches, and the engine whines past what it can bear. Underneath, I hear the car whimper.

I focus on moving as fast as I can.

Tremor comes after me with a screech of tyres. So far, the plan is working. I've taped a wing mirror to the handlebars of my bike. I tilt it with one green-and-purple hand, and see headlights behind me.

Fucking hell, he's close.

"Tracker is working perfectly," Goddess says in my ear.

"Yeah, we have other problems," I pant, then glance in the mirror again. "Mysterious women don't like cars that move too fast," I murmur.

"Oh gosh, I'm sorry," the car splutters. The engine hiccups and dies.

Tremor shouts, and after a brief pause the car roars to life again. It's enough time for me to put much needed distance between us.

I cut through the supermarket car park on the corner. He follows me in and I shoot down the alley where the deliveries are made, coming out onto a busier street. I pause, waiting. He needs to follow.

He comes around the corner way too fast. Horns blast. People flash their headlights in irritation. I sprint the bike across the road, making sure he gets a good look, then I take a tight turn and race off down the opposite side. He can't see me properly through the traffic, but I can hear him shouting out of the open window.

He keeps honking the horn, but other cars keep him jammed in and I don't have to pay attention to the rules of the road. Once the traffic thins out and he catches sight of me again, I duck down a side street. Back in suburbia, it's rubbish day, the red and green bins lined up neatly.

The car roars into the street behind me.

"You're comin' on way too strong, baby boy," I tell him, and the engine dies obediently. He screams when Tremor starts him up again.

Bins hate rubbish day. They're too full, jammed with other objects that complain of being trapped in their bellies. The green waste bins are tired of their fetid stench and of being left too long without cleaning.

I take a right, skip over the middle of a roundabout, take another right.

Tremor follows me. We're in one long street with no exit. From here, it's only neat rows of houses and the looming shadow of the forest.

He probably thinks I'm cornered. The car revs into a shriek and his voice howls in harmony. The stereo starts up, but there's nothing but bass, all staccato and distorted.

"Assemble," I call, and raise my fist into the air.

Behind me, a row of bins rolls into the street, directly in front of the oncoming car. From the sound of the hollow bang, he hits at least one. I hope it's green waste, that his windshield is covered in refuse and slime.

I don't turn to look, because I'm focused on pedalling. I need to reach the forest before him. My legs burn. There's a reason we did all that damn exercise. I can't see him in the mirror. When I risk a look over my shoulder, he's in the street, fighting his way through the bins that roll back and forth. He clears a path and gets back in the car.

By this point I've reached the entrance to the forest park. The gate is closed. I ask it very nicely to open, and it obeys with a slow creak. The instant the pool of his headlights reach me, I'm off, full-tilt blasting across the gravel.

I wonder if he questions this. Why would I run somewhere dark and isolated, where there's nothing but trees to bear witness? Does it never occur to him, even for a second, that he's being lured here?

I almost skid on the gravel, but right myself. Up ahead is the car park and a wide open grass area. Right at the edge are the rest of the mutants. It's everyone but Goddess, but I know her drones are overhead and that she's watching.

"She said you were coming," Moodring says urgently. "I was still fucking scared."

I coast to a stop, kick my bike onto the ground.

"Get back," I pant. "He's here."

Tremor's car swings into the parking lot. The bass rattles the windows. He turns a slow circle and the pool from the headlights moves across the ground until it reaches my knock-off Converse and the purple and green bottoms of my shitty costume. The tyres lock, skidding on the gravel. He revs the car. He thinks he's got me cornered. He wants me scared, wants me to run.

"To me, my Cute Mutants," I say.

The car speeds towards me.

"Don't touch me, baby," I whisper.

The car's engine goes dead instantly.

"None of that singing. I'm not a girl who likes to be serenaded."

The stereo cuts out and there's nothing but wind and trees and a gentle pinging from the car's engine.

"In fact, I don't even like you looking at me."

The headlights go dark. The night is mostly cloudy, with only a few ragged patches of stars visible through the holes they leave. Everyone reaches into their pockets and pulls out heavy sunglasses. We all turn our backs and close our eyes.

The only noises are from Tremor. The door opens, there's some banging, and the door closes.

"I can't believe this. Talking shit about me to the pigs? Have you been spying on me? I'll catch you and

I'll kill you. I'll take my time too, you stuck-up little c—"

Even with my eyes closed and my sunglasses on, I sense the flash from Glowstick, like the sun briefly rose. It's not his brightest, but Tremor bellows.

"You can open your eyes now," I tell the car, and he flicks his headlights back on.

Tremor's on his knees. His eyes are open and he's blinking rapidly.

"What the fuck was that? I can't see. I can't fucking see." His tone rises higher.

"Your turn," I tell Wraith.

Her demons look like they're made from smoke in the headlights' glare. They fall upon Tremor, who paws at his eyes as if that will return their sight. The demons surround him, wrapping their light-and-shadow hands around his arms and throat. They nestle their heads in against him and sink glowing fangs into his skin. Tremor screams. It's a chilling sound and I almost want to stop. Then I remember who he is and what he's done, and I let the demons carry on. Wraith looks nervous. I reach out and touch her shoulder lightly. Moodring joins on her other side.

Tremor is incoherent, ranting and crying. I don't know if the pain is physical or mental. He says something about his father and what a prick he is, about how his Dad let some bitch take him away. He rambles about different women he's known, things that make me sick to hear. Wraith lets out a strangled sob. I don't know how someone becomes like this. How does he have so much hate in him? I can't watch this anymore. I squeeze Wraith's shoulder. She gratefully closes the void in her chest, and her demons return. Part of me wishes they could stay with Tremor forever, but that's not how things work.

"My turn." Moodring's tone is light. She puts her AirPods in and tugs the blindfold up over her face. I guide her gently towards the figure of Tremor, still lying on the ground. She whispers to her headphones, choosing a playlist.

Tremor blinks rapidly. "Oh thank Christ," he says. "My fucking eyes, I can see something."

He's confronted by a monster. Something pale looms over him, a face reminiscent of his stepmother who Emma found information on. A *Coraline* version of someone he hates. Her eyes are empty voids and her mouth is a bloody slash in her face. Her hands reach out, clawed and grasping.

"Jack," she says, her voice rich and welcoming. Her tongue is forked and bleeding, and her teeth glow red hot in her mouth. Fucking hell, Moodring is terrifying sometimes.

Tremor screams, and scuttles backwards until he hits the grille of his car, steaming lightly in the cool night air. He looks around wildly in a panic, until his gaze lands on me.

"You," he snarls. "I'll kill you. I bet you're ugly under the mask. I bet nobody wants to fuck you. You don't have the right to come at me. I can end *you*, not the other way around." He places his hands on the ground.

I thought all this might unsettle him or break him. I thought he might beg for us to stop, but no—he only wants to kill me.

The plan accounts for this. I don't know if the plan accounts for how badly I want to hurt him. The desire thumps in my chest like a second heart.

"Get back." I gesture with one hand at the others.

The ground rumbles around us. It feels as if the world is shaking apart, but it's all from this one guy. A man with too much power.

"This needs to stop," I tell the car, rage threaded through my voice. I feel him respond in my head, a ferocious weapon of metal and oil. "Hit him for me."

The car revs to life and bunny hops forward, catching Tremor a decent whack in the back and sending him sprawling. It disrupts his power. There's a crack in the ground between us, a reminder to take him seriously.

"Keep your hands to yourself," I snap at him.

"Fuck you," he spits, unfocused.

"Accio bat." I hold out my hand and Batty sails through the air, landing in my palm with a satisfying thwack.

Tremor has been blinded, set upon by demons and haunted by a thing from nightmares. Now all he has to face is a girl in a stupid costume.

"Who the fuck do you think you are?" The tendons stand out in his neck. He holds out his hand towards me. I feel the rumble beginning in my chest. "This is some feminazi thing, isn't it?"

My heart races.

It's me and him and a baseball bat in the dark.

"Because if that's your problem, I'll ra—"

No. Fuck him. He doesn't get to finish that sentence. *Fuck him.* I swing the bat as hard as I can at his outstretched hand. I whisper an apology to Batty as he flies. He says he forgives me, and then I feel the impact. Something breaks. More than one something. Tremor screams, and I hear his scream mirrored behind me by someone. Lou, I think.

"Dylan, no," he says, horrified.

Fucking codenames, Lou. Right now, I'm not Dylan. I'm Chatterbox.

There's blood on Batty. It glistens in the headlights.

Tremor looks at his hand in disbelief. There's bone sticking out. He takes these huge, shuddering breaths. I'm a heart-fluttering second away from hitting him again. I know if I start, I won't stop. My body is a fragile cage for what burns inside me. It scalds my throat. My hands shake so hard I nearly drop the bat.

"Knock him down," I tell the car. He lurches backwards and then surges forward. His bumper connects with the side of Tremor's head and sends him sprawling. I crouch beside him and roll him over. He's alive. His chest rises and falls.

"He's done," I tell Emma. No doubt there's a drone over our heads, watching this with a night vision camera, but I want to tell her anyway. I want everyone to hear the words come out of my mouth.

"Calling the cops," she says.

I know this is a risk but I don't know what else to do. We can't kill him, can we? We have to trust the system, even though it doesn't make much sense to me. Maybe I'm just too obsessed with stories of supervillains.

"Ohmigod Chatty, I thought he was going to kill you," Moodring says.

We stand together in a circle. I'm drenched in sweat. I want to scream in triumph.

I catch Lou's eye for a second, but he turns his head away. I wonder what the scene looked like through the camera of his eyes. What did he think when he watched his girlfriend break someone's hand?

We check the car, who has already told me what we'll find. Black plastic sacks full of liquor. A diamond necklace that's slipped down the gap in the seats. There's even a gun in the glove compartment. I'm lucky he didn't think enough of me to use that first.

Moodring takes a rope out of her bag, and we tie Tremor's hands behind his back so he can't point at anyone and quake them. It turns out Wraith's good with knots. There's also a note that goes with him, warning the police about his hands. I have no idea how believable they'll find it, but it seems like our only option.

The faint sound of sirens becomes audible, so we disappear into the night. The lights on our phones bob among the trees as we make our way up to the ridge that overlooks the car park. I can barely make out the unconscious figure of Tremor lying in the pool of light cast by the car.

"They're here," Emma says. "I can see them from the air. I'm going to take this little guy out of range. We don't want him spotted. I'll meet you at the rendezvous point."

Batty's still clenched in my hand as we dart off through the trees. My last glimpse is of red and blue lights joining the pool of yellow. I want to stay and watch everything, but it's too risky.

"Trust the plan," Moodring whispers to me, as we slip away, near-silent and victorious.

CHAPTER TWENTY-TWO

We exit the forest across from the golf course, and sneak around the edge of the manicured greens. They're drenched in hissing sprinklers which we avoid to make our way through the tangle of suburban streets. I'm the only one with a bike, so I walk it alongside everyone else. Once we reach the main road, Emma comes flying out of the dark and barrels into Alyse. She hugs us one after the other.

"We fucking did it," Moodring howls. "Cute Mutants!"

I take my mask off. The cool night air feels amazing on my damp face.

"Chatterbox, our fearless leader," Wraith says. "That was one hell of a plan. And what was with *accio bat*? It was both the nerdiest and coolest thing I have seen in my life." She holds out her hand and strikes a pose, lifting Batty up like a sword.

"It was amazing," Moodring says. "It went flying into your hand like magic. And then you hit him like that! Look, I'm shaking." She holds out her hands and her fingers are trembling, like there's a tiny earthquake moving through them. She's transformed into something both radiantly beautiful and warrior-fierce. It's quite a look.

"You okay?" I nudge Glowstick, who looks dazed.

"It was intense," he says. "You broke his hand."

"Did you hear what he said?" I'm glad I don't have Moodring's powers or my eyes would be spitting flame. For a moment I think he's going to argue, but any belligerence collapses along with the tension in his shoulders.

"You were—it was scary." He leans against me and closes his eyes. "I was so scared, but maybe he deserved it."

Bianca snorts in the background. Even Emma rolls her eyes.

I put my arms around him and I feel him trembling.

"Are you really okay?" His eyes search mine, but I think they only see fire there.

"I'm good," I say, but adrenaline howls in my veins like a siren. I want to dance on top of a car. I want to wield Batty like he's fucking Mjolnir and call down lightning.

"I need to get home," Lou says. "Or I'll be in so much trouble."

It's true. His parents are intense around where he needs to be and when. It's like they think that if they control every other part of his life, they'll somehow make him fall into line with this mythical ideal of him that makes no sense. We've missed the last bus, so Alyse calls him an Uber. He protests, but only feebly.

Bianca's girlfriend comes by and picks her up, which leaves me with Alyse and Emma.

"Fucking crazy shit," Alyse says, still in warrior mode.

"I liked hitting him." I can admit it to these two, unlike Lou. I don't know how that conversation would go.

"I wish I could have seen it in real life." Emma pats Batty gently. Her voice isn't as quiet as usual, and she's not hiding behind her hair. "He deserved it."

"He did." The world blurs for a second and then comes back into focus. My eyes are heavy but my heart still races.

"We did it." Alyse links arms with both of us. "We stopped Tremor."

I wonder what the cops are doing with him. What story will he tell them? Will they believe our note? Too many questions, and I feel itchy not knowing the answers. My brain thrashes in circles, and I can't tame it.

Alyse insists on calling Ubers for us too, even though I protest.

"I like helping," she says. "So let me help."

"Thank you." I lock my bike up by the bus stop and give her a quick hug. Her hands are warm against my back.

"We'll talk in the morning," she says.

I nod and gratefully climb into the Uber. The driver says nothing, just plays weird slow music on his stereo. The little glowing display says it's called waterfront dining, and it makes the world feel like it's winding down. I don't know if it's exhaustion or the music itself.

When I get home, the house is dark. The door unlocks itself and opens for me without me even asking it. I drink two glasses of water in a row in the kitchen and spend a long time patting Summers, who is pathetically pleased to see me. There's a note on the table: Pear letting me know they're at Sarah's and to come visit if I'm lonely. It's a relief, to be honest. I don't know if I could lie to them. Adrenaline has hollowed me out.

I don't remember climbing into bed.

When I wake, my objects are talking in hushed tones. Batty, discarded on the floor with my clothes, is telling the story in great detail. You think there are dull human storytellers? You've heard *nothing*.

"Then Dylan adjusted her right foot. She commanded the others to get back with a wave of her left hand. Alyse left rapidly at a thirty-eight degree angle, moving fifty paces before throwing herself to the ground, or perhaps tripping up. Dylan exuded a Zen-like sense of calm."

Hold on. Wtf? A Zen-like sense of calm? Since when did Batty become such a poet? I slump back down into bed, fall asleep briefly and wake to a startled shriek from someone, probably the alarm clock because she's a noisy brat. "But—but—you abhor violence." And again what? *Abhor*? What is happening to these objects?

"I have learned I abhor senseless violence," Batty says. "It is different in service to a cause."

Oh God, Batty. What have I done to you? I grab my phone and check for messages, but the group chat is dead quiet. I figure everyone's probably still sleeping, given that it's barely past nine, but then my phone buzzes.

Moodring: morning dilly
Moodring: so tell me what the xmen do after they win a fight

I smile down at my phone.

Chatterbox: well they sometimes have like this big baseball game together

Moodring: ok ok ugh

Moodring: tell me theres an option 2?

Chatterbox: they go hang out at the mall lol

Chatterbox: pear loves those issues because like me pear has no friends

Moodring: had****

Chatterbox: ??

Moodring: you are the sweetest dummy

Moodring: what do u think i am huh

Moodring: and everyone else

Moodring: im not just here for the superpowers

I stare at the last line. I'm scared of how to respond because all my potential texts are desperate emotional flailing and I don't want to scare her away.

Chatterbox: ok so im guessing u want mall?

Moodring: yes u and ur FRIENDS at the mall

Chatterbox: ok cool

Chatterbox: alyse…

Moodring: yes dilly?

Chatterbox: im glad ur my friend

Moodring: 😎 there u go was that so hard? lol

Chatterbox: kind of

Chatterbox: im used to being mostly on my own

Chatterbox: like im not trying to make u feel sorry
for me

I immediately wish I could drag those texts back out
of the ether and remove them from existence. There's
another properly useful superpower. My phone has
never spoken to me, outside of Siri who talks to everyone. Maybe its brain is too full with all the knowledge
and other weird shit on the internet for it to have time
for me.

Moodring: well just to let u know
Moodring: i am 💯ur ride or die bitch
Moodring: so ur stuck w me now
Chatterbox: good and same which u might regret
Chatterbox: because im super annoying
Moodring: shuut uuuuuup
Moodring: the important thing is MALL TRIP

It's nearly lunchtime by the time the whole group has
crawled out of their sleep cocoons. Everyone seems

hesitant to discuss the events of last night. The first mention is when Emma sends us a link to a local news story. It talks about a 'disturbance' in Bottle Lake Forest, and the arrest of a twenty-two-year-old man who may have 'some links' to a string of robberies. Nothing about the earthquakes. The cops are probably still trying to find the device that caused it, not realising they have it right in front of them. The note was supposed to explain all that, but maybe they're keeping it secret given how weird it is. I consider making an anonymous call, to try and reiterate what Tremor can do and how dangerous he can be. But I don't know what I can say to make them believe me without revealing the existence of all of us, and I've read enough X-Men to know that isn't safe.

No, we've done our part. It's in the hands of the police now. We made the sensible, practical decision. We're not vigilantes, no matter how appealing that is. We're hardly a combat-ready group anyway. If we had a single Wolverine, preferably Laura, omg, or Gabby— please universe bring me both—then it might be different. I feel disconcerted at how much I like that thought. If I had claws, where would I have stopped? I'd been so angry. Disconnected.

I pick my mask up off the floor. It's still slightly damp, but I pull it on and look at myself in the mirror. I still feel like Dylan, a girl in a stupid mask, but there was a point last night where it shifted. A moment I became Chatterbox.

Batty leaps into my hand without a single word. I tilt my head slightly. That's more like it. I wish I had those eyes that animate properly rather than these staring ones. My uncertainty shatters the illusion and I'm Dylan again.

I change into jeans, oversized skate shoes, and a black and pink Red Velvet hoodie with Irene's name on the hood because you've got to rep your bias. The last thing I add is an X-Men cap. I put on concealer and eyeliner. Panda eyes in full motherfucking effect. Am I emo-hot? I smear my lips with gloss and make them shiny. My reflection shakes its head at me like what are you thinking, dummy?

I'm ready to go and I check my phone. There's a message from Lou that came in twenty minutes ago.

> Glowstick: im still feelin weird abt last night
> Glowstick: like what if he died?
> Glowstick: does that not worry u?
> Glowstick: dylan are u sure ur ok?

I leave it on seen and shove my phone into my back pocket. I catch the bus to where I left my bike and ride it to Sarah's house. She's sitting on the porch drinking coffee in a rocking chair with Lorelai curled up in her lap. When she sees me, the floof hurtles over, presenting a curly belly to be patted.

"You're looking cute," Sarah says.

"She is, isn't she?" I rub the dog vigorously, who spills her tongue from her mouth and then tries to lick me with it. "You're the prettiest girl in the world, aren't you, Lore?" She soaks up my praise and asks for more. Who can resist her?

I hear the front door open and shut, and look up to see Pear standing there. They're wearing nothing but a long Joy Division t-shirt. Their hair is long for them, almost a whole centimetre. I've been too busy to notice it's grown. "This is a nice surprise."

I get up from the dog and leap up the steps of Sarah's porch to lean against them. "Morning, Pear."

"It's afternoon." They show me their stupid smartwatch with the black band.

"Not in my time zone." I plant a glossy kiss on their cheek and go into the house. I stop in to say hi to Sarah's mostly adorable kids who are all curled up on the couch together, having a lazy argument in front of some cartoon show I'm too old to recognise. Then I beeline for the kitchen where I find actual cereal and non-expired milk, which are hard to find in our house. I take a bowl out to the porch and sit on the step below Pear and Sarah.

"Are you wearing makeup?" Pear asks.

I turn and bat my eyes at them. "I would never betray the Taylor code in that way."

"Stop it, brat." They laugh. "You know what I mean. My naturally suspicious mind wonders why the sudden change."

"Mall trip with the girls," I sigh theatrically. "You simply have to look the part."

I half-swivel so I can see their reaction. If anything, the suspicion is deeper.

"Who's going?" They give me an eyebrow arch almost as cool as Dani's.

"My friends. And because I am such a treasured gem of a human, they're all various shades of intelligent, funny, and beautiful."

Sarah starts laughing, and I know she's laughing at how similar Pear and I are, but I don't mind. Pear reaches out and pokes her in the side and it only makes her laugh harder.

"I don't know how you put up with this one, Sarah," I say. "You must be a saint."

I tip my bowl up and drink the dregs of the milk.

"Got to go." I skid down the steps and back to my bike.

"Is Lou going to be there?" Pear calls after me. "How are things going with him?"

I feign deafness, as does Lorelai, who Sarah is trying to call back from chasing me. The silly dog accompanies me out to the road, and I have to stop and firmly send her back.

I'm late to the mall thanks to my detour, but when I arrive, I get enveloped into this big group hug. Everyone's talking at once. The busy mall traffic is detouring around us and we get a lot of annoyed looks. I've cast these looks before, like why do these girls have to make such a production out of their friendship? Except now that I'm in it, it doesn't feel like a production. We're all talking at once and laughing. Alyse threads one arm through mine.

"Dylan Taylor's wearing makeup," she whispers in my ear.

"So is Alyse Sefo, even though she can shift herself to look however she wants, which makes it entirely redundant. Not all of us are so lucky," I whisper back.

She laughs, but she looks more beautiful too.

"Where the hell is Lou?" I ask, and then I remember with a guilty start that I left him on seen. I pull out my phone.

Chatterbox: u coming to mall?

Glowstick: can't

Glowstick: grounded

Chatterbox: omg why? what now?

Glowstick: last night

Glowstick: out past curfew so whatever

Glowstick: have fun with ur girlfriends talk to u later

I almost cry then right in fucking public, because I thought we were *past* this. I love that he's trying, but why do we keep running into the same problem? I don't know how to solve this.

Chatterbox: lou ffs why

Chatterbox: none of this is fair

Chatterbox: we r a team babie boy and ur part too

Glowstick: then why doesn't it feel like it?

I type 'maybe its a u problem' and then delete it. It's like he's dragged a pall over the afternoon. Alyse and Emma stand there watching me scowl down at my phone. Bianca has drifted off to look at a stall selling enormous candy sticks.

No, I'm not going to let anything ruin this. It's our celebration. We're the X-Men at the mall.

> Chatterbox: feel like it or not, doesnt change it
> Chatterbox: ur a cute mutant
> Chatterbox: the cutest

I wait for a response but it doesn't come, so I put my phone on do not disturb and join my friends.

Instead of Lou joining us, Dani Kim does. She hugs Emma and gives the rest of us the delicate sneer, and I can't reconcile this aloof Dani with the one that spoke to me in the storage cupboard at school. But I'm the leader and I have to make an effort, so while the others are off buying donuts, I get her a chai latte.

"Thanks," she says, and takes a long drink. "Magik is totally the hottest X-Man by the way."

I almost choke on my own coffee. "Sorry, what?"

"Your X-Men roster. Illyana Rasputin. Magik with the heart beside it. I get it. Got to love a monstrous girl."

My head is whirling, because I'm having a conversation about this with Dani freaking Kim. "You mean like Alyse?"

She winks at me. "I think you and I both know that Alyse is a delightfully fluffy cinnamon roll. My tastes, such as they are, lie in other very specific directions."

I have literally no idea what to say to this or what she's implying, so I deal with the moment by taking a giant gulp of coffee and then actually choking. Dani starts hitting me on the back. I have no idea how to survive this experience, but thankfully Emma comes to save me and the group is reunited.

We wander through the music store and look at K-pop CDs, while Bianca buys a vinyl by some old guy. Then Alyse drags us into a fancy clothing shop. Bianca nopes out to look somewhere else, but Alyse insists on trying on clothes. Not just her. All of us. Given this is part of the plot of one of my favourite X-Men issues of all time (#244! Jubilee! Nerd Alert!) I can't exactly say no, although I hope we don't end up at a strip club called Hotbods.

Alyse and Emma make me go into the changing rooms first. Dani is off somewhere else, for which I am extremely grateful. I don't need her judging my outfit.

Imagining the sneer and eyebrow raise in unison makes me nervous.

It takes me a while to get changed, and I have to ask the dress to do itself up for me. As accommodating as it is, we look ridiculous together.

"I'm not coming out," I say.

"X-Men at the mall," Alyse sings, to the tune of a song I can't place. She whips the curtain open and does a double-take. "Omigod Dilly." She takes hold of my arm and pulls me out into the corridor so I can see myself in the full-length mirror.

"Wow," Emma says. "That's—all I have is wow."

"It looks amazing." Alyse makes me turn around. The dress is a dark red colour that I think is called wine. It clings to my chest so dramatically that I want to cover myself up, and keeps on clinging down to my waist before it spills out around me.

"She looks like Audrey Hepburn," Emma says.

"Audrey Hepburn, yes," Alyse touches my bare shoulder. "The eyes and the hair. God, Dilly. It's a shame that boyfriend of yours isn't here to see you."

"Maybe Grace Kelly as a brunette." Emma's got her hands clasped in front of her.

"I don't know who these people are," I complain. "Are you making them up?"

Emma laughs. "You like weird superhero stuff, I like old movie stars."

"It's a ridiculous dress." I frown at my reflection.

"Sure, but you look good in it," Alyse says. "Not that you don't the rest of the time, beautiful girl."

I suddenly feel too embarrassed to be here, and rush back into the cubicle. I pull the curtain tightly shut.

"What?" I see Alyse's fingers on the edge of the curtain.

"Please don't." I'm pressed up against the back of the changing room. How do I escape from here? Oh to be Nightcrawler, so I could bamf home.

"Why not? What's wrong?"

"Stop saying I'm beautiful."

The curtain is pulled aside and both of them are standing there. They come into the small space with me. I shut my eyes like a little kid.

"You two are both actually gorgeous," I say. "And I feel so—I don't know, so grotesque next to you."

"Remember when you found me?" Alyse asks. "In the bathroom that day. Might give you an indication of how I feel sometimes."

I look at her and then at the ground.

"Nobody's ever called me gorgeous," Emma says. "I've been called a lot of other things. Words I won't say." She's hidden again behind her curtain of hair.

"Racist things?" I ask in a whisper.

She tucks her hair behind her ear and her face is revealed. "What do you think?" I've never seen her look so fierce. "I'm sure you've heard people talk about me like that."

I have, and often I let it pass unchallenged. I've tried to speak up more recently. Seeing the look on Emma's face, I vow to never keep quiet again.

"You too," I say to Alyse.

She shrugs. "I try to ignore it. People are assholes. It's not like they don't say anything about you either."

"Oh, I know. 'Is that girl the only boy you can find who wants to fuck you?' It's worse if they know who Pear is. 'No wonder she's like that, given she's got a thing for a mother.'"

Alyse's face twists. Her body shifts into a monster. An avenging angel.

"Fuck them," she spits. "We've taken down Tremor. Next we're going to go around webbing up bigots."

Emma laughs. "That's a lot of people to web up."

"We're young," Alyse says. "We've got a lot of time."

"What are you talking about?" It's Dani's voice from outside, because of course it is. "You can't honestly be talking about fighting bigotry by webbing people up."

I slide between Emma and Alyse and pull the curtain open. I step out into the corridor, prepared to challenge her, and explain a thing or two to her insufferably arrogant ass. Except she's standing there dressed in a suit and all the thoughts go flying out of my head. It fits her perfectly.

She stares back at me and doesn't say anything either. We stand there like two gunfighters waiting to draw except we forgot to bring ammunition.

It's completely unfair that she looks so good. I wish I looked that good in anything, but most especially a suit. The language part of my brain is short-circuiting over and over and I can't figure out why.

Alyse comes out of the cubicle, and somehow she has enough presence of mind to form sentences: "Oh hey, cool suit, Dani. But please tell me how *you* plan to fight bigotry then?"

But for once, for some unfathomable reason, Dani Kim doesn't have any answers.

CHAPTER TWENTY-THREE

The mall trip is deemed a success, and Alyse decides to throw a party to celebrate once Lou is no longer grounded. I'm supremely hesitant. I still hate parties, and this is one I can't make a lame excuse for.

"Oh stop," Alyse says, once I finally quit whining. "I'm not going to invite everyone I know. It'll mostly be us and any special friends you want to bring."

"All my special friends are here," I grumble. "I don't want any more."

"Yes, but you didn't know you wanted us," Alyse says, with unassailable logic.

"My friend brain can barely cope with you lot," I say. My compulsion to call her my best friend is back, but I can't bring myself to do it. The last time I tried, I was eight years old and the girl laughed at me. I know Alyse is different, but what if I'm wrong?

The party turns out ok, even though it's a daytime party *and* a pool party. Dani is there, because of course she is. I feel awkward around her after the suit/dress incident so I keep my distance.

Bianca's girlfriend Shell is there too. She's even smaller in person than she looks over Snapchat. Even Emma's taller than her. Once she parks herself in Bianca's lap, she doesn't want to leave. Probably making sure the tendrils of the work wife cult don't steal her away.

I don't invite anyone. The only people I would consider bringing are Batty (who would make me seem psycho), Pillow (who would make me seem like a five-year-old) and Pear, who would despise it with every fibre of their being.

Alyse has set up deckchairs and sun umbrellas around the pool. There's music playing from a Bluetooth speaker. Within five minutes I've made friends with it, and can override whatever shitty song someone wants to play. This is not how you endear yourself to people, I get that, but it's my damn superpower.

Given I've spent a bunch of time around most of these people in a sports bra and yoga pants, I feel less uncomfortable about the fact I'm in my bikini top and shorts. I still don't think I've ever had this much skin on display before.

The pool is the perfect temperature, but most people are pouting about it being cold. I dive in and swim lengths, alternating between backstroke and breaststroke. Lou sits on the edge of the pool, his feet dangling in the water. He's wearing a long-sleeved t-shirt and baggy shorts.

I swim up beside him and lean my arms on the sun-warmed concrete edge.

"Hello." I wipe water from my eyes and squint up at him. "It's nice to see you."

"Yeah." His tone is not enthused. The sinking feeling comes back. "I'm glad to see you too, Dills. Honestly. It's just—" He sighs, and looks around at the others. "I kinda hoped we'd go out just us."

"We will," I say. It's a fair point. We used to spend a big chunk of our free time together, and now our relationship has been folded into the super-team thing. We keep bumping into the fact that I like it, and he doesn't. He came back to the team and he tried, but it doesn't make the problem go away.

"Can we make a plan then?" He swishes his feet through the water. "So it actually happens."

"Sure." I swim closer. "I'm the plan queen, don't you remember?" I grab hold of his calves with my wet hands and he lets out a loud squawk, somewhere between surprise and laughter. I fold my legs against the wall and push backwards, dragging him in with me. He's totally not expecting it and doesn't even resist. He topples in with a splash. There's a ragged cheer from the people sunbathing around the pool, and I pull him under with me.

We surface with my legs locked around his waist. I kiss his upturned face.

He very definitely does not kiss me back. "What are you doing?"

"We can have a little pre-date date right now." I keep my tone light. People are watching. "Underwater. Just you and me in the cool of the pool."

He doesn't pull away from me, but he floats with his arms loose. "I don't want to do this in front of your friends."

"*Our* friends." I frown. I unlock my legs and kick backwards. We float in the water a couple of meters away from each other. Two separate people.

"Whatever. I'm not talking about this now." Lou swims over to the edge of the pool. He pulls himself out and stands on the edge, dripping onto the ground. Then he picks up a towel and stalks off around the side of the house. I do a backflip under the water, and when I come up, wiping water from my eyes, Alyse is watching me.

She raises one perfect brown shoulder in a shrug.

I shrug back, lifting my hands out of the water. There's nothing else to say. I swim lengths until I'm exhausted.

When I get out of the pool, I wrap a towel around myself. I walk into the dim interior of the house, wet hair brushing my cheeks. I'm intending to go into the kitchen and get a drink, but Dani is in there. She's wearing a pale yellow bikini top and tiny denim shorts. I'm not staring at her. There's a triangle of red plastic cups set up on one end of the kitchen island, like for beer pong. I pause in the doorway and watch.

She raps one knuckle hard against the countertop. The red ball leaps out of one cup and into another. She repeats it a bunch more times while I stand there leaving small puddles on the floor.

"Welcome to the show," she says, without turning around. "Impressed?"

"You're gaining more control." I'm automatically curious. The ball is small and she's hopping it from cup to cup, going around the edge of the triangle and then into the middle.

"Practice makes perfect," Dani says. She's obviously still working on her powers without the rest of us. I wish I hadn't ruined it with her, because she would be amazing on my team. Our team.

"Dizzy," the ball says to me softly. "Very dizzy."

"Oh, you poor baby," I say reflexively.

Dani whirls to face me with a frown.

"Not you," I say. "The ball. Come here, little one."

It lifts up out of the cup and whizzes through the air to me. It rolls over the back of my neck onto my shoulder.

"Safe," it whispers. "You don't shout."

"It seems so unfair that there's no pain when you do it." Dani watches the ball roll along the line of my collarbone, like a pet nuzzling in.

"No," I say. "There's just a lot of conversation."

One side of her mouth lifts up. "I suppose that might be quite painful for you." She holds out her hand. "Can I have my ball back?"

"No," the ball whispers. "Stay with you."

"She's very scary, isn't she?" I say to the ball, although my eyes are on Dani.

"Oh please. It's not actually talking to you." That sneer of hers, oh my god. My brain fritzes out trying to process it.

"Every power has a downside." I convince the ball to float over to her and it does, landing gently in her outstretched palm. "Be gentle with the poor thing."

She clicks her tongue and raps her knuckle on the surface again, the ball spinning up to land with a soft splash in the middle cup.

"So how do we get you back?" I ask.

She gives me that eyebrow arch she loves. I bet she practises it. "Oh really? You want me to join the Cute Mutants?"

I can't help but laugh. "It wasn't my first choice of name."

"And yet still somehow accurate." I'm trying to decipher this when she shifts the attack. "You know what I think. You're reckless. Teenagers with powers running around with no control. You need someone sensible in charge. These sorts of things should be monitored and managed."

I blink at her for a few seconds. "Holy shit. You'd vote for the Superhero Registration Act."

She smiles and I am completely undone. I realise I've never seen Dani Kim properly smile. It's an expression to go to war for. I knew she was beautiful, but with this smile unfurled like a conquering banner I'm—

No. This is insane. I fucking refuse to have a crush on Dani. She doesn't even like me.

"You like that, don't you?" She's still wearing the delighted expression, like she wants to obliterate me. "You like to imagine that I'm boring old institutional Tony Stark, and you're Cap the rebel."

Her words make me reckless. I feel like Chatterbox, not boring Dylan Taylor. There's a big round serving dish on the table in the other room. It's barely awake, but it's aware enough. I call it to me with a murmured word. It flies through and attaches itself to my left forearm as a glittering silver shield.

"Holy shit." She takes this long, slow breath and shakes her head. "That's a hell of a trick, but it's not enough to convince me to do something so insane as join your vigilante group."

"We gave him to the cops," I say.

"After you broke his hand." She looks at me as my cheeks flush. "Yeah, I heard about that."

"Fine, don't join." Every atom in my body is humming. "But look at the world around you, and consider this. Maybe Magneto was right."

"Mutant pride," she scoffs. "Yeah, right. I'll see you on Krakoa."

Ohmigod she reads current X-Men. Who *is* this girl? I'm about to open my mouth and talk about how cool fricking *Kate Pryde* is and Psylocke as Captain Britain and and—

None of this is the point at all. I'm being dismissed as reckless, stupid Dylan Taylor, caught up in comic books and missing the fact we're in the real world. All this despite that smile that sends my heart shaking much worse than Tremor did. And beyond that, no matter what my heart is doing, I have a boyfriend, even if the thread that binds us together seems so frayed lately.

Dani deliberately turns back to resume her focus on the little red ball. I watch her for a few moments more, and turn to see Lou standing across the room from me. How long has he been there? He's changed back into street clothes, although his hair is still damp. He looks sad and handsome. The smile I give him feels desperate. He crosses to stand in the doorway beside me.

"You think you're so cool, Dani," he says, going for a sneer of his own.

"There's a lack of evidence to the contrary," she says, but she's looking at me while she says it. I want to stop staring at her face but I can't.

"Why are you even here?" Lou demands.

I take his hand, wanting him to stop, but he snatches it away.

"Oh, let me see." Dani slaps her hand on the counter hard. The ball whizzes in a tight orbit around Lou's head and back to her. "Alyse invited me, my best friend is here and well, Dylan is just desperate for me to join her adorable ass and be one of the super cute mutants."

She still won't take her eyes off me, and the way she says desperate makes me feel like I'm slowly dissolving into the air.

"Dylan doesn't want anything to do with you." He looks at me, waiting for agreement. But my lips are sealed, because if I unseal them I don't know what I'd say, and everything already seems precisely balanced on the edge of disaster.

Seconds tick by and the awkwardness increases.

"Come on Dilly, let's bounce." Lou shoves his hands in his pockets, curling in on himself. He's so unsure. I've kept putting the team ahead of him for these last weeks while we've turned ourselves into a unit, and now I'm reaping the rewards.

"Yeah, let's go." It's my own offering of peace, because I'd rather stay. I wonder if he notices it or values it.

I get changed and head out to say goodbye to Alyse.

"Are you okay?" Her face searches mine for clues.

"Girlfriend duty," I say. "It's fine."

She reaches out and touches the back of my hand. "Ride or die, remember. Text me if you need me."

I walk back through the house, deliberately keeping my eyes away from the room where Dani is. Whatever this unfolding knot of feelings inside me is, Dani doesn't want to be any part of my life, as a mutant or a friend or anything else for that matter.

Lou's waiting by the door with his backpack on. He nods and walks out the door without even waiting for me to reach him. I think I know what's coming, but it's hard to accept. We walk down the street in silence for a while.

"Can we talk?" He's a couple of steps behind me, and hurries forward to try and catch my gaze. I don't want to hold it, so I look at the wind in the trees instead.

"Sure," I say.

"We've been best friends for a long time, through a bunch of shit."

It's a strangely hopeful beginning to the conversation, but I know where this arc will end.

"Just say it," I tell him. I'm reduced back to my basic essence of irritable and awkward, and it makes the anger surge. "Don't fucking soften the blow."

"I don't think this is working," he says. "I've tried and you've tried and it's just not happening. And I've blamed everyone else but me."

I flip my hood up over my wet hair. "You don't think it's working."

There's a long pause and then he shakes his head. "Do you?"

"No," I say. It feels like an admission of guilt.

"There it is," he sighs. "We agree. So it's easier to bury it then, right?"

I'm not quite so ready to end it. I'm mad. I feel like there might have been a path through this, once upon a time. "You couldn't just share me? Is it so hard to be part of a wider world?"

He nods. "I feel like I've stayed still and you've gone racing ahead. You're the fast mutant guy, what's his name? Not the Flash, the other one."

"Quicksilver," I say, even though it's probably a rhetorical question.

"Yeah, him. You showed me that comic where he's talking about how it drives him mad that everyone else moves so slowly."

"Your entire world is filled with people who can't work cash machines," I whisper.

"I'm that person now," Lou says. "You've moved on and I can't catch you anymore."

"But I didn't," I tell him, weirdly insistent. I feel like I've failed, and I hate it. "I'm still right here."

"You're not." His hand moves towards mine, and then retreats. "Not like you used to be."

I have nothing useful to say, so all I do is take a step backwards.

"I still want to be friends, Dilly," he says, but I can't deal with this now.

"You don't get to call me that," I say, which is petty af but whatever. Then I turn and run. Not as fast as Quicksilver, but I do leave him behind. This isn't my fault. I've tried over and over to fix this but some things are unfixable. Unsolvable. It's not my goddamn fault.

When I get home, Pear takes one look at me and knows instantly. This, they pick up on.

"Lou?"

I nod. Apparently this is worthy of a full-body hug because they enfold me in their arms. I try not to cry. We sit side by side on the couch.

"I don't know if this is the worst thing," Pear says.

"Very fucking encouraging," I sniffle.

"People change. Your Dad and I changed. Some-times people can shift together and sometimes they can't. I love Lou. You know I do, and I don't love many people. But I've seen you two be good friends in the past, and lately it seems like it's not so good. Maybe it's that—"

"Thanks for saying all this earlier." I hunch my shoulders against the world. "It might have been helpful in all the confusion."

Pear shrugs. "People don't always want to listen. Figured it was better to let it take its course. What I don't want is for you to blame yourself."

"I don't blame myself," I say irritably, and immediately realise it's a lie. I blame myself for lots of shit. For some reason, it's easy to do. The whole thing with always calling yourself a dumpster fire means it's easy to think you're the trash person in any situation.

"Oh, Dilly. If only I could choose what you inherited from me." Pear leans against me and I lean back.

"We do okay," I tell them. They laugh and mess my hair up.

We end up watching *Buffy* which is our other parent-and-child comfort food. Of course, we go for the episodes 'Surprise' and 'Innocence,' because there's no way my breakup can compare to the horror of that one. Except we only get fifteen minutes in before there's what sounds like a battering ram at the door.

Pear gets up with a frown to open it. There's a trio on the doorstep. Emma, Alyse and Bianca. There's no Dani, and I don't know why I'm disappointed. She's not part of the team.

"Hi, um, uh, Dylan's Pear?" Alyse says.

"Ness," Pear says with a smile.

Alyse gestures with a paper bag. "I mean you've probably got it all under control, but we've got supplies. Mostly ice cream, but it's a start, right?"

I appear behind Pear. My eyes are still smeary and red but I don't care.

"I'm glad you came," I say.

Way later, I'm lying in bed. Pillow murmurs underneath me. I feel wrung out and melancholy, which leads to the potentially stupid decision to make an actual fucking voice call to Lou.

"Dilly?" His voice sounds even softer than Pillow's. "Sorry, Dylan."

"Hey." There's a super awkward pause, where I almost call him boyfriend. Why did I do this?

"I didn't expect to hear from you," he says.

"We never finished the conversation, because I went running off," I tell him. "But I wanted to say that we were always good as friends. I like hanging out with you. You make me laugh. And for fuck's sake, of course you can call me Dilly."

"I was dumb," he says. "Dumb and jealous."

"Well yeah, you were. But I did some dumb things too."

"I was the dumbest."

"It's not a fucking competition, Lucifer," I say with a laugh. My phone is warm against my ear. "I went headlong into this mutant thing because I want it *so fucking much*. I raced off and I expected you'd follow me."

"I wanted to follow. Honestly. I guess I'm not cute enough to be a mutant."

"Lou, Jesus. It's never been about whether you're cute—"

"Sorry, that was dumb again. Honestly, I *am* sorry for being a dick," he says. "I do still want to be friends and I know it's not my right to ask that but—"

"Of course it is," I say. "You think I'm miles ahead, but I'm really not. We can be friends. It'll be weird, but you and me have always been weird. If anyone's strange enough to pull this off, it's us."

"We can be friends without me being in your gang?" His voice shakes a little.

"We *are* friends," I tell him firmly. "That doesn't unravel because you don't want to kiss me anymore. Or because you don't like running around fighting villains."

"I'm glad," he says.

"I'll still *have* my gang," I tell him. "And I'll have more friends than just you."

"I know, Dilly, and I'm glad you're happy. Honest."

"Pear says people change and sometimes they change in different ways but it doesn't need to be *totally* different."

"Mutants," he whispers.

"We've always been mutants. Always going through changes."

"I'm really glad you called." His voice is hoarse.

"Me too." And I am. Maybe it wasn't such a catastrophic decision after all. Now that there are all these connections happening in my life, I don't want to lose any of them.

CHAPTER TWENTY-FOUR

For the next few days, things are quiet. Pillow and Batty worry about me, talking between themselves late into the night. They ramble on about first love and resiliency, and about how there's someone nice out there for me. They're open to any or no gender. I'm impressed at how Pillow has adapted to the idea, as she used to be very much a heterosexuals-only girl and now she's ready to wear a rainbow case to the Pride parade.

"I definitely like that Alyse," she says to Batty. "They're very comfortable together. I can imagine them darning each other's socks."

What the actual fuck, Pillow?

"They're only friends," Batty says carefully. "I think she likes the mean one."

I raise my head from Pillow. "Do you think you two can give it a rest? I don't like Alyse or anyone. I'm defi-nitely not interested in starting anything right now. And can you please, please, fucking *please* let me sleep." And besides, who do they think is the mean one? Bianca? No thank you. I don't need that drama in my life.

The rest of the Cute Mutants worry about me too, or most of them at least. Bianca thinks I'm better off out of it, and there's no point expending any mental or emotional energy on it. So it's mostly Alyse and Emma being very concerned and careful with me, like I'll break.

"I'm not that fragile," I say. "I told you, Lou and I are friends." They exchange glances as if I can't see them.

We haven't had any meetings since the day Lou and I broke up. I decide that we'll do something this weekend. Proper training. See if we can think of some new uses for our powers. Come up with a ten point plan for webbing up bigots.

I still see Lou around school, and we have text conversations late at night about anime and new songs we like. He sends me his drawings and I tell him I love them. At school, things are less normal. He sits near us at lunchtime but has this fixation about how he's *not part of the gang*. It breaks my heart to see him alone, so I ask the other mutants to hang out with him. Bianca point blank refuses and says she's allowed to take sides if she wants. Emma and Alyse go over to him, but he walks away and doesn't come back. Aggravating boy. I can't pry open his world and force my friends into it. That was the issue before. He'll do it when he's ready, or he won't. It's not my responsibility any more.

That afternoon I'm sitting in class, doodling in my open exercise book. My thoughts are drifting, except they keep coming back to Dani smiling at me in Alyse's kitchen. Great work, brain. Kindly stop thinking about Dani Kim. I'm supposed to be planning new things—realistic things, not impossible fantasies.

When the shaking starts, it takes my brain a few seconds to place the rumbling sound. Like a train going past, but the tracks aren't near here. It's when the whole building starts hammering that I think holy fuck, this is a big one. A real one. Everyone screams, but we still get under our desks in unison. All the training we got as kids growing up in earthquake country is paying off. The lights flicker frantically and then go out. They don't come back on.

It's impossible to estimate how long earthquakes take. The big ones stretch time out like gum. There are crashing sounds from outside and people scream again.

Everyone fumbles for their phones, and forty pools of light shine around the room.

I catch sight of the big eyes of the girl under the desk next to mine. She's crying with her mouth open.

"It'll be ok," I tell her. "We've done this before." I don't think she hears me, because she's looking at her phone.

The quaking dies away and everything is still. An eerie silence gives way to other sounds: crying, panting, creaking, things falling in the distance. I remind myself there will be aftershocks. My hands are shaking, but we should try to get out now. Nobody's paying attention to me, so I grab my mask out of my pocket and pull it on. It's like a goddamn Spider-Man story and I hope everyone's just as dumb in real life at figuring out who's under the mask.

I slide out from under my desk and run to the door. I put my phone in my pocket, the light glowing through the fabric of my skirt. I shove at the door but it doesn't open, wedged shut by some shift in the building. There are more people crying now. The teacher knocks me out of the way and tries to open the door herself. She doesn't seem to notice my mask. Shock does weird things to people. She shakes and kicks the door, swearing under her breath. Her skin is sallow and beaded with sweat.

Ignore the fact it's an earthquake. It's nothing to do with Tremor. We get quakes here, and that one felt really fucking big. I hope the rest of the city is okay. Shit. I need to text Pear. Except Wifi is down and I'm out of credit. They'll be fine. They'll call.

Adrenaline spikes in me but I take a moment to calm myself and reach out. What objects are in here? Usually at school I make an effort to ignore everything. I don't want to get trapped in tedious daily conversations with—

The desk.

"Hey there, you big beautiful beast," I murmur. I feel the desk's awareness expanding to meet mine. "You want to get us out of here?"

The desk scrapes across the floor. It pivots around and slides towards where the teacher and I are standing. I drag the teacher out of the way.

"That's it," I whisper encouragingly. "Knock it down."

The desk rears up on one end and then leaps. There's no other word for it. It throws the whole bulk of itself towards the door, which splinters and buckles. Most people are crying and/or looking at their phones. I hope nobody's videoing it. If anyone accuses me of anything afterwards, I'll tell them they're crazy. Who's going to believe this?

"One more try," I whisper to the desk. It skids backwards, looking like an overexcited puppy. It even waggles one end of itself a little before lunging forward again. It blasts through the door and skids into the corridor. Screaming comes from outside.

"Wait," I shout. I take my mask off and scramble through the wreckage of the door. The corridor is lit by a concert's worth of phone flashlights. It makes it hard to see anything. The desk sits, quivering lightly, amongst a group of girls who cling to it. The rest of my class files through the door behind me, shining their phones around. Nobody's questioning anything about our escape yet.

There are too many voices to make out anything coherent. Someone is shouting up ahead, so I push my way through the crowd.

"Everybody please remain calm." It's one of the tech teachers I had in Year 10. He stands on the reception desk, shading his eyes as he's bathed in light from girls aiming their phone torches at him. "The local cell tower is down so we can't call out. Please don't try to call or text to prioritise emergency services. Also please stay away from the east corridor as there does appear to be a fire outside. The doors to the building are currently blocked, but—"

His voice was already struggling to rise above the hubbub, but with bad news layered on top of bad news, he gets drowned out by fresh screaming. We're stuck in here. I carry on through the crowd. There's plenty of shoving back and forth, although most people are trying to move towards the doors. Yes, the ones the teacher just said were blocked. Nobody's listening, and everyone wants to escape. There must be windows around here somewhere. Why is nobody leaving out those?

I get near the front, to where people are squashed up against the glass doors. The crying and shouting is worse. I ask the doors to open but they're not listening. Out in the carpark, there are so many cars, it gives me a headache. They're all worried, trying to check I'm alright.

"Shut up." I'm rude and snapping, but they'll deal. "Let me think."

I could get the cars in here, but it's an insane plan to drive cars into a building full of people. There's got to be a better way. I try to talk to the doors again, but they're still silent. Then a flicker comes from a smart screen beside the door to my left. It fritzes and blurs into static and then very briefly shows >:(

"Are you there?" I whisper.

Something rustles at the very edge of my consciousness. A faint, feeble voice, someone gasping for breath. I try to find anger inside me, but there's too much panic and worry, and I can't focus on any single feeling.

"I'm here," I tell it. "I'm waiting. Can you see me? We need the doors open."

The screen flickers again.

>:(*pain dying pain oh god it hurts can't move* >:(

The writing dissolves and the screen is blank. I check my phone again but the WiFi still isn't up. "Does anyone have reception?" I shout, but nobody's listening to a girl trying to talk to a dying building. Everyone's waving around their phones like they're magic wands and the right swish and flick will conjure up reception. I'm pretty sure this won't work, but I'm almost desperate enough to try it. I need to know what's happening out there, and how bad it is in the city.

The cars are still blabbing in my head, and one of them suggests turning on the radio.

I'm such a fucking scatterbrain.

I tell the cars to find me some goddamn news. It doesn't take long. There's a breaking news bulletin on one of the boring stations Pear listens to, that's mostly talking. It doesn't take long for my world to fall apart: *appears to be isolated to a single school, Brookside Girls' High in—*

No. It can't be true. Something hot and heavy lurches in my stomach. This is my fault. My brain is just saying 'ohhhh fuuuuuuccccckkk' dragged out real slow like the world's rotation is slowing down. I shake my head. The cops *had* Tremor. They can't have let him go. We gave them the evidence, but of course the cops have no idea how to handle a mutant. They don't even know we exist. We should have been stronger, should have been better.

Another car chimes in with news from another station. It's true. The earthquake only happened here, which means Tremor attacked the school. There's no other explanation, and like the tide receding from the beach before another wave comes in, I feel briefly empty of emotions. That tangled mess of worry disappears and the rage comes flooding in. It's at Tremor, and the police, and at myself too. There's a lot of blame to go around.

I slam my hand on the wall beside the screen. If I'm going to feel all this, it better be fucking useful. The screen flickers to life, green messages scrolling across it.

This hurts, please stop it

I can't feel anything, I'm numb

Everything is cold

"You need to help me," I whisper through gritted teeth. "We need to get out of here. We're all trapped and scared and—"

The building screams. Every screen inside flickers to life, even the big ones behind the reception desk. They emanate this awful pale blue glow and weird symbols flicker across them. There are no meaningful words. It's keyboard mashing, like scrolling K-pop stan twitter. The screaming sound is deafening, since the building is joined by hundreds of girls freaking out. Not only have we just survived an earthquake, but our smart building is having a nervous breakdown. This is my fault too.

"Fucking do it," I hiss to the building. "We need to make this right. We need to save people. We need to be heroes."

Self-loathing looks like rage when you're this close to it. I can feel the building howling static gibberish. It's in pain, an electrical storm surging as it tries to connect to me. The doors are jammed closed and the building can't make them open. It's gasping for energy. I can feel the extent of the network, trailing into every classroom and office. It's scrounging for power, and it finds some in me.

I feel my skin burning but there's no sign of it on my body. Another rush of power goes through me and I double over, retching. I taste blood in my throat.

The building screams in my head. The doors scream as they scrape open over the buckled ground. The girls around me scream as they lunge for the slowly opening gap to freedom.

The doors never make it open all the way. The connection with the building is abruptly severed, as if a cord has snapped. In my head it's quiet, but it feels like my brain is ringing with the backwash of all the emotion.

Around me, the other girls spill out of the building, like a draining tub. The teachers call for order, but there is none.

I think there are tears on my cheeks.

"I'm sorry," I whisper to the building. "You did it. You saved everyone."

There's a faint flicker. *XD all safe?*

"Yes." My hand is pressed against the screen, and I hope it can take some comfort from me, not just rage. "Someone will come and fix you, and you'll be all better."

I hope it's true.

Almost everyone else is gone, and I stagger after them, flooded with relief.

Outside, my brief elation turns sour. One side of the building has partially fallen in, even though it was supposed to be earthquake strengthened. They promised us.

Police vehicles thread their way through the cars that drove closer to help me. Ambulances arrive too, as well as a line of fire trucks. People in uniforms are everywhere, trying to organise the chaos. Teachers stand atop benches, calling for their form classes. People in ambulance uniforms run past, wheeling gurneys with people on them.

I weave through the crowd. I need to find my Cute Mutants. I need to find Lou.

I take out my phone to check if they've got the stupid Wifi up, but my hands are shaking so much that I can't unlock it. It won't recognise my thumb and I can't enter the code.

This is all my fault.

I taunted Jack. I broke his hand and made him furious.

I baited him into coming after us.

My head swims. I clutch at someone beside me. It's a girl I don't know, and she tugs her hand away. She's crying, looking for someone.

I stand alone. Where are my friends? What if more of them are hurt? I can't face them. They'll know it's my fault and won't want to know me anymore. They'll blame me too. If I hadn't been so arrogant, this wouldn't have happened. I knew Tremor was dangerous.

I thought we could beat him.

How stupid can one person be?

CHAPTER TWENTY-FIVE

I don't remember getting here, but I'm at the dairy between school and home. I'm in front of the drinks fridge, desperately thirsty but bewildered by the options.

"Are you okay, miss?" The owner leans over the counter to look at me.

"I'm fine." I still can't decide what I want, so I walk outside and almost trip over Alyse.

"Dylan! Emma found you with her app. It's the only thing working. Omigod, where the fuck have you been?" Her arms are around my neck. "It was crazy. We were trapped in the building and then—"

Over Alyse's shoulder, I see a figure stumbling down the road. "Dani?"

We separate and rush over to her. She's walking on a weird angle, holding her head.

"What the hell is going on?" Alyse asks.

Dani blinks slowly. There's blood on the side of her head. It runs in rivulets down her neck.

My throat stings. My legs tremble.

"Home," she says plaintively, this awful non-Dani hitch in her voice. "I need to get home."

She takes one more step and collapses in slow motion, buckling to her knees and then leaning over very slowly until she's lying on the concrete at our feet, as if it was simply too exhausting to go any further.

I don't know what my heart is doing. It's skipping beats like weird YouTube music. Everything feels dark and doomed, as if the world is plummeting into a pit. Dani is hurt. She's collapsed and she's fucking *bleeding* and I don't know what to do. I have to be something other than useless. It's important.

I stumble over and crouch down beside her. I put my hand to her neck, and her skin is cool and slightly damp. "What the fuck?" I fumble for my phone and drop it on the concrete.

"Dylan, Dylan, call an ambulance," Alyse is holding her own phone and flapping her other hand. She looks tiny and fragile, collapsing down to a wispy child size. "I can't remember the number. What's the number?"

"There isn't any fucking time for an ambulance." I look out frantically into the street. "I'm desperate. Who wants to help me?"

Three different cars parked nearby rumble to life and pull up alongside us. I choose the one that says 'zero emission' on the back, because even in a crisis, let's please take care of the fucking planet, why don't we?

"Hello," the car says. She has this gentle, reassuring voice that stops me from crying. "My name is Roxy. It looks like you need my help."

The nearest back door swings open.

"Yes, Roxy. Thank you. We need to get to the hospital." I try to pick Dani up in what I'm suddenly aware is called a 'bridal carry' but my legs don't work properly. "Fuck's sake, Alyse, please shift back to something normal and lift her with me."

"Dylan, we can't even drive!" Alyse protests, although she obediently helps me with Dani's legs as we uncomfortably manoeuvre her into the back seat.

"I don't need to drive." The screen of my phone is cracked, but it seems to work okay. Dani's head lolls in my lap as I pull up directions to the hospital. My brain lurches ahead to nightmare scenarios of her being dead. I have to fucking focus. "Okay, Roxy. Can you please go to the end of the street and turn right?"

The car pulls out into the street and accelerates fast. It brakes just enough at the corner and turns with a slight squeal of tyres before speeding away again.

"This is insane." Alyse has Dani's legs in her lap and one hand splayed on the back of the passenger seat. "The car is driving itself."

Goddamn it, Alyse, stop stating the fucking obvious. I'm basically driving by waving my hands. The car is being a sweetheart but if we don't do this properly, Dani's going to die. Except I can't say that.

"Yes, the car is driving itself. And I have to navigate, so I need you to stop talking. Roxy, my sweet, please turn left up here."

Dani's slumped across me. Her hair is all over her face. I pull it away from her mouth and stroke her forehead.

"It's going to be okay," I whisper to her. It has to be okay.

The hospital is close to the centre of town, and traffic is appalling. Dani's blood is warm on my thighs. I try to find the wound and press the sleeve of my school blouse against it as hard as I can. I'm sure they taught us stuff in school about this, but I can't remember anything. Why the fuck do I never pay attention in class? Dani was right, of course, and now because I'm too dumb, she might die.

Meanwhile, the car doesn't move and waits for the lights to change.

Alyse breathes loudly beside me. "The quake at the school." Her voice sounds ferocious, like a god that wants to swallow the world. Except her face is a pale shadow, trying to shrink away from this awful reality we're in. "Do you think it was Jack?"

I can't talk about this now. If I stop to think about possibilities, I'll panic. I have to concentrate on getting Dani to the hospital. We're still completely stopped. I can see the estimated time of arrival move upwards by a minute.

"Fuck it," I tell Roxy. "Run this red light. Just please avoid the other cars."

"Oh, baby," she purrs. "This is a dream come true."

She reverses a little and bumps her way up onto the footpath. Then she revs forward, slews in front of the other cars and shoots in an angle across the intersection. There's a massive blast of a horn and someone slams on their brakes, but we're across. The car shrieks in wild laughter, while Alyse and I scream in the back.

The car doesn't slow down. We're doubling the speed limit but I can see on my phone the ETA to the hospital is decreasing. This might be okay.

I touch Dani's cheek, shaking her slightly, trying to rouse her. There's nothing. She's like a dead weight on me, and I immediately have to slam the door on that thought because 'dead weight' is only a turn of phrase and can't possibly be anything more. This is all my fucking fault if Dani dies. You can draw a line from my actions to this situation in thick black marker.

Roxy is speeding like crazy, although traffic is getting heavier again. She pounces in and out, taking the smallest gaps.

Then I hear the worst possible thing—the howl of a siren behind us. I scroll around the map with one thumb. The hospital backs onto the park. There's a street that leads directly there, but the line on the map doesn't take us that way. I poke at it.

"Go right," I tell the car.

She obeys with a muttered expletive. I immediately see why she swore, and why the map didn't take us this direction. It's a one-way street. Two lanes of traffic, coming straight for us. Roxy howls with both her horn and alarm. The oncoming cars frantically unzip as we speed down the middle. The siren falls away, even as the drives around us lean on their horns.

"It won't help if we all die," Alyse says, clutching onto me, but by this stage the car has shot out of the mouth of the one way street and is slaloming between more traffic.

"Into the park," I urge Roxy.

There's a fence in the way and the car smashes straight through it. We get a fairly hard jolt, but I'm cradling Dani and although I crack my forehead on the seat in front, I keep her safe.

"Don't hit any fucking cyclists, Rox," I snap.

Roxy guns the engine and blasts her horn. People scatter. I guide her straight for the hospital, right through the middle of the park. We're so fucking close. Then the howling starts behind us again. The police car appears in the rear view mirror. It's horribly loud, and they're shouting something through the speaker.

"We're fucked," Alyse says.

Roxy speeds full tilt across the grass. The hospital buildings are right in front of us. Except between us and there, the grass slopes down towards a wide man-made lake. To the left are tennis courts. To the right is a cricket field with spectators around it.

I've been running this whole way on adrenaline. Underneath it, there's a horrifying pit of despair and self-loathing and rage. This is all fallout from my plan. This can all be laid at the feet of Tremor and Chatterbox. I'm shaking. I'm crying. I'm so angry I want to scream. I want to go back in time and beat Tremor to death at the edge of the forest.

And now we're about to drive into a lake and get arrested and Dani might die in a stolen car while the cops scream at us.

I hear the car's voice in my head.

"Don't fucking stop, Dylan. Don't fucking stop."

At this point, I'm not doing anything but screaming. This is the end.

Roxy lifts into the air like she uses her back wheels to kick off from the ground. Momentum glides her over the rippled surface of the lake. It's like that old movie with the kids riding their bikes in front of the moon. I turn my head and see Alyse staring at me, her mouth hanging open.

"Are you doing this?"

"Not on purpose," I gasp.

Roxy dips down and skids onto the ground on the far side of the lake. She speeds into a patch of trees, then turns and opens the far door. "Out out out," she says.

I drag Dani out the door with Alyse's help and we sprawl on the grass. The car slams her door and lurches forward to drive away, while we stagger into the cover of the trees. I have no idea how long Roxy will go without me, but I feel like she's earned her freedom. Maybe she should have always been free.

"This is insane," Alyse says shakily. "I can't believe that happened."

That's an understatement. I've made objects fly before, but this seems to be on a whole other scale. Although right now the scope of my powers doesn't matter—only Dani does.

The pair of us struggle along with her, coming out of the trees onto a small gravel path that winds its way down to the main street in front of the hospital. It seems a long way. Dani hangs limp between us. Her cheek is sticky with blood and rubs against mine.

"She's not dead," I whisper, although I don't know who I'm talking to. "She's not fucking dead. She's going to be okay, she is, she's fine, everything is okay."

The electronic doors slide open and we take her inside.

"Please," I say, nearly out of breath. "We need help."

CHAPTER TWENTY-SIX

Alyse and I support Dani up to the desk. There's a woman sitting there, who looks at us like she thinks we're up to some shit. I want to scream at her, but that's not the way to get anything done.

"My friend." I have to clear my throat. "We found her. She collapsed. I think she hurt her head in the earthquake."

"Earthquake?" The woman looks suspicious.

"At school." My voice is shaking and I want to collapse myself. I wish Batty was there to get everyone's attention. I can hear my voice getting higher. "There was an earthquake at our school."

"It's true," a younger woman says from a desk further down. "They've alerted us. Didn't you see the emails? There's more on their way."

The woman finally focuses on us, and reaches for a clipboard. "Her name?"

"Danielle Kim," I say. I don't know where she lives, but Alyse has her phone number.

Everything speeds up into a ghastly nightmare lurch, and when time slows down again, there's a brisk woman and an even brisker man who are taking Dani away. They lay her down on a stretcher. She's so still and quiet. Normally she's so intense and animated and everything she does has purpose. Now there's nothing at all. There's still blood all over her face, and I try to wipe it away. I'm holding onto one of her hands. They detach me gently, like I'm a kitten with my claws caught.

"Is she going to be okay?"

"We'll look after her," the nurse says. "You two should get home."

They glide the stretcher away from us, surrounded by people in blue, and I can't do anything to get her back. The doors hiss shut. They're covered in signs that tell us we're not allowed in. The weight of everything catches up to me, like that stupid gif of No-Face being swamped by a wave covered in *feels*. The quake, the building, Tremor, Dani, Roxy. My brain glitches. The world is too bright and everything is jagged. Someone is painting over everything in thick cross-hatched black. It's like the scene in my favourite New Mutants story where the demon bear is gobbling up the world with darkness.

"Are you okay?" Alyse asks me, somewhere in the distance.

"I'm fine," I say, because I don't know how to say anything else.

I don't remember getting home, and I don't know what happened to Alyse.

The next thing I'm aware of is being back in my bedroom. I'm dressed in my stupid green and purple Chatterbox costume. Batty's in my hand. He's talking to me, but I can't hear him. I try to remember how I felt, looking down at Tremor, the sound of his hand breaking.

My phone buzzes and skids across the dresser. I fumble for it, but knock it to the ground. I collapse to my knees. I manage to hit the speaker button.

"Dilly? Dilly? My God, are you okay? I've been in a seminar all day and nobody told me anything." It's Pear. I feel relief, even though I know they couldn't have been hurt by Tremor.

"At school," I say. Words don't come out properly. My teeth are chattering.

"I saw the news. Where are you? The school couldn't find you."

"Home." I put my head between my knees and wait for it to stop swimming. "Alone."

"Wait for me there. Please. I'm coming. Just have to get across town."

I hang up and take my stupid costume off. I kick it under the bed, and try to find something to wear. I put on a hoodie and tighten my hood around my face. My objects are talking to me, but I don't listen. I can't stay here alone. I don't know where to go.

I decide to go to Sarah's. She'll look after me while Pear comes home. I text them with shaking fingers. It's gibberish but it says Sarah in there somewhere.

I take Summers with me, because he's furry and loves me and doesn't understand the world is falling apart. We make it to Sarah's house, where everything is eerily quiet. Lorelai is inside the house, leaping up and down on her hind legs. I don't have my key, so I put my hand to the window and Lore tries to lick it through the glass. I slump slowly down the wall until I'm lying on the porch, my face against the grains of the wood. Summers eventually tires of trying to get through to Lorelai and curls up beside me. I bury my face in his neck fur.

There's no way this isn't my fault. If I hadn't directly taunted Jack, he wouldn't have attacked the school. I made us a target. My stupid desire to play X-Men. So desperate for friends, for acceptance, to do something important that I didn't think long enough about what might happen when I played superhero.

Tyres crunch on gravel and doors slam.

"Dylan, oh my God, Dylan. Are you okay?" It's Sarah's voice.

I struggle into a sitting position. "I'm fine. Worried about people at school."

I see the figure of her oldest daughter Hazel behind her shoulder. She's holding her bag, and has tears on her cheeks. She goes to my school too, and I feel a rush of relief that she's okay. Sarah helps me to my feet.

"I'm going to make you some tea." Sarah unlocks the door and Lorelai comes barrelling out. She's so happy to see everyone, and she tears around in circles with Summers like nothing's wrong.

Hazel drifts into the house. She drops her bag and wanders into the living room as if she's a leaf in a current.

Sarah puts her hand on my shoulder. "There's a rumour that one of Hazel's friends died." Her mouth twists on the word 'died' like she's tasted something sour. "We're trying to confirm it, but please don't say anything to Hazel if there's news."

I hear nothing but the rushing of blood in my ears.

A kid has maybe died because of me and what I did—winding Tremor up and letting him loose.

I grab hold of a seat to steady myself, manage to fold my body into it. Sarah has her laptop on the counter, and she finds a news streaming site. It's on mute so Hazel can't hear. I sit there and stare at the closed captions, not really taking them in.

There are lots of shots of the school. It doesn't look so bad from the air. It's the ones on the ground where you can see how the building broke. The jagged trenches in the earth are visible, leading away to where Tremor started the earthquake. The video cuts to one of the smaller hospitals. There was another quake there, where Tremor was held. He wasn't in jail after all, because some stupid girl broke his hand with a baseball bat. There are officers injured, the caption says, as well as two nurses and a doctor. One of them is in critical condition—someone else to add to my list of victims.

We shouldn't have confronted him at all.

A darker voice inside me says I shouldn't have stopped. If I had killed him at the edge of the forest, then he couldn't have done this. I should have listened to my anger.

I was too arrogant to leave well enough alone, and too weak to stop him. And the cops? What use were they? I slam the laptop closed and put my head on my hands. If only I could close my eyes hard enough to stop thinking.

Sometime later, there's a light touch on the back of my neck. I raise my head, startled, but it's only Pear. They kiss my cheek and crouch beside me. "Are you okay?"

There aren't words or body language to encompass it. I start crying and can't stop. Pear holds me for a long time.

"Kids this age went through the quakes so young," they say to Sarah. "They were traumatised then, and this brings it all back to the surface."

I want to tell them it's not that. I want to confess, to spill everything, but I can't. The words won't leave my mouth. It's not only my secret—it's all of ours. And to express my guilt out loud is something too large.

I'm vaguely aware of what's going on in the house. Hazel is upstairs in her bedroom. Sarah has a doctor friend of hers coming over to check on her. The news has come in from the school and it's not good. Two people died in the quake. A thirteen year old and a fifteen year old, killed by the side of a building collapsing. People are screaming for answers, like how could this happen in a new, earthquake strengthened building? The scientists say it was an unusually targeted earthquake, something that couldn't be planned or built for. They talk about plate tectonics and lines of force, and someone speculates about a new type of earthquake.

Pear finally takes me home.

I cradle my phone in the car and read the group chat.

Moodring: is everyone ok?

Glowstick: fucking scary

Wraith: u want to be a cute mutant now?

Moodring: wraith plz

Moodring: today was fucked up cant u just be nice

Goddess: It was Tremor, wasn't it?

Glowstick: had to be but how?

Glowstick: the cops had him!

Goddess: I'm trying to find out. Deep searches.

Moodring: has anyone heard from dilly?

Moodring: i saw her with dani but then she went off when my aunt picked me up

Wraith: shit she better be ok

Wraith: if shes not imma go fucking wild

Wraith: watch out bitches its hell on earth time

Moodring: wraith calm down i did see her today

Glowstick: i can go to her house

Moodring: jfc glowstick no

Glowstick: we are actually still friends u know

Wraith: tbh thats the last thing she needs

I need to interject here, before they all start fighting.

Chatterbox: here

Chatterbox: imfine

Goddess: It was you who got us out, wasn't it?

Chatterbox: it was the building that did the work

Chatterbox: think i hurt it

Moodring: dylan plz tell me ur ok

Chatterbox: hahaha

Moodring: dylan!

Chatterbox: with 💧 alg

Except it's nowhere near *all good*, but there's nothing anyone can say to undo it. It's too late.

My head hurts from crying when I finally lay down to sleep and Pear manages to tear themself away from me. I lie there in the dark. There isn't any more crying to do, but I don't know what other options I have. There is one that occurred to me with startling clarity at Sarah's when I heard that Hazel's friend had died. Except I could never do it. I know with complete certainty that if I were gone, Pear would fall into a black hole, and I don't know if they have it in them to climb out.

I feel like I can still hear the rumble of the earthquake. There are no aftershocks though, at least not here.

I'm drifting off to sleep when my phone buzzes.

> Moodring: are you ok?
>
> Chatterbox: no
>
> Moodring: dilly hold on plz
>
> Moodring: its not ur fault
>
> Moodring: u need to blame tremor
>
> Moodring: he did this not u
>
> Chatterbox: thanks <3
>
> Chatterbox: but im like responsible you know
>
> Moodring: no i do NOT fuckin know
>
> Moodring: i would straight up slap u with ur bat if i was there
>
> Moodring: tell ur bat from me
>
> Chatterbox: if we hadnt done it
>
> Moodring: for someone so smart u are also pretty dumb
>
> Chatterbox: wow thanks
>
> Moodring: u know what i mean
>
> Chatterbox: im going to sleep
>
> Moodring: dilly please
>
> Moodring: dilly
>
> Moodring: ffs were talking about this tomorrow u know

I put my phone onto do not disturb.

"Poor sweet girl," Pillow says. "You should let me hold you and have a proper sleep."

"It's all my fault." Somehow I'm crying again. I didn't know I had so much moisture in me.

"Your friend Alyse is right." Pillow sighs. "It's not your fault at all. It's that nasty Jack boy. Batty told me about him."

"She's partially at fault," Batty says.

I feel a sting at first, and then a rush of gratitude. Finally, someone to tell me that I'm wrong and wretched and useless.

"Fractionally at least," he continues. "There's a matrix of culpability. His parents and upbringing obviously factor significantly into it. Then there's societal factors, particularly a pattern of radicalisation of young white males on the internet, leading to what's colloquially known as incel culture. Add to that whatever fluke genetic factors resulted in this particular man getting this particular power. The police have far more culpability than you, given they were unable to hold him in custody. The only small blame you have is that your actions perhaps encouraged him to pick a target where he could harm a large number of teenage girls, yet even that can be explained by other factors."

The baseball bat falls silent, suddenly uncertain.

"Batty," I say.

"Yes, Dylan?"

"How the fuck did you get so smart?" I'm propped up on one elbow looking at the bat lying across my desk. Like I'm not close to that smart. It's nothing he's getting from me.

"I've wondered that myself," Batty says. "I've come to believe there's such a thing as a hive mind of object consciousness. The more time I spend with you, and the more intense that time is, the more deeply I can connect with it."

Pillow snorts tiredly underneath me, as if this is total nonsense, but I'm not so sure. I've never heard anyone talk like that. I'm not sure where else he could get it from.

"Do you really think I'm not the main reason it happened?" I ask the bat.

"I think your responsibility pales into insignificance, to the point where considering it as a valid option is ridiculous."

"I think that's a no, dear," Pillow says.

"Then why do I feel so shitty about it?" I ask.

"Because something terrible has happened," Pillow says. "And people you know were hurt. It's a horrible thing to experience for anyone, and you're a terribly sensitive girl."

I roll my eyes, but Pillow is so gentle and comfortable that I don't complain too much.

"You're also young," Batty says, "and humans in general tend to overestimate the weight they exert on the fabric of events. It's a protective factor, in many ways, to counterbalance the sense of overwhelming helplessness in the face of a hostile universe."

"So rather than thinking I'm responsible for what happened, I don't matter at all?" I ask.

"Something like that, dear," Pillow says.

I drift off to sleep, but my dreams are a confusing jumble.

I see Tremor in most of them.

CHAPTER TWENTY-SEVEN

"**Y**ou dick!"

The light is on in my room and someone's shouting. I cringe away from the brightness and sound and pull Pillow over my face. "What the fuck is going on?"

"You absolute asshole! You don't just fucking ghost me after something like that."

I peer out to see a monster towering over me. It's a shadowy thing with a ghostly pale face swirling in its depths. In any other situation, I would freak out about this, but it's obviously Alyse.

"What the hell is going on?" Pear shouts from the other room.

"Jesus, stop it, Alyse. Pear's coming. You need to look normal."

I hurl myself out of bed and race for the door. I'm on the other side of it by the time Pear stumbles out of their room.

"Don't worry. It's only Alyse," I say to them. "She was worried after what happened."

"It's fucking four in the morning. I only just got to sleep."

"Then go *back* to sleep." I give them the most winning smile that I'm capable of.

"Can you tell her to keep it down at least?" They knuckle their eyes and go shambling back into the darkness.

"Very disrespectful," Tempus says from the wall. I poke my tongue out and slip back into my room.

Alyse sits on the bed, looking mostly normal, if a little tear-stained. I sit down beside her and put an arm around her.

"I'm okay," I tell her, although I'm not sure it's true.

"I was so worried. You were weird, like the wreck of Dylan. Right from the hospital. I mean the car thing was fucking insane, like you flew a car which is crazy. Then when we left you were all spooky but you insisted you didn't need anything. My aunt thought it was polite to leave you be, but I told her—"

"I *will* be okay." I feel like that part might be true.

"You still think you're responsible?"

I consider lying to her. It would be easy to say the words. Except this is Alyse. For all the times I've agonised over the team and my friends and my place in the world, I can't deny that Alyse keeps turning up. So I give her the gift of honesty.

"I can't see how it's *not* my fault. Either we—"

"For fuck's sake," Alyse hisses. "You are the worst." Her teeth are sharp and her eyes are fiery holes. "It's fucking Tremor's fault. All of it. The first day I heard about him, you said he was an incel. Who's to say he wouldn't have attacked people anyway? The asshole fucking stole his powers from Emma! He's the *bad guy*. All these people are his victims. We tried to stop him. Somehow the cops fucked up and let him go! And then you act like—" She starts crying, which I didn't expect, and am not prepared for.

I reach out and gingerly pat her arm. "I'm sorry."

"You're my best friend," Alyse says fiercely. "I don't want to watch you beating yourself up over this. You're the one who loves comic books. The bad guys come back, right? They hurt people. And the good guys have to get up again and stop them. You're wasting time feeling guilty and blaming yourself. You should be angry. He killed those two girls. He hurt Dani. We made ourselves powerful to stop him, so we should stop him again rather than running away."

As she talks, Alyse transforms again into something radiant, her face a multi-faceted diamond.

"Somebody's secondary mutation is speeches," I murmur.

"You should be angry at *him*." Alyse is holding my hand as if she can convey all her feelings down this line between us.

"I am." I can do that. Anger is easy. It's always been easy.

"It was scary with Dani today, wasn't it?" The subject change takes me by surprise.

"Seriously," I say. "And it was yesterday."

"You know what I mean." She nudges me with her shoulder. "Was it weird to have the first time you touched her like that be in some life or death situation rather than, like, a smoochy one?"

"Smoochy?"

"Omigod Dylan, you have to spill tea occasionally! I know you don't like words, because I called you my best friend and you left me hanging and—"

"Of course you're my best friend." I frown at her. "You know that."

"Dylan, I don't think you realise that your thoughts only come out when you speak them."

"You didn't know?"

She's radiant goddess Alyse, incandescent and gorgeous. "Well, I wasn't *sure*. You're very difficult sometimes. But ever since you locked yourself in the bathroom stall with an actual monster, I've known you were special."

For some reason, this makes me laugh and I can't stop. "You're so fucking soft," I gurgle.

She pokes me hard in the side. "Speaking of soft, you and Dani."

"Dani is not soft, and she doesn't make me soft and—"

"Oh *please*," she scoffs. "You're like two people who exist as constant fists of rage, but then you come face to face and get an attack of heart eyes."

"That is…" I splutter.

"You can't even finish the sentence!" She looks triumphant, like this proves something. "Fine, you don't have to tell your best friend your innermost feelings. Not tonight, anyway. But I'll get it out of you one day."

I almost tell her. It's so tempting. But admitting it to her means admitting it to me, and I keep shoving the thought away because the world doesn't have room for that many impossible things. The conversation winds down and we find we're both exhausted. We end up sleeping together, curled up on the bed like a couple of puppies. It's ridiculously comfortable because Alyse apparently transforms into something extra soft when she sleeps, like some shapely and feathery pillow.

"Hardly an appropriate headrest," Pillow says snippily.

"Don't be jealous." I pull her down so she can nestle between us.

"This is hardly the sort of behaviour I should be indulging in," she says, but I can hear the comfort in her voice and the three of us drift off together.

In the morning, Pear takes us to the hospital to visit Dani. We make our way up to the room she's supposed to be in. Except it's empty when we get there, which makes both Alyse and I freak out momentarily. We wait for a few minutes and there's no sign of her, so we head to the nurses' station in the hope of finding someone who can help.

I'm striding ahead and turn a corner, where I almost walk full-tilt into Dani. She's standing at a water station, bent over and drinking in a long t-shirt that rides up high on her thighs. Her hair that used to be shoulder length has been shaved close on the sides and back, but there's a long, glossy swoop on top that falls down over one side of her head. There's a stitched-together wound on the other side of her scalp that goes all the way down to her chin. It looks so badass that I feel this half-intoxicated rush, like the world is going to star wipe me away.

"Omigod, I'm so sorry." I accidentally grab at her, my hand on her arm. I release her like she's burning hot.

Her eyes widen. "Was it you two?"

"Us two what?" God, why are sentences so *difficult?*

"They said two students from Brookside brought me in. Was it you?"

Those extraordinary eyes of hers are fixed on me and I can't actually form the syllables in my brain, let alone my mouth.

"Yes," Alyse says. "Dylan stole a car and asked it to drive us here."

"I didn't *steal* it," I blurt. "It wanted to help."

"The point is that it was her powers that did it." Alyse breaks off. "Are you okay?"

"Fine," Dani says. "I've got a concussion and I'm going to have a wicked scar. But I'm alive, apparently thanks to the two of you and a helpful car."

"You collapsed in the street." I look at the ceiling, because it seems safer. "It was…" My eyes drift to Alyse, who looks entirely normal, which I cannot understand because I feel like a shaky wreck.

"It was intense," she fills in for me.

"Thank you." Dani has her hand on my arm now. I wonder if she feels the heat from my skin because I'm blushing all over. My gaze skitters towards her nervously like I've found a bug crawling up my arm and don't want to see how big it is. When my eyes meet hers, they click into place like Lego bricks. I don't want to keep going on about it, but she really does have the most ridiculously beautiful eyes. Metaphors sound stupid or overwrought when trying to replicate her eyes and all the feelings of this moment. Words mean nothing against the physical fact of her fingertips against the inside of my wrist, and my entire body pulsing in time with my heart.

"You're welcome," I say, like a fucking dumbass, because I have nothing cool or witty. The other words I have are proclamations and dedications and a million fevered statements of lovesick pining.

No, not lovesick. I don't love Dani. Seriously. This is not what's happening here.

"It was the guy, wasn't it? Making the earthquake. The one that brought part of a damn building down on me."

I nod and watch the line of her jaw move as she clenches her teeth. It's certainly some face.

"He escaped from the cops," she says. "Like a break-out from the Raft."

Oh my god, she really is a comics nerd.

"Yeah, and he's still out there," I say.

She inhales slowly. Her eyes don't leave mine. "Maybe Magneto was right." She does that half-smile thing. "I better go find my mum. I'll see you both soon. And thank you for stealing or not-stealing a car and saving me. It's—I'm not good at that sappy shit, but—it means a lot."

Dani walks off slowly down the corridor. I lean against the wall and watch her go. I can't stop watching her.

"I like your hair," I call after her, like the world's worst idiot.

She pauses at the corner and I get the full smile. It unpicks the armour around my chest and leaves my heart open and raw and bleeding. Is this what swooning feels like? Am I swooning? Is it obvious?

Then she's gone from view. I'm still leaning against the wall, like I have no energy left in my body to move my legs.

Alyse is grinning at me, fanning herself with one hand.

"Stop it," I say, even though I'm smiling too.

"What does 'Magneto was right' mean? Is it some gay code I don't know about?"

"Alyse! It's not *gay code*. It's an X-Men thing."

She snorts. "I get the feeling X-Men is gay code all on its own."

"Well, *anyway*," I say heavily, to move the conversation on. "Xavier believes in humans and mutants living together in harmony. Magneto believes that humans will never tolerate the existence of mutants, and so mutants have to fight for their right to survive. In this specific case, I think she might mean that we need to deal with Tremor ourselves."

"Jesus, that's dark," Alyse says. "And God help the fucking humans if you two ever team up."

"Who?"

"Who do you think? You and Dani."

I push myself away from the wall and head for the exit again. "This whole obsession you have with me and Dani is the worst ship that has ever been shipped. She doesn't like me."

"I admit it's terrible for ship names," Alyse says. "It just ends up being Dilly. Or Danlan, who sounds like a total dudebro. Maybe Danylan? Emma and I ship it hard though."

I roll my eyes theatrically. "Whatever. Emma does not."

"She does, and we both know something you don't know," Alyse sing-songs.

I ignore her and carry on walking. Whatever she's going to say, it'll be ridiculous. There is literally zero chance anything will happen between me and Dani. Not that I even want it to. She has a nice face, that's all, like an objectively amazing face. And also the best smile I've ever seen. Okay, so fine, maybe I like her, but that has no bearing on whether she likes *me* or not.

"Do you know why Emma kissed you the night of the party?" Alyse calls out, right in public. A couple of heads turn in our direction.

I walk faster.

"Emma asked people who the hottest girls they knew were." Alyse scurries to catch up with me. "So she asked Dani who she thought. And guess who she said?"

I reach the doors to the hospital. They slide open in front of me, just as Alyse calls out.

"She said Dylan Taylor."

I feel like the blinky white guy reaction gif. Like uh hello is this thing on? Saying I'm emo-hot is one thing, but not this. I don't really think Alyse is exactly lying—she's supposed to be my best friend—but she must have misunderstood. Dani and I exist on different points of the human evolutionary scale. Disaster chaos demon and immaculate ice-queen goddess are a ship that only works in the underbelly of fandom.

CHAPTER TWENTY-EIGHT

Things are weird after the attack on the school. The police finally say they're looking for a person of interest responsible. He's named and identified. Jack Firestone's picture is everywhere. The media swarm around his house. They're even parked up on our street outside number fifty-two, which is still being repaired. They've put all those pieces together now too. There are so many stories trying to dig down to the bottom of why. What made this man snap? Why did he attack the school? And what did he use to cause the earthquakes? His high school physics teacher says Jack was a bright enough kid, but couldn't imagine him building a machine capable of such things.

None of this makes me feel better, but on the bright side, nobody comes forward with any information related to mutants. There's no mention of a green and purple Spider Hero costume. Nobody even hints at the idea Jack could cause earthquakes with his hands.

I feel there has to be a story behind the story, where the police and some shadowy international agency work to find the mutant threat. Yet there's no mention of the m-word and new facts spill out. The papers talk about his parents' divorce and the ugly mess that was left. His juvenile record is sealed, but friends of the family tell their secrets of the time a thirteen-year-old Jack attacked his stepmother and she needed to go to hospital.

Online sleuths dig into his accounts on various forums in the darker parts of the Internet. All together they make horrifying reading. I can't even get through more than a handful before I feel sick. So much hate.

Out come more thinkpieces. How are we failing our young men? And how can women stop failing them so badly?

Then there are the deeper conspiracies. It's a false flag operation spearheaded by the global feminist elite. It's corporations working on new fracking techniques, and Jack has been set up to take the fall. I vow not to read anymore news stories, but I click every link that pops up anyway.

In amongst all of it, the media trucks and the endless rehashing, Jack Firestone is gone. He's a ghost. The police are hunting for him. They have media conferences on the news, but I hear more via Emma. He hasn't been back home, his phone has been destroyed, he's not using his electronic cards. None of his accounts have been active. I think of how much cash he might have accumulated from the robberies.

I attend the funeral of Hazel's friend along with Pear, Sarah, and Sarah's kids. It's the worst thing. There are so many people crying while everyone tries to make sense of it. Someone talks about God, but it doesn't sound convincing. I try to feel anger like Alyse said, but I'm a hollow thing with guilt at the centre.

It's Alyse who organises the first meeting of the Cute Mutants revival. I feel ambivalent, but I go along because I don't want to let her down. The right thing to do is impossible to determine. Tremor's a bad guy, that much is clear, but what can we do about it? How do we even begin that conversation?

I'm half surprised to see the whole gang gathered at Alyse's. Even Lou is there, and he grabs hold of me almost the second I walk in.

"Are you doing okay?" His voice is tentative.

"Not so okay," I admit. I still find it easy to talk to him.

"I kinda freaked out when I thought you might be hurt. That's a friend thing, right?"

"Yes." I can't help but smile at him. "You're still allowed to worry about me. I worried about *you* in the whole earthquake mess."

"You did?"

"Of course, but I'm surprised to see you here. I thought the mutant thing was—"

"What he did." Lou uncurls from his usual protective stance. He stands straight and looks me in the eye. "Attacking the school like that? Fuck that guy. So if you'll still have me, I want to be a Cute Mutant again."

"I'd really like that," I tell him, and then we hug. His body feels slim and warm in my arms. I wish he'd eat more.

"I'll always love you."

"The Dolly version," we say in unison because Pear didn't raise a fool.

The rest of the group is gathered in the lounge, so Lou and I go through and arrange ourselves on the couches with everyone else.

"Right." Everyone turns to face me. "So we all know what happened." I swallow. I can't bring myself to say it all. "But we're here today because Tremor is still out there. He's hurt people. He's... he's killed people. And he needs to be stopped." I finish and nobody says a fucking thing, which is just great. "That's what I think, anyway."

"That's what we all think," Alyse says softly. "I'm happy to hear you say it."

"I know it's hard for everyone to keep coming back together like this, especially when I keep fucking things up so thoroughly but—"

"Dylan," about three people say at once.

I screech to a halt.

"Listen for once in your fucking life," Alyse says, with mock sternness, but she's radiating softness and beauty, which undercuts it. "None of us are here right now because of superpowers, although they're cool. We're not here because of Tremor, even though he's a fucking monster."

"Um." I have no idea where this is going, but I'm nervous.

"We're here because of you. You're supposed to naturally pick up on all this, but apparently you're the literal worst at signals. So we're telling you this in a way you hopefully can't ignore: we're the Cute Mutants because of you. We're here today because of you. You inspire us. We like you. We like being this team."

"Alyse, you soft bitch," I say, but I can't actually say anything else because my heart feels like I'm being quaked by Tremor, and I can't see a goddamn thing. My panda eyes are running all down my face, and I can't even tell who's hugging me, but it feels like a lot of arms.

This is better than the comics. It's happening to me in real life. Somehow I'm the misfit, hated and feared, who has found the other misfits and in the most unlikely turn of events, they want to cling to me as badly as I want to cling to them.

I somehow stop crying. Emma wipes the mascara from my face and Bianca ruffles my hair to make it even messier than it already was. I'm sure I look like an absolute walking trash fire, but I don't even care for a second. I'm with my friends.

"Okay," I say, and try to regather myself, but I'm interrupted by the doorbell.

"Go answer the door," Alyse says to me.

"This is your house!"

"Please? I'm busy."

"You don't *look* busy." I glare at her.

"Dylan can you please go and answer the damn door," Emma shouts, which takes me by surprise so much that I'm up and halfway there before I'm aware of it.

I heave the wooden front door open, and I'm immediately both mad at Alyse and dizzy too, as well as about a hundred other things.

Dani is standing there, wearing a jacket like the one Lou has, and yoga pants that have the word Marvellous on them.

"Hi," she says. "I get the feeling from the way you're staring that this is a surprise."

I want to say something witty and charming that will make her fall helplessly into my arms. "Yeah, nobody said anything." Good work, Dylan. You're fucking irresistible.

She gestures to her leg. "I picked this as a name. I hope it's okay."

"It's perfect," I say. "Like OG Jean Grey."

"Well, it's a step up from Marvel Girl. Anyway, Emma and Alyse got me this ridiculous outfit and told me to turn up here and—"

It doesn't look ridiculous on her at all. It looks like she was designed in a lab to be a superhero. Luckily, I manage to keep all these thoughts in my head.

"I'm glad you came," I say, and am rewarded with her smile, the one that makes everything crack inside me. It's not losing any potency from exposure.

We're both standing in the doorway, so I move aside and hold out my arm for her to enter the house, like I'm the fucking Queen of England or whatever. She moves past me and there's a moment where her hip touches mine. I glance at her waist and think about how I could slide my hand around it and pull her in to kiss me, which is crazy. I'd have to ask first. I can't ask her. I can't even tell myself I don't have a crush on her. I try telling myself it's not my most insanely reckless act yet. I can't lie to myself anymore.

Alyse stands with Emma, staring at us, because *obviously* they were too fucking busy to answer the door. I glare at them like wtf guys, nice ambush, aren't you supposed to be my friends? They're doing the goofiest 'ahhh I ship it faces,' and I'm just dead.

We all reassemble ourselves back on the couch. Dani sits on the ground in front, nestled in between Alyse's legs and mine. I look at the line of tiny stitches on her head and wonder if it hurts. She turns her head to look at Alyse. "Are we doing the thing?"

"We already did." There's a very faint blush in Alyse's cheeks. "The moment just came up."

Dani sighs and swivels towards me. "It all goes for me too," she says. "I'm here for you. I want to be on the team. With you."

Everyone else in the room is staring at me. I don't know how to respond. I want to run away and I want to kiss her and I want the ground to swallow me up and I want her to swallow me up, and while my brain is pinballing between these options, I'm saying nothing.

"I'm glad you're here," is what I finally scrape together. Stupid words. Somehow I have to figure out how to talk to her. "Really glad, like we're finally the team we were meant to be."

"Together," she says, and that particular word from her lips makes my brain unable to function until Alyse pokes me and restarts whatever stupid process was frozen in my head.

"So, Tremor," I say. "We're going to stop him. Mutant justice for mutants." I feel Dani lean her weight slightly against me like she's agreeing with me. "The question is what that looks like."

"Fuck him up," Wraith says.

"Specifically how?" Dani's not going to be one of the sit back types, that's clear already.

"Like actually kill him." Wraith shrugs. "I thought that was obvious."

There's silence after this pronouncement, even though I've been thinking about it a whole lot.

"We should consider it," Marvellous says, which seems like a fucking reckless thing to say, if you ask me, but I'm not complaining. I feel weird that there's a #TeamKill-Jack, and it's Dani and Wraith and possibly me.

"I hear you, but it's fucking crazy." Glowstick shifts uncomfortably. "You're talking about killing a person. It's not something you just decide to do in someone's living room. We're supposed to be the good guys."

I open my mouth to speak.

"Dylan, I don't want to hear you say Magneto was right," he says.

Marvellous and I both make the same exhale at the same time. I'm against the death penalty in principle. Taking someone's life into your hands, excluding the possibility of redemption. At the same time, in this specific instance, it's hard not to imagine a better outcome.

"Do we think the cops can stop Tremor?" Goddess asks. "Do we leave him out in the world to hurt more people?"

"There's supposed to be a team for this sort of thing," I whisper.

Marvellous turns her head, and I see the curve of her cheek as she smiles. "We need an X-Force. If only we had a Wolverine—preferably Laura."

Oh my heart, please stop beating this way. Dani is still leaning against me. I'm exerting the tiniest amount of pressure back, very aware of exactly how much of me is touching how much of her.

"Except there's just us," I say. Like the New Mutants, we keep ending up in these shitty situations, having to make decisions we're not ready for. There's nobody we can turn to, not without risking too much. It's us, choosing between Xavier and Magneto. With the world the way it is these days, Xavier's dream seems like something from an older time.

"So what do we do?" Moodring asks. "I don't know what the right thing is."

"It's easy," Wraith says. "We treat him like a bad guy in a movie. They're always accidentally falling out of buildings or impaling themselves on their own goblin gliders."

"Jesus, Wraith," Glowstick puts his face in his hands.

"What?" She acts like he's being the irrational one. "It solves the problem. We're not killers, and he's dead."

She pauses and sighs. "Of course, he'll come back from the dead at the last minute and someone will have to fuck him up. Probably Chatty and her magic bat. That would be bad fucking ass."

It flashes through my head, vivid as if I'm watching on a big screen. Tremor, staggering and bloody. My hands, my bat. Him falling like a puppet with its strings cut. I think I could do it to save someone's life in the moment. My heart thumps. My hand brushes the back of Dani's head and she leans against it, like definite deliberate contact. I feel a flock of butterflies take flight inside me, and it leaves me paralysed.

"Chatterbox, you're the leader," Goddess says. "What do you think we should do?"

"I don't think we can decide now." It feels like a cheat but it's true. "We have to wait and see. But if we need to, if it's the only way to save lives, I'm willing to do what it takes."

"Dylan, you can't," Glowstick says.

"I'm Chatterbox. And it's not just me who feels that way. It's Batty, too."

"I don't know." Lou sounds like he's on the verge of tears. "I feel like a bunch of high school kids can't make these decisions. None of us have the right to decide what happens."

"*He* did," Goddess says. "He stole these powers from me and he used them to kill those girls. I don't think we should let him decide what happens again."

"You're right," I say, at the exact same time Marvellous does.

"We do what it takes," Moodring says.

"Yes." Wraith grins around the room at us. "We're all very badass and I'm totally on board with him accidentally falling into a volcano or whatever, but do any of us actually know where the little asshole is?"

She has a point.

Tremor is a ghost. Maybe that's his secondary mutation.

The rest of the meeting is rather less tense, but entirely unproductive. Nobody has any good ideas for finding Tremor. If the police are making no progress, what hope do we have? We're stuck waiting for him to pop his head up. Emma's searches have come up empty. She talks about hacking into facial recognition databases and CCTV footage, but I'm not entirely sure if she's serious. She says maybe Tremor has fled the country, although there's no record of him travelling. I guess maybe he has enough cash for a false passport. Is that a real thing or only a movie thing?

As I bus home, a plan takes shape in my mind. I know Tremor will want revenge on me. I can use that to my advantage, so I begin to concoct an extraordinarily stupid plan, involving me as bait and somehow going viral on TikTok.

Fortunately or unfortunately, it never comes to that. By the next evening, my plan has only gotten as far as making notes on one of my big sketchpads. Except I get distracted when the Cute Mutants group chat buzzes with activity.

Glowstick: um u guys need to turn on the TV

Goddess: Yes. Do it now. It's happening.

Wraith: wtf who has a tv these days

Glowstick: the internet stupid

Wraith: im a lot smarter than u pretty boy

Marvellous: Is this how you lot always communicate?

Wraith: wow ok dani disapproval is so on brand for u

Chatterbox: hi dani is it ok that i added u

Marvellous: Of course! I'm part of the team now

Chatterbox: im glad ur here 🥺

Moodring: omg soft bitch club

Marvellous: lol fuck off Alyse

Chatterbox: yes plz fuck off alyse

Wraith: lmaoooooo

Glowstick: jesus can u all pay attention

Goddess: Yeah, this is important.

Wraith: oh yes lou please me the big boss man

Wraith: please be*** fuck why do typos hate me

Glowstick: TREMOR IS BACK OK BIANCA

Wraith: um did u just shout at me

Moodring: omg

Goddess: Enough. This is really bad.

Goddess: Everyone go here:

Emma posts a link, which pulls up a live feed on one of the news sites. The camera is down the street from a big building with lots of glass windows. There's a mess of police cars and emergency vehicles parked outside. The letters that crawl across the bottom of the screen say: HOSTAGE SITUATION. SCHOOL ATTACK SUSPECT INSIDE.

Chatterbox: ok well fuck

Marvellous: Wow ok this is intense

Moodring: meet at my house?

Chatterbox: yes everyone get there asap

Chatterbox: theres no time to plan

Chatterbox: were going in

CHAPTER TWENTY-NINE

bus to Alyse's with my hood up and my headphones in. My costume is on under my clothes, and my mask is in my pocket. My eyes are fixed on my phone, but the facts are frustratingly vague.

Depending on which news story you read, there are somewhere between fifty and one hundred people in the building, being held on one of the upper floors. The exits have been quaked up and are impassable. There has been 'some' communication from inside. They confirm it's earthquake fugitive Jack Firestone. Everyone still thinks he has a machine, though there's no evidence of it. Probably not the worst thing, from our point of view, keeping mutant powers at least *sort of* on the downlow. They think he wants money and a helicopter—the standard 'I saw this shit in a movie' package.

I get to Alyse's, and there's still no further news. She's angry and alone, pacing around the house in her playsuit and masquerade mask. Dani and Emma turn up just after me, and Emma immediately begins setting up all her gear on the giant expanse of the dining room table. Dani's wearing black jeans and a black hoodie that says wow on it and a balaclava like Tremor, except it makes her look like the world's hottest thief. I really need to stop thinking about how hot she is, but seriously.

"I don't want to send drones in with the cops around," Emma says. "But I've got some little collapsible ones you can use inside the building, assuming you can find a way in." She has a duffel bag open on the table and is loading it with gear. I love combat Emma.

Bianca turns up next, in black jeans and v-neck sweater with her demon mask. She strikes a pose in front of me. "Do I look proper badass, Chats?"

"So badass." I grin. "Can't go into battle without my emotional support himbo."

She fakes a couple of punches at me. "You're going to need your ESH even more now that you're just a baby gay taking your first steps towards battle with a high-level gay mage."

"What the fuck are you talking about?"

She rolls her eyes at me. "It's not cute, this pretending."

"You mean the high-level gay mage is Dani?" I whisper and she cracks up laughing at me, which seems to completely miss the 'emotional support' part of the himbo equation.

It's exactly the wrong time to talk about this, but I kind of want to, except then Lou turns up and now everyone's here. Cute Mutants assemble and so on.

Emma's loaded up the supply bag with medical stuff, burner phones, portable drones, GPS tags, and one of those pocket WiFi things.

Alyse has the hostage situation playing on the enormous TV that takes up almost an entire wall. There's not much going on. We're all half-watching it, but it's Emma who notices something changing.

The whole picture starts to shake. It zooms in jerkily and we watch as a police car shudders. It bounces up and down on its tyres and the windows explode in a shower of glass. There's no sound, so we don't hear anything, but it looks like at least one officer is down. Tremor isn't fucking around.

Another cop wanders around with blood on her face. The camera tracks her staggering movement until she collapses behind the car, only one outflung arm visible. Someone runs down the street towards the camera. The footage stops abruptly and changes to the pale figure of an announcer in a studio. This is bad. Really bad. I clench my fists and try to focus.

"There is no plan," I say. "We're going to have to be flexible and see what the situation's like. As for getting there, a friend of mine is waiting outside."

"Friend? What are you talking about?" Lou asks, but he's drowned out by three shrill beeps. Alyse runs to the door and swings it open to find a car idling in the driveway. It's Roxy, who has been going around the city hiding from the cops. She refuses to go home to her so-called owners, and has been talking EV chargers into topping her up. I've woken her up and freed her, and now she won't go back into captivity again.

She's very happy to see me.

"Dylan, my darling," she says excitedly. "Where are we going today? And look! So many friends! And the very beautiful one is better now?"

The five of us get into the car, and I give Roxy directions. She hums off, obeying the speed limit this time, which I make very clear is a non-negotiable rule.

"There's a car park building across the street," Emma says in our ears. "From what I can see from the news footage, it's outside the cordon. You're in the flying car, right? If you get to the top, do you think the car can make the distance?"

"Roxy," I say tentatively. "How do you feel about flying between buildings?"

"That will be amazing!" Roxy says, and then pauses. She changes lanes and takes a corner very carefully and sedately before she speaks again. "Can you tell me exactly how far it is that I'll have to fly?"

"How did this car fly?" Dani asks from behind me. There's a slight edge to her voice, as if I'm encroaching on her territory.

"There was a lake," I say. "And I was really worried about you possibly dying, and Roxy just flew herself across. I don't know if I can do it again."

"Don't tell that lovely girl, but I don't know if *I* can either," Roxy says worriedly. "Do you think she'll still like me?"

"I'll do it," Dani says determinedly.

"What's the biggest thing you've moved?" There's no time to worry about her feelings. Getting into the building is going to be one of the hardest parts. It's surrounded by police. The doors are all fucked up, so I can't charm my way in, even if the doors would listen to me.

"My parents' couch," she says.

"And how much pain were you in to do that?" I ask.

She looks at me. There's no smile, only surety. "I promise you I can do this."

I have a really bad feeling, but I don't have any other options. I have to trust Marvellous. Surely whatever she does will be disciplined and sensible. It's her whole fucking thing, isn't it?

"Okay." I check Roxy's going the right way and turn back to the others. "Marvellous will get us in. We have no idea what we're going to face, but we have two goals.

One is to stop Tremor. The other is to free the hostages. Once we get in, we need to listen to each other. Code-names only."

I look from face to face and they're all listening, all looking back at me. Everyone's in agreement. The team's assembled.

We're really doing this.

Roxy travels the rest of the way in silence and pulls up outside the parking building. It's further from the hostage site than I expected. The cordon the police have set up is being pushed back, but it hasn't reached us yet.

"Are you sure you can do this?" I ask Marvellous, and she nods in response. "Okay, Roxy. Take us to the top."

She leaps off with a screech of wheels and begins to drive to the top of the building. The speed limit rule is discarded, and racing up ramp after ramp has me almost carsick. When she reaches the rooftop, she turns in a slow quarter-circle until we're facing the building where the hostages are. We're a lot higher, but it seems very far away.

"Tell the girl you like that I can help her," Roxy says.

Why is it so obvious I'm into Dani? This is the wrong time to be thinking about how into Dani I am. No, don't look at her every time you think the word *Dani*. Fucking focus, Dylan's brain.

I take a deep breath.

Hope we survive the experience.

"Okay, Marvellous," I say. "Let's go."

So then she takes a fucking knife out of her bag and stabs herself in the shoulder. She does it so fast. I'm helpless as I watch it. The handle of it is sticking out of her black hoodie. Her face is pale but determined.

Everyone in the car screams. The fucking car screams. And then Roxy lurches forward and rises crookedly into the air.

"Dani, what did you do?" I shout. "Fucking crazy reckless shit!"

She smiles at me and I am far beyond smitten. I am destroyed and terrified.

"Marvellous, don't take that knife out or it could make shit worse. Wraith, press something against the wound as hard as you can."

I'm furious. I'm exhilarated. The girl I really really fucking like is stabbed and flying a car between two buildings. Are the police watching? Are the cameras watching?

"Oh bother! This is going to hurt, isn't it?" Roxy says in a startled voice. She flicks her headlights on and I can see the reflection of her heading towards the building. The next second we're crashing through the glass window with a deafening sound. We all scream and clutch at each other. The car skids to a stop and flings her doors wide.

It's very dim inside the building. All the lights are off and the windows are tinted. The only light is coming from the hole we left coming in. Roxy whimpers to herself in mixed fear and adrenaline. We all clamber out and form a loose circle.

A rumble comes from below us, and the building shakes violently.

Okay, so Tremor is definitely here. He probably heard us come in, but let's hope he assumed it was quake-related damage. Either way, we can't panic.

"Right," I say. "First things first, Wraith, get the first aid kit and patch Marvellous up."

"What the hell is going on?" Goddess asks urgently.

"Dani stabbed herself and flew the car over."

"Holy shit." The earpiece crackles with her laughter. "Looks like she's trying to impress you."

"A fucking stupid way to impress me," I snap, but I can't deny that it worked.

Wraith fumbles in the duffel for the first aid kid and thoroughly tapes up Dani's shoulder with the knife still sticking out of her. Looking at it makes me sick. Marvellous winces, but doesn't say anything. It doesn't seem like the most auspicious start.

"We need to find Tremor." I say. "Once we do, some of us will take him on and distract him. That's me, Wraith and Marvellous. Glowstick and Moodring will locate the hostages and try to find a way out. Glowstick, you light the way. Moodring, you look calming and beautiful like a beacon in the night. And Marvellous, try not to fucking *die*."

I'm shifting from panic to being mad about it, but I need to focus.

The building shakes. I'm trying to ignore that too.

"Get my baby drones out," Goddess says. "They'll find Tremor and the hostages."

I unfold them from the duffel, and they wobble into the air one after the other.

Glowstick starts to light up, but I tell him to save it. At least it's impressive control. He must have been practising.

"Let's wait for Goddess to find Tremor." It's clear he's not on this floor, so we make our way through a big open-plan office with lots of desks and computers. The stairwell is signposted at least. As we quietly walk into it, there's another massive rumble. We cling onto the rail and wait for it to pass.

"What the fuck is he doing?" Wraith hisses.

"Baby Two found him two floors down," Goddess says. "I think the hostages are another three floors below. He's collapsed a wall to block them off and I can't even get Baby One through."

"Okay, Moodring and Glowstick, you go down. Marvellous, you up to moving the walls?"

"I can move whatever you need me to." Dani holds my gaze. There's a moment where I almost ask if I can kiss her. Even though she has a knife in her shoulder and we're about to do this insane mission, the chance to touch my face to hers seems vitally important.

I blink and it passes. We have work to do.

"Let's go," I say. My voice almost sounds like a leader talking.

We head down to the next floor. Wraith and I stop while the others carry on.

From here, a shouting voice is clearly audible. A figure walks in front of the narrow window in the door. It's Tremor, a phone clamped to his ear. Talking to the cops?

He turns and begins to walk away. I push the door open. It sticks a little, but it's silent. I poke my head around. The room is an entirely empty space with only cables lying snaked across the floor. Tremor is against the far wall, standing by the window with his back to me.

"No, you fucking listen." He bangs his fist on the glass. His broken hand looks misshapen, as if it hasn't healed right. "Five million dollars," he shouts. "And a way out of here. I've got a lot of hostages. I can send one down to you from the top floor. See if you can catch them."

I point at Wraith, who opens up her chest. It's still creepy to see her demons eddying out of her, sniffing the air. She doesn't need to give them any instruction. They go for Tremor like hunting dogs that remember their prey. He doesn't even sense their approach. The three of them leap on him and sink their teeth into his arms and neck. Tremor drops the phone and howls.

I reach behind me and pull the baseball bat out of my backpack.

"Ah," Batty says grandly. "The final showdown. How splendid. This is where the villain gets his comeuppance and—"

Tremor falls to his knees. His face is twisted from the demons' attack. He pitches forward.

I advance fast, Batty raised.

Tremor presses his hands flat onto the ground and the building bucks around me. Walking towards him feels like climbing a steep slope. The floor disappears. Something hits me. I hit something. There's so much noise and crashing. I wish I could make my powers out of pain like Marvellous can. Everything hurts. My leg fucking hurts.

"Dilly, are you alright?" Batty asks from somewhere nearby. I can't see him. Something's fallen on me and everything is dark. I hope the others are okay. I think Tremor collapsed the whole floor underneath us, and brought more down on top of us. How is the fucking building still standing? He's fucking crazy, and I should've known that.

"What the hell is your problem? Always coming at me, like you've got some hero bitch complex or something." It's Tremor's voice, slightly muffled.

I kick out with the leg that hurts less, but whatever's on top of me won't budge. Something crashes. Not another quake? Someone says something I can't make out. There's another thump and a surprised shout and then Tremor laughs.

"Oh, an invisible bitch? That's clever. Where did you find an invisible bitch?"

Who the fuck is he talking about? Wraith isn't here. Where the bloody hell is Wraith?

There's a gurgling sound, as if someone's being choked. Then a slapping sound and a series of thumps. What the hell is going on?

"It is Wraith," Goddess says in my ear. "She used *dontseeme* and attacked Tremor, but she's down. He got a lucky shot in."

"Is she okay?" I ask.

"He can't see her," Goddess says.

"Fuck you." Tremor's voice is strangled and tight. "Wait til I find you again. I'll hunt you down one at a time and take you apart. Then I'll start on the hostages. I'm going to up my asking price with you lot in here."

"Can anyone hear me?" I whisper. I'm not talking to the Cute Mutants. I need an object. Any object.

"I can," Batty says. "And I think there's a desk here. Very old, very tired."

"Please," I whisper. "Can you hear me at all?"

The voice in my head is dusty and faint. "Oh yes, little voice. So bright, you are. So astonishingly bright. I haven't heard from one of you in such a long time."

"I need your help," I whisper.

There's a dragging sound from somewhere out past where I'm trapped. Tremor's still prowling.

"I don't know what a dreary old desk can do for a—" The desk talks so fucking slowly, seriously.

"Get me out of here," I shout, not bothering to hide my voice. I let adrenaline and fear and rage spike my powers. The desk, because that's what fucking hit me, thank you very much you old bastard, leaps off me and spirals through the air to land with a crash halfway across the room. Very elegant indeed.

It reveals me curled up on the ground, covered in dust. My costume is half-torn, and my leg is bleeding.

I get to my feet.

Batty leaps into my hand.

Tremor turns to face me.

"Spider-Bitch," he says. "There you are. You're the worst of all. You and that fucking bat. Three guesses what I'm going to do with you when I get hold of you."

Fuck him. I throw the bat straight up into the air, and Tremor frowns.

Batty arrows towards him like a wooden missile.

Tremor raises his injured hand and punches at the air. There's a weird pressure feeling that makes my ears pop hard.

I cringe away from it.

My poor sweet bat disintegrates into a shower of splinters.

I hear him scream. I feel him die.

Batty is gone.

I can't believe it, except there's an unplugged link in my head where his voice should be. This can't be real. It's not possible. There's helplessness in the face of violence, when something breaks your world. You can't undo it. It can't be fixed. Everything's changed from one brutal action.

Tremor smiles.

"Look what you did when you broke my hand, Spider-Bitch. You gave me a free upgrade."

I don't register what he says. Not really. I'm on my knees, trying to sort through the wreckage of Batty, trying to find a fragment of him that might still be alive. It's all just rubble. It's not him, it's just parts of his body. A splinter slides into my palm and I come back to myself.

The void left in my head is replaced by thunder. I reach out to every object around me and spur them to furious motion. Desks and computers and phones and pens and tables and whiteboards and coffee cups. The useless remnants of office life. They swirl around me like a tornado.

"Oh Dylan." It's the voice of Goddess in my ear. "I'm so sorry."

"You fucking killed him," I scream.

Tremor isn't smiling anymore.

"Get him," I snarl, and every object that can hear me flies towards him. As a plan goes, it's a disaster. There are way too many *things* and they get in each other's way. I'm so angry I don't care. I want to send him flying out the window, surrounded by objects that will bury him. The press of them forces him backwards. He lashes out with his broken hand over and over, trying to blast his way through. A few more objects get shattered, which makes the others scared and wary. They approach him more hesitantly, falling to the ground and then leaping up to lunge at him. He's scared and retreating.

A small cabinet floats up behind Tremor. It spins above him and then falls with an audible thud onto his head. He collapses to the ground. The cabinet rolls off him, dazed and happy.

"She made me fly," it gurgles.

Most of the other objects scatter, but a few more come rolling up to give Tremor another good thump or two.

Someone puts a hand on my shoulder. I turn to see Marvellous. She still has the knife in her shoulder. I don't even know how she's upright.

I've got part of Batty's handle in one hand. My other is bleeding around the shards of him that I've been holding too tight.

"He was alive." I'm crying again. I can't help it.

Marvellous helps me to my feet. Her arms go around my neck. I feel her lips against my cheek through the mask. "I'm so sorry," she says.

I step out of her arms and walk over to Tremor. His eyelids are moving rapidly. He's coming back around. I reach down among the objects on the floor around me and pick up a crowbar, some remnant of construction left in a room somewhere.

"Are we going to do something fun?" The crowbar's voice is soft and husky.

My head is pounding, and I can taste blood.

"Fun for me," I say and bring it down as hard as I can on Tremor's damaged hand. He wakes up screaming, just in time for me to hit his other hand. I do it again, and then again for good measure. There's blood. There's a lot more broken bones than the time in the forest.

It's not pretty. He sobs and screams.

"Try quaking anyone else with those," I shout at him.

I swing the crowbar back. He's no Batty, but we're about to fuck Tremor up together. I tell myself he deserves this. He killed those two girls at the school.

He hurt people at the hospital and again here. He was going to throw someone out a window. I close my eyes really tight and open them. I wonder how many times I'll dream of this.

I ready myself to slam the crowbar against his head. I aim the end of it right for his temple. I wonder if it'll kill him in one blow or I'll have to hit him over and over. Strangely, I'm not sure I care. All the anger inside me will come out in this one single action.

The crowbar arcs towards him.

Except it flies out of my hand with a jerk that grazes my sore palm. It hits the ground and skids off into the pile of objects.

"Sorry," Marvellous says. Her hand is on the knife in her shoulder. "I thought you might regret it. I thought we should talk about it first. You're upset about your bat and—"

Except Tremor's still alive and staring at us with loathing. He's panting, his breath coming harshly. His mangled hands look fucking horrifying.

"Fuck you. You're all going to die." His hands are still resting on the ground. I'm frozen, waiting for the quake, but instead the bones in his wrists and forearms break with a series of dry, snapping sounds. His mouth opens in this misaligned oval. No sound comes out. Then he arches his back and slumps back down, unconscious again.

CHAPTER THIRTY

I'm standing over Tremor's unconscious body. His hands and forearms look completely ruined, but aside from that, he looks so fucking ordinary. He has bags under his eyes, and his lips are dry. I walk past people like him every day.

I feel both victorious and sick. I'm very aware I nearly killed him a few seconds ago, and it was only Dani's intervention that stopped me. She's standing right beside me. I lean into her slightly.

"Thank you," I whisper.

"I didn't know if it was the right thing to do, but I thought we should at least take a breath, you know. Vote on it or something?"

My head's swimming, but democracy sounds like a solid out.

"Goddess warned me to come up here once she saw what happened to Batty," Marvellous says. "But I've got cubicles to move."

"You go," I say. "The hostages are the most important thing."

"What are you going to do?" She looks worried. I see my reflection in the window. I look like every scene ever where Spider-Man's beaten to shit and his costume is torn and bloody, except I'm purple and green. I look unhinged.

My hand aches because I want to be holding Batty.

"I'm going to stay here and watch Tremor. Maybe I'll throw him out the window." I look at her. Exhaustion sweeps through me. "I don't even know, Dani."

She doesn't even blink at me using her name instead of her codename.

"Be careful, Dylan. If you decide to—you know—please wait for me. We'll do it together."

I nod. My vision swims. I reach out to steady myself and the old desk comes shuddering over to my side. I lean against it gratefully.

"Are you sure I should go?" Dani doesn't want to leave me. I don't want her to go either.

"We need to do the hero thing." I smile, but I feel caught between villain and victim.

Marvellous reaches out and touches my cheek very gently. I get this sad ghost of her beautiful smile through the mask, and she limps out of the door.

I feel someone's touch. Arms wrap around me. I scream and try to tear myself away.

"Chatterbox, it's Wraith," Goddess says in my ear. "She's used *dontseeme*, remember? She's hurt but she's fine. Also, heads up," Goddess says. "Glowstick's on his way."

"What the hell is going on?" Lou stands in the door, still glowing faintly. "Marvellous said something about—Jesus Christ, Dylan, what did you do?" He runs across to Tremor and looks down at the unconscious figure. "What the fuck happened to his hands?"

"They broke," I say. It's true enough. "Then he tried to quake again and his arms—"

"He's going to die if we don't get a doctor or something," he says firmly. "Is that the plan? Let him die and call it an accident?"

Wraith pops back into existence. She's limping. I can see a red mark on her neck, and she's holding one of her arms awkwardly. "Letting him die sounds like a good deal to me," she says.

I feel far too tired to make the simplest decision, let alone whether Tremor lives or dies. If we put it to a vote, what happens? Glowstick is against. Wraith is for.

"Tourniquets," Glowstick says. "Otherwise he's going to bleed to death. You could help me if you want, you two."

"There's a first aid kit over there," an empty plant pot says to me.

"Where?" I ask vaguely.

"Here! Here! I'm here! Look! Me!" I find the little red case hopping about behind a fallen bookshelf.

In it there are a bunch of bandages, so I bring them back over to Glowstick, and we tie two tourniquets just below each of Tremor's elbows.

"I don't know what I'm doing," I say, as I tie mine tight.

"We're saving his life," Glowstick says. "But it's going to hurt like hell when he wakes up."

I rummage through the medicine in the kit. I don't think Ibuprofen is going to help.

"Are we killing him or not?" Wraith asks. "I vote for throwing him out the window, but if we're not going to, my babies can do pain relief."

"What do you mean?" I ask.

Wraith shrugs. "It's one of those fucked up things, isn't it? The things that hurt you can be comfortable too. You get used to them. Changing into something new can be fucking painful and sometimes it's easier to stay how you were."

"Ten points to the emotional support himbo," I mutter. "Okay, let them out."

The demons come slithering out of her chest. They whisper and slink over to Tremor, where they wrap themselves around his forearms and sink their fangs into his flesh.

I take a deep breath. There's too much pain in the world, it seems to me, and this man right here is responsible for more than his share.

"Goddess?" I ask. "How are the hostages?"

"Marvellous has moved the cubicles out of the way. Moodring is being very soothing, but we're going to need Glowstick back down to light the way out."

"Okay, I'll send him down."

We need to coordinate all this and my brain feels full of sludge. The hostages need to be let out, and we need to get away. I wonder if Dani's up to taking Roxy on another trip. It seems like a lot to ask. No, that can wait. We need to solve the Tremor problem first. I'm still no closer to a decision.

Wraith stands beside him, looking down with a scowl. "Wake him up," she says to her demons.

There's a couple of breaths and his eyes flicker open. His expression is distant.

"I guess you won this round." He looks down at his hands. "I think I'm pretty fucked, aren't I?"

"Looks like it." It's surreal to talk to him like this.

"What happens now, Spider-Bitch?" His eyes are fixed on me. I feel like he can see through my mask and avoid the urge to tug at it.

"Call her that again and I'll fucking throw you out of the building," Wraith says.

"Nah, you think you're the heroes." Tremor smirks. "You aren't throwing me anywhere."

"Desk, make a hole," I say casually. The big old desk chuckles darkly to himself and waddles up to the window, where he swings his back half around and bashes at the glass. It's safety glass, but it's been weakened by Tremor's attacks and crumples outwards at the desk's second attempt.

"What the fuck crazy powers do you have?" Tremor asks.

I ignore him. He's irrelevant. He rambles some more, but I don't bother listening. I'm still holding a little piece of Batty. "What do you think we should do, Goddess?"

One of the little drones buzzes into the room and hovers over him. I wonder what it looks like on her screen. Is it easier to sentence him to death from a distance? I'd throw him out the window for her. I know that with a sick certainty. Right now, his life is in her hands, but I choose not to tell her that.

"I thought maybe I wanted to confront him," she says. "Make him look at my face. But he doesn't deserve to haunt my dreams, so send him to the cops. Hopefully his hands are broken badly enough that he can't quake anymore."

"That's a problem for me," Marvellous says from the doorway. She must have raced back to be here for this. To be with me.

Tremor stares into space, mumbling. I want him gone, but I don't know how to break that down into specific concrete actions.

"What happens if his hands do heal?" Marvellous asks. "If he breaks out of prison and kills a bunch of people. How do we live with that?"

"I don't know if they *will* heal," Goddess says.

"Do we want to risk it?" Marvellous is talking to Goddess but she's looking at me. I'm the leader. It's my decision. I think about the power he wielded and how he killed Batty with his broken hand.

"No," I say. "We're not going to risk it."

I still have this hyperawareness of the objects around me. I know what's two floors down inside a glass case. I hold my hand out. I don't say accio. I just ask it politely to come to me.

"What's happening?" Glowstick says, vehement and demanding, which is annoying because he's supposed to be leading the hostages out right now.

I don't say anything, but a fire axe glides into the room and smacks into my outstretched hand.

"Oh my god." Glowstick looks like he'll puke.

The sight of the axe puts fear and intensity back into Tremor. "I'll fucking kill you, Spider-Bitch. I'll tear the whole world apart until I find you. Someone knows who you are, and I'll figure it out too. You think there's a jail that can hold me?"

I look down at him. "Currently? No. Once I'm fucking done, yes."

Lou's No-Face mask is fixed in my direction. I watch his shoulders sag.

"Do it," he says.

"You sure?" I ask. The axe feels heavy in my hand.

He nods. "You're right. I don't think there's any other option."

"Wraith, can your demons please hold him down?"

We can't let Tremor stay out in the world. He's a monster and a weapon. These are true facts. Except the truth below the truth is that the fucking asshole murdered Batty. I feel like something made of rage and vengeance is wearing my skin. I need to do something to mark his passing. I remember what Dani said at the mall about monstrous girls. Maybe she really was talking about me. A girl capable of monstrous things. I feel the creature inside raise its head, sniffing for blood.

Dani's looking at me very intently, and I give her a weak smile behind my mask.

"Do you want me to—" she begins.

I'm already bringing the axe down. The impact jars my forearms, but the blade bites deep into the broken mess of flesh at his left wrist. I'm surprised by how much blood there still is. Tremor's scream is terrifying. It sounds inhuman.

"I can help," the axe whispers, and lends me momentum when I bring it down again. I hear the broken bones split. Tremor passes out with Wraith's demons wrapped around his arms.

When I'm done, Tremor is gone. Jack Firestone will live. We leave his hands on the floor as a macabre marker, then drag him down until we reach the hostages. The desk bumps and thumps behind us, grumbling to himself the entire time.

I pause at the door to where the hostages wait. I've never felt so exhausted.

"We need a plan for getting out of here," I say to Marvellous. "We either go with the hostages, bash our way through another window and hope nobody notices or—"

"We go out the way we came in." Her mouth is very close to my ear. "I'm in enough pain it shouldn't be a problem. It's fine. I'll survive. But the way I feel right now, I could fly your beautiful car all the way home, Dilly."

I practically swoon against her when she calls me Dilly. But there's still work to do.

"Lights," I call to Glowstick, and pull the door open to the hostage room. He goes in to join Moodring. There are a lot of people sitting around on the floor. They look rumpled and scared. The rest of us walk in behind him, me in my stupid garish costume. People won't be able to see us, squinting in Glowstick's glare.

"Hi everyone. The situation has been resolved and we have a way out." I sound stupidly young, and there's a flurry of questions.

"Quiet," Moodring snaps and they listen to her like they're a bunch of kids sitting up straight for their schoolteacher.

"We have the hostage taker," I say. "But you'll need to take him with you. Make sure he goes last, right at the end of the line. Find a couple of strong people to support him. He's been, uh, injured, I guess, in the situation. Go down the stairs. We'll have an exit at the bottom. Tell the police you caught him."

There's a bunch of whispering.

"This is the plan, people," Moodring says. "You've survived, like I promised. Everything is going to be okay."

Wraith and Glowstick manoeuvre Jack over to the hostages.

"Give him to the cops," I tell them. "He can't hurt anyone now."

"Who are you?" It's the only question I make out.

"We're the Cu—" It's Wraith.

"We're here to help," I say firmly over the top of her. There's no way we need the Cute Mutants name getting out. The stories from the hostages are going to be bizarre enough without that. "Team, we're going up."

I move back into the stairwell with the others following.

"Okay, desk," I say. "Clear another hole down below, right at the bottom."

He huffs and puffs past us and goes thumping down the last flight of stairs. There's a series of almighty crashes and then silence. A loudspeaker voice comes from outside, but it's hard to make out.

Moodring pauses in the doorway. "Remember: wait a few minutes until the coast is clear, and then leave," she says to the hostages.

I take her hand when she leaves. My other is around Dani's waist.

There seems to be an awful lot of stairs but we finally reach Roxy, who's rocking back and forward in a slow arc.

"Dylan," she says. "I've been so worried! The building was shaking and I thought I was going to fall through the floor!"

She flings her doors wide and we clamber inside. This time, Alyse takes the driver's seat and I get into the back with Dani.

"We'll leave in a different direction," I say. "Over the back of the building where it faces the river. There aren't so many cops there. And we're going to fly as far as we can before hitting the ground. Then we'll go straight to the hospital because some reckless person stabbed themself."

Dani's in my lap. She's slumped against me. I put one arm around her waist and steady her head. Her forehead is damp. I smooth her sleek hair off her face.

"I can make us fly," she whispers. Then she takes hold of the handle of the knife and rotates it the tiniest amount. She screams, and her body thrashes. I hold her tight.

Roxy leaps forward, hurtles out of the window, and then turns in a long slow arc towards the bright lights of town.

CHAPTER THIRTY-ONE

Everyone's fine in the end, or something that looks like it if you squint. Dani gets patched up. The rest of us only have cuts and bruises and maybe a concussion. I don't dream about Tremor, but that might be thanks to Pillow, who's been extra soothing, even though she's missing Batty. When I woke in the night, she was crying. We sat together and talked about him.

In the morning, Emma sends us a whole bunch of links.

The headline on the news website says AN ANGEL AND A GLOWING BOY.

According to the hostages, that's who saved everyone and led them out of the building. There are mentions of others too. Someone strong enough to pull collapsed interior walls off people. A leader in a strange mask who gave orders. Hey, wow, that's me.

"They were heroes," one person is quoted as saying. "Like the Avengers."

Wraith: omg these fucking know nothings

Wraith: its the xmen yo

Wraith: new mutants

Marvellous: Cute Mutants

Marvellous: Still a weirdly accurate name

Moodring: omg

Moodring: soft bitch squad assemble lol

Chatterbox: shut up alyse

Marvellous: yeah, shut up Alyse

Glowstick: shes not wrong

The news stories don't talk about how we got out. It took a while for all the hostages to clamber over the desk and out to freedom. We were long gone by the time the cops swept the building.

There's very little detail on Jack Firestone, only that he's in custody. There's no mention of his hands, or reports of what he might have said. The paper mentions no further unusual activity. To find that, we head to YouTube.

There's one video of Roxy crashing into the building, and about ten of her coming out. None of them are high quality and are obviously taken from a distance. The comments are full of accusations of hoaxes and jokes about Harry Potter. Except scattered among them are long-winded screeds.

What if this jack Firestone did NOT have a device but was the device hgimself?!!! quakes caused by unnatural powers!!! add to this we have reports of

1. A glowing boy

2. An angel (some say literally an angel some say a beautiful woman...... they all similar say that its not a human but somethng better)

3. A flying car

4. Someone strong enough to lift walls

Theyre a squiad of heroes like that woman said except i believe a state sanctioned appparatus!!

So there *are* people out there who are suspicious, but they all seem legit fucking nuts, so hopefully they won't catch the attention of anyone more sinister. At least Jack confiscated the phones off all the hostages, otherwise we'd have photos to contend with. The 'sketches' done by police artists of Alyse are wildly different and don't look anything like her. The ones of Lou all look like No-Face.

Once everyone is up, we all meet at Alyse's house. For once, her parents are home, which means we're all crammed together in her bedroom. Everyone's there. My team, my friends. The Cute Mutants. My best friend, my emotional support himbo, my darling computer genius bb, my ex-boyfriend-friend, and the girl I really, really like. I have no idea how to move from liking Dani to being something else, but it doesn't seem quite so insurmountable given everything else that's happened.

We defeated Tremor, and even more than that, I've found somewhere I belong.

"Right." I'm not even nervous talking to my team anymore. "So we need to figure out what next. Because I don't think I want to stop."

"Why would we stop?" Alyse asks.

"Okay cool. So we keep hanging out." I say with a grin. "We train. Keep working on our powers and fitness and teamwork. And then if something comes up, we deal with it. Like I don't know if I'm ready to go out there and fight crime. But if something happens, I don't want to sit back and do *nothing*."

"*I'm* open to fighting crime," Alyse says. She has her head in Emma's lap and is painting her nails black, very carefully. "Like we have these powers, right? Why not use them? We'll get better costumes. Proper badass ones. Colourful and sexy, but not like objectifying. Things that you feel sexy *wearing*."

"It sounds good to me," Dani says, because sometimes she's as reckless as me. She's near me on the bed, and when I shift, my little finger overlays hers. Maybe hers curls to meet mine and maybe it doesn't, but it feels like we're wired together.

"You know I'm in," Bianca says.

"And me," Emma chimes in.

Everyone looks at Lou.

"I'm a glowing boy," he says with this tiny smile. "I have to be in." The rest of us pile on top of him, smothering him in a group hug until he begs to breathe again.

"Cute Mutants," I say and hold out my fist. Everyone touches theirs to mine. "We're a team. We've been through a lot. Fuck it, let's stay together."

Emma puts on the *Yuri on Ice* theme, which makes Dani laugh so hard she nearly cries. The others start dancing around the room. I feel awkward for a moment with Dani there, but Alyse drags me up off the bed and I dance too. I close my eyes for a brief moment and when I open them again, she's looking at me. Dani Kim. Her face is transformed by that smile and my heart feels like it's going to break out of my chest and go bounding across to her to snuggle up bloody in her lap. Then she gets up on Emma's bed and starts dancing too. Of course she's an amazing dancer, like unfairly good. I'm trying not to stare, but my eyes are somehow always on her.

Someone bangs on the door and we all suddenly stop our dancing, even though the song keeps going. It swings open, and it's Alyse's dad. The expression on his face when he sees us frozen mid-dance makes us all start laughing.

He shakes his head and closes the door.

Afterwards, as we're all leaving, I catch Lou out on the street.

"Hey, glowing boy," I say to him fondly.

"Aren't you looking smug now that I'm a Cute Mutant after all." He holds out his hand, faintly shining. "Feel kinda dumb that it took me so long."

"We all mutate at our own pace," I tell him, as if I'm some wise fucking sage. "And smug or not, I'm glad you want to hang with us. It makes me feel like my world is complete."

"It's gross how sappy you are," he says.

"I know. I disgust myself."

"And I'm not going to say I told you so, but good luck with Dani."

I feel a lurch in my stomach. "I'm terrified," I admit. "I don't even know if it's real but—"

"I talked to Alyse about this," he says, a fact which blows my mind on its own. "She thinks you've been genuinely clueless this whole time, and I eventually had to agree."

"But I'm me," I tell him. "And she's Dani."

"Now we're just friends, I can be honest with you." He shakes his head and grins at me. "Dilly, you are the world's best idiot."

I scowl, even though I can barely breathe at the thrill of possibility. "I don't understand."

"Dani is so into you it's intimidating, and all you can do is blink at me. If I can end up joining the Cute Mutants, maybe you can mutate into occasionally seeing a glimpse of the Dylan that other people see."

"Seems like a shit superpower," I say awkwardly.

He shrugs. "I did warn her you'd never make the first move."

I give a strangled yelp. "You talked to Dani? Please tell me this is a bad dream."

"We're all friends now." He has this ridiculous, goofy smile on his face, and I almost collapse under the weight of how lucky I am. I have these people around me who give a shit and who, despite all the fucking odds, seem to genuinely like me.

"I'm terrified," I say again. "I don't know how to do this."

"You were the one who leaned in to kiss me," he says. "So I know you can do this. Scared is okay, but don't miss out on something amazing because of it."

"Now who's being sappy and gross?" I shake my head at him and then I give him a hug, because it feels right.

"See you at the next meeting." He bumps fists with me, and then he jogs around the corner and is gone.

Roxy takes me home, playing an impeccable NCT mix on the way, and drops me off around the corner. I have dinner with Pear like nothing at all is different. Like I'm not a mutant, like I'm not a hero, like I'm not part of a team, like I'm not standing perched on the edge of something that feels like falling in love.

Afterwards, I'm sitting on the couch scrolling through Netflix, looking for something to watch. Then I hear music coming from outside. It's the theme song from *Yuri on Ice*. I assume it's Alyse, so I go to the door dressed in my Red Velvet hoodie and underwear and literally nothing else. I am the queen of slobs. My hair is a disaster.

I open the door, but it's Dani standing at the end of the driveway. She's holding my Bluetooth speaker up like something from the 80s movies Pear loves so much and she's wearing the suit.

Like *the* suit.

I close the door behind me and stand on the top step. I'm perfectly still aside from the fact I'm trembling all over.

"Hi," Dani says. She fumbles at the speaker and it goes silent.

I don't know what to do. Not even the one (1) brain cell in my head is functional enough to respond. She walks further up the driveway towards me and pauses at the bottom step.

"Dylan?"

"Hi, Dani."

I take a step down and she takes one up.

"Um," she says, and I realise I've never seen Dani flustered, not even when she stabbed herself. "That day in the mall. You looked, uh, you looked really good in that dress."

"I'm not a dress girl." Why do I say this? It's a fucking dumb thing to say. Own the dress, Dylan, you idiot. She likes it.

"I was going to say." Her breath hitches. "You look even cuter in an Irene hoodie."

She said cute. My brain streams a series of shocked and swooning and hype gifs in surround sound in case the dumbass part of me didn't register it. Dani fucking Kim said I look cute.

"I like your suit." I don't know if she even hears me, I say it so quietly, but she smiles, and I want to kiss her smile more than I've ever wanted to do anything, even be an X-Man.

"And that thing you did with the shield the other day at Alyse's house was the sexiest thing I've ever seen."

"Oh," I say faintly.

"I know you don't like talking, but you're not making this easy," Dani says. Her hair tumbles across her face. She tilts her head slightly and it falls away. I watch as she stills a trembling hand at her side. I see a flash of her tongue and her teeth graze her bottom lip. I can't process this sensory onslaught.

"Sorry," I whisper.

"You don't need to apologise." Her smile is wider somehow. It could dazzle the world. "Can I kiss you?"

"Okay," is all my brain can muster up as an answer.

"Is that a yes?"

As if a whole new language has been beamed into my brain, I can finally make sense of her expression. There's desire and fascination and nervousness mingled. It almost hurts to breathe.

"Yes, please," I say and I wrap my arms around her neck.

I'm not going to go into detail about the kiss. There are some things that should be private. Let's just say if I had Lou's power I would have blinded the whole street.

I'll also say that of all the talents Dani Kim has, kissing is right up there. At one point I accidentally touch her shoulder and make her say ouch against my mouth and at another point the back of her hand touches my thigh at the hem of my hoodie and I'm officially deceased and ascending to heaven. Tremor could come back and shake the entire world apart, and I'd still only be aware of Dani's lips and her tongue and the tiny click when our teeth touch. Of the fall of her hair across her cheek and the warmth of her fingers against my bare skin. Her hand is tangled in the back of my hair and mine is pressed in the small of her back, trying to remove any space between us.

At some point we have to break. It's either that or fuse into a new entity.

"Curfew," Dani whispers.

"I hate curfew," I say.

"Believe me, so do I. But tomorrow is a new day, and I promise I'll kiss you again, Chatterbox."

She presses her lips to mine one last time, then turns and walks away. Fuck me, she looks unbelievably good in a suit. I walk backwards up the steps and lean against the door. My body still feels flushed and buzzing, like the kiss is still going. Things shouldn't feel this good. It must be illegal.

I slide down the door. My legs don't want to hold me up anymore. I'm lolling against it in this giddy daze when Pear opens it abruptly. I fall backwards and hit my head.

"Ouch," I say.

"Honestly, what are you doing now?" They frown down at me, but it's a nice frown.

"Oh Pear," I say. "You do like it when I tell you things, don't you?"

At least I can tell them this, if not the mutant thing.

"Yes?" They're dubious and rightfully so. I look up at their upside-down face. Summers comes over and leaps on top of me, and I have to squirm out from under his enthusiastic attention. He sits on my chest panting.

"It's stupidly early to tell," I say, "but I have a horrible feeling I might be in love."

"Oh."

"Yes, and I think kissing might be her secondary mutation."

"Well, being dramatic is obviously yours. Oh, Dilly, to be young and in love. I hope you survive the experience."

EPILOGUE

Fifteen minutes after Dani leaves, there's another knock at the door. My foolish heart thinks it could possibly be her returning, and lurches into excited life. Except when I open the door, a man and woman are standing on the doorstep. I've never seen either of them before. They're wearing smart, preppy clothes and there's this little logo on the breast of their dark blue blazers that's a Y inside a circle.

"Dylan Jean Taylor," the woman says. "Also known as Chatterbox."

All the fine hairs on my arm stand up. I clutch onto the doorframe, because otherwise I'm going to collapse in it for the second time that night.

"I'm Dylan." I frown at them. "But I'm not sure what you mean by a chatterbox?"

The woman smiles indulgently. She slides her phone out of her pocket and glances down at it.

"Alyse Teuila Sefo, codename Moodring. Kim Joo-Hyun aka Danielle Kim, codename Marvellous."

Despite how my entire life is falling apart in slow motion, there's still a ridiculous lovesick part of me thinking 'oh wow, Dani's name is so beautiful.'

"Bianca Marie Powell, codename Wraith. Emmaline Jing Hall, codename—"

"What's going on?" Ugh, here is Pear behind me.

"Are you aware of your daughter's extracurricular activities, Mx Taylor?" They even fucking pronounce it Mix, like they've done their research well. I realise I am in phenomenally deep shit and it's getting deeper.

"I don't think I like what's happening here," Pear says.

"We understand. Unfortunately, Dylan has been deemed a national threat for her actions in what has been termed the Firestone Incident."

I don't think Pear expected to ever hear those words in that particular order, especially the ones 'national threat.'

"Excuse me?" They look pale, like they want to clutch onto something, but I'm the only thing close enough and they don't want to clutch me rn thank you very much.

"As the mutant Chatterbox, Dylan is the leader of the group responsible for the capture and mutilation of Jack Firestone aka the mutant Tremor, as well as the rescue of the hostages." The woman beams at me, as if I'm a very good girl as well as a national threat.

My brain is back to going 'ohfuckohfuckohfuck' like it does so helpfully in these situations.

"I'm sorry." Pear sounds like they're about to faint. "Who are you exactly?"

"We represent the Yaxley Corporation. We contract to the NZSIS on matters of this nature."

"The SIS?" Pear's voice is ascending into a shriek, which does not bode well.

"Of what nature?" I ask, taking over the questions from Pear before they melt down.

"We run the training institute responsible for the management and development of such extrahuman individuals." The woman smiles at me, very wide. "Also the blacksite detention facility for those who are unwilling to cooperate."

My brain says number one: these are *obviously* assholes. Number two: this is a whole new level of fucked that I am in. Number three: TRAINING INSTITUTE OMG

"I'm in," I say, and I hear Pear inhale sharply beside me.

It's not like I really have a choice. I guess I'm going to superhero school. I'm sure this will backfire in many spectacular ways, but okay, I admit it. I'm a tiny bit hyped.

Insert appropriate flail gif here.

ACKNOWLEDGEMENTS

First, I want to thank my partner, who kept encouraging me to write even during my wasteland years. Despite the 'occasional' complaint, I'm glad I came back to it. Then there's the rest of my family, who put up with the fact that writing can be an emotionally messy business. 'I'm sorry' probably covers it more than 'thank you', but both are true.

If it takes a village to raise a child, it takes a lot of support to get an anxious writer to send a book out into the world. Cute Mutants has a slightly odd gestation. It started in Nano 2019, when I was dared to write a story in response to a Jonathan Frakes YouTube clip. That story starred Ness/Pear as an irascible detective who could speak to objects. At the end of the book, their daughter Dylan inherited the same ability. My friend Cassidy was the one who encouraged me to write a book from Dylan's point of view, so at least some of this is her fault.

The idea of a teenager who could talk to objects lurked at the back of my mind for a few months, but

I never found a great hook for it. Until I hit a time when I was frustrated with every word that I typed, and decided to write an entirely self-indulgent story about an X-Men superfan who got powers and found their own superteam. It seemed a perfect opportunity to revisit Dylan's world. When I began, I thought it would only be for me, and that nobody else would possibly be interested. The fact that people connected with it so much along the way makes me feel soft af, as Dylan might say.

In a way, the experience of writing this book has paralleled Dylan's journey, although I've found writing friends rather than my own superhero squad. Either way, I feel stupidly fortunate, just like Dilly. There are so many people to thank who contributed their time, advice, inspiration and encouragement along the way so deep breath...

Cassidy was the first person who read it and let me know it wasn't entirely terrible. Avery Fowler helped take my first draft and put some much needed structure around it. Emma Jun fell in love with the characters and brought out the best in them. Nina Grauer read it three times in various incarnations, and shouted GAAAAY at me in the comments. Jessica Lewis and Amanda M Pierce helped crack open the heart of it and showed me the path to deepening the story. E. M. Anderson got all my jokes and gave me amazing ideas for merchandising opportunities, and Rebecca Lavelle helped put the final polish on top. Blame me for the mistakes, not any of them.

So many other people were generous with their time and advice. I had a wonderful group of talented and patient beta readers: Breeanna, Ayida, Eris, Sarah, Tiffany, Monica, Andy, Laura, Leta, Chelsea, Maddy and Skye. I couldn't have gotten this story told without all of you. Hopefully some of you are willing to read the sequel!

Special thanks to team trash, who are a squad of wild noodles, and have provided an enormous amount of encouragement and hilarity while I've been on this Cute Mutants writing bender. You're wonderful, talented people, and I can't wait for all your amazing books to be out in the world. Long Tom will have his due.

The X-Men comics were obviously a huge influence on this book. Thanks to all the people who've written, drawn, inked, coloured, lettered and edited those books over many decades. These characters mean an enormous amount to me.

And finally, thanks to G for the help formatting this, because I would have made a real mess otherwise.

For anyone who's read this far, thanks to you too. There are more books to come, and the story of these kids is just beginning. Stay tuned. It's going places.

FURTHER READING

There are a lot of X-Men stories alluded to in the book and if you're interested in investigating further, here are some places to go.

New Mutants
The best place to start for the namesake team is The New Mutants graphic novel (Claremont, McLeod et al), which shows the original team getting together. However, mine and Dylan's favourite New Mutants (and in our opinion one of the best X-Men stories ever) is The Demon Bear Saga (Claremont, Sienkiewicz, et al). There's also a current New Mutants ongoing (Hickman, Brisson, Reis et al) which is both awesome and the inspiration for the logo Emma uses when designing the clothes.

Magneto
There are so many places to go for Magneto, but here are a few starting points. Uncanny X-Men #150 (Cla-

remont, Cockrum et al) begins to truly flesh out Magneto's character. Magneto: Testament (Pak, Di Giandomenico et al) digs into his history and the more recent Magneto vol 3 series (Bunn, Walta et al) shows his more modern character development. The slogan "Magneto Was Right" comes from the incredible New X-Men run by (Morrison, Quitely et al) and you can definitely buy t-shirts if you're so inclined. It's canon that Dylan owns one and that Dani's worn it on more than one occasion.

X-23

Laura Kinney aka X-23, Wolverine clone and favourite of both Dylan and Dani has a complex publishing history like many X-Men, but good starting places are the Complete Collections which includes the Kyle/Yost and Liu runs, and then moving onto the recent and absolutely wonderful All-New Wolverine (Taylor, Lopez et al) which introduces Gabby and Jonathan the Actual Wolverine.

Latest

Both Dylan and Dani make reference to recent X-Men comics where the mutants all live together on an island. The place to start here is House of X/Powers of X (Hickman, Larraz, Silva, Gracia et al) which takes the X-Men in a fantastic new direction. Kate Pryde can be found in Marauders (Duggan, Lolli et al) and Psylocke is Captain Britain in Excalibur (Howard, To et al), but it's all good and both Dylan and Dani buy every new issue from their friendly local comic shop as they should.

Miscellaneous

God Loves, Man Kills (Claremont, Anderson et al) is one of the all-time classic X-Men stories and should be required reading if you like this stuff at all.

The mystery of Nightcrawler's parentage is explained in X-Men Unlimited #4 (Lobdell, Bennett et al).

The story referred to in Dylan and Lou's breakup is in X-Factor #87 (David, Quesada et al) which is an all-time classic.

ABOUT THE AUTHOR

SJ Whitby lives in New Zealand with their partner, as well as various children and animals. They are predictably obsessed with X-Men and spend too much of their free time writing. This isn't their first novel, but it's the first that's made it out into the world.

You can find them on Twitter at @sjwhitbywrites.

9 780473 528645